P9-DFU-953

CAROLE WILKINSON

# DRAGON MOON

Dᴉꜱɴᴇᴘ•HYPERION BOOKS

NEW YORK

If you purchased this book without a cover, you should be aware that this book is stolen property. It was reported as "unsold and destroyed" to the publisher, and neither the author nor the publisher has received any payment for this "stripped" book.

First published in 2007 by black dog books
15 Gertrude Street, Fitzroy Vic 3065 Australia.
Text copyright © 2007 by Carole Wilkinson

All rights reserved. Published by Disney • Hyperion Books, an imprint of Disney Book Group. No part of this book may be reproduced or transmitted in any form or by any means, electronic or mechanical, including photocopying, recording, or by any information storage and retrieval system, without written permission from the publisher. For information address Disney • Hyperion Books, 114 Fifth Avenue, New York, New York 10011-5690.

Printed in the United States of America
First Disney • Hyperion paperback edition, 2009
10 9 8 7 6 5 4 3 2 1
Text design by Michael Yuen
Map by Julian Bruère

Library of Congress Cataloging-in-Publication Data on file.

ISBN: 978-1-4231-1174-0

Visit www.hyperionbooksforchildren.com

TO MOM AND DAD
WITH LOVE

# CONTENTS

# CHINESE EMPIRE IN THE HAN DYNASTY

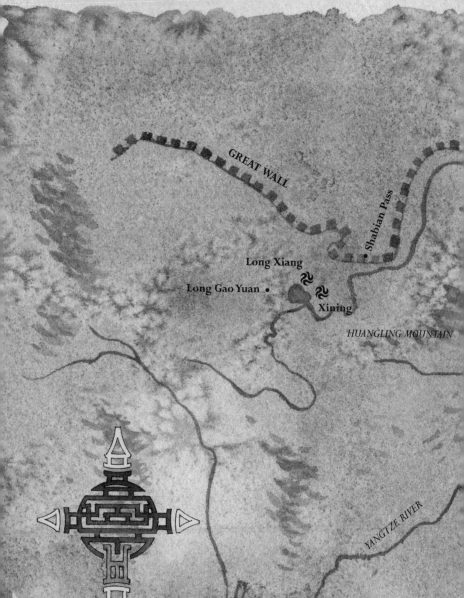

GREAT WALL

Shabian Pass

Long Xiang

Long Gao Yuan

Xining

HUANGLING MOUNTAIN

YANGTZE RIVER

Xiong Nu Camp

Ji Liao Garrison

GREAT WALL

YAN

Beibai Palace

YELLOW RIVER

TAI SHAN

OCEAN

YELLOW RIVER

Ming Yang Lodge

Chang'an

# CHAPTER ONE

# ATTACK

It was raining hard, but the sky was cloudless. It wasn't raindrops that were falling on Beibai Palace, but arrows. They pelted down, bouncing off flagstones and walls. The inner courtyard of the palace was usually a quiet, peaceful place, but today the wind brought sounds of war—the battle cries of soldiers, the rumbling of drums, the clash of weapons. People were shouting. Hurried footsteps echoed around the courtyard as a squad of the Duke of Yan's soldiers ran across the flagstones, trying to buckle their blue-and-gold tunics with one hand as they held shields over their heads with the other. Arrows fell around them. One managed to hit a target, digging deep into the thigh of a soldier. He fell to his knees, clutching his leg.

Ping watched from a doorway as a crossbow bolt tipped with fire soared across the square of blue sky above the courtyard and struck a watchtower. Flames erupted from the wooden structure.

It was all her fault. She should have left Beibai Palace months ago. Ping tried to run out into the courtyard, but Tinglan held her back.

"It's too dangerous," the servant said, clinging to Ping's sleeve.

An arrow ricocheted off the flagstone in front of them and bounced through the doorway. Tinglan flinched. Ping yanked herself free and ran out into the courtyard. An arrow pierced the hem of her gown, narrowly missing her leg.

"Please, madam," cried Tinglan, "come back inside!"

But Ping ignored her. She flattened herself against the wall and crept around the edge of the courtyard. She didn't even glance at the wounded soldier as his companions dragged him into the shelter of the palace. He wasn't the one she was rushing to help. She moved as fast as she could, inching crabwise along the wall, protected from the rain of arrows by the overhanging eaves.

The flames were spreading. The roof of the dining hall was already burning. Ping knew how quickly fire could spread through a wooden building. She wished she could see how the battle was progressing, but the only place where it was possible to see outside the palace was from the top of the walls.

The shouts of the Duke's soldiers had woken Ping early that morning. She'd thought it was a dream until Tinglan rushed in, tears streaming down her face, babbling about sentries dead on the ramparts.

"Is it the barbarians?" Ping had asked.

"No," Tinglan had sobbed. "Imperial soldiers are attacking us!"

Ping didn't believe her, but frightened kitchen hands and ladies-in-waiting soon confirmed it. The Duke of Yan had recently made peace with the Emperor's enemies, the Xiong Nu who lived beyond the Great Wall. He had set up direct trade with them, making it easier and more profitable for the barbarians than trading with the Emperor. But that wasn't what had provoked the attack.

Imperial spies had infiltrated the palace and informed the Emperor about the dragon living there that was bringing great good fortune to the Duke. An envoy had arrived two weeks earlier, with a message saying that the dragon was an imperial dragon—and the Emperor wanted him back. The Duke had replied that he would not give up the dragon. Ping imagined the Emperor's fury when he received the reply. Imperial troops had attacked at first light. The fact that his sister, Princess Yangxin, was married to the Duke and lived in the palace hadn't stopped the Emperor.

The battle had gotten off to a bad start. The Duke's men were outnumbered ten to one. To celebrate the recent peace with the Xiong Nu, the Duke had given most of his soldiers leave to spend the winter with their families. The remaining soldiers had been taken by surprise.

It was too dangerous to climb up to the ramparts to see what was happening, but everyone had seen the dead and the wounded in the Peony Hall. Panic had quickly spread as the palace inhabitants imagined the worst.

"Thousands of soldiers are gathered outside the walls," Tinglan said. "Whole companies of them, so one of the stable boys said."

The Emperor had been unpopular with the people of Yan even before the attack. They didn't like paying higher taxes to fund his expeditions to foreign lands to look for the fungus of immortality and the water of life.

"What sort of person puts his own sister at risk for one small dragon?" Tinglan said.

"The Emperor will lay siege to the palace," one of the cooks predicted. "He'll slowly starve us to death."

Tinglan shook her head. "The luck of the dragon will protect us."

Ping knew the Emperor wouldn't have the patience for a siege. His attack would be swift and deadly.

"Liu Che wouldn't do this," Princess Yangxin had protested as Lady An, her head lady-in-waiting, coaxed her toward the safest part of the palace. "My brother wouldn't risk harming me."

The Emperor had recently sent his sister a gift—a gilt statue of a horse almost two feet high. The Princess was convinced this was a sign of his love for her. She was sure that the attack was the work of a rebel general. The passage of time had made her forget how her brother had ill-treated her—sending her away from her home to be the Duke's wife in order to keep the peace with Yan. But Ping hadn't forgotten. She hadn't forgotten what he'd done to her, either. He had imprisoned her and sentenced her to death. She didn't believe he'd suddenly changed.

Ping knew she should have been helping care for the wounded, but she had another priority. She finally arrived at the doorway on the opposite side of the courtyard and ducked inside. The sharp smell of dried fish mingled with the aroma of honey. Baskets of vegetables were piled high alongside sacks of grain.

In the center of the storeroom there was a well about four feet wide, the one well in the palace that didn't freeze in winter. She leaned over the low wall that surrounded it, peering into the water even though there wasn't enough light in the storeroom to allow her to see below the surface. She took a mirror from the sleeve of her gown. One side was polished bronze, the other had an etched image of a dragon circling a raised sphere that served as a handle. Ping angled the mirror so that it collected the rays of morning light that reached inside the doorway and reflected a beam of pale light into the well.

The water soon began to ripple. The ripples became waves. A paw broke the surface, and then another, each armed with four sharp talons. The paws felt around the edge of the well until they found a grip. Two sturdy legs clambered up. A head emerged, covered in dark purple scales. It had a long snout, drooping ears, and brown eyes that blinked away the water. A purple body with a row of spines down its back followed, and was heaved out of the well onto the storeroom floor with the aid of two powerful hind legs. Water ran off the creature, splashing Ping's gown and soaking her silk slippers. She touched the dragon's purple head and heard a sound like tinkling bells.

"Is it spring?" said a voice in Ping's mind.

"Almost," she replied.

The dragon shook himself. Now Ping was wet from head to foot.

He looked around the storeroom. "Did Ping bring birdies?"

Ping laughed and scratched the dragon around the bumps on his head where, one day, his horns would grow.

"No, Kai, I didn't bring you anything to eat."

The dragon's brow creased. "Why did Ping wake Kai?"

Her smile faded; she put an arm protectively around his scaly shoulders. "The palace is being attacked. It's Liu Che. He's found out that we're here."

"Does Ping's second sight warn of danger?"

Ping shook her head. "No, but the palace is on fire. We must get to safety."

Kai stretched to his full height. It was more than two weeks since Ping had last seen the dragon. He'd grown. His head came up to her waist. She tried to pick him up. He was now about the size of a goat—a rather fat goat. She couldn't lift him.

Angry shouts came from outside the palace walls.

"Quick, Kai!"

She tried to push him toward the doorway.

"Dragons may not have good hearing," he said, refusing to move, "but Kai knows those aren't the cries of imperial soldiers."

Ping went to the doorway. Kai was right. The shouts were in a language Ping didn't understand. The shower of arrows had stopped. Men were clambering onto the roof with buckets of water to put out the blaze. The flames died down as she watched, until a few plumes of smoke were all that remained of the fire. Other voices rang out from within the palace. It was the Duke's soldiers cheering. Ping ventured out into the courtyard, keeping close to the walls in case another volley of arrows rained down.

Lady An ran toward Ping, her face beaming. "The Xiong Nu have come to our aid," she said. "The imperial troops are retreating!"

"Can we trust the barbarians?" asked Ping.

"They're better friends to us than the Emperor," Lady An replied. Ping had never heard her speak so sharply.

Ping wanted to see for herself. She climbed up a flight of steps that led to the ramparts on top of the outer palace wall. Kai followed her. Others had had the same idea. Ping pushed to the front of a crowd of cheering people. A band of perhaps a hundred barbarians was gathered outside the palace, together with the Duke's foot soldiers. The barbarians were dark, rough-looking men wearing clothes made of leather and fur. The Duke's men were mingling with them, raising their spears and bows, and shouting in triumph. To the west, a cloud of dust was all that could be seen of the retreating imperial army. Several men on horseback rode out of the palace gates toward the soldiers. The Duke was among them.

Kai looked at Ping, his eye-ridges wrinkling in a frown.

"Did Ping sense that Kai was in danger?"

"No, I had no sense of foreboding. I just wanted you to be safe."

"Kai *was* safe." The dragon's voice was unusually stern. "The well was the safest place to be."

Ping lowered her eyes so that she didn't have to meet the dragon's gaze. He was right. She'd panicked. The well would have hidden him from imperial soldiers and protected him from fire. If there had been a real threat, she would only have led him into danger.

"Is it dinnertime?" Kai asked.

· CHAPTER TWO ·

# SEVEN CUNNING PIECES

Ping spent the rest of the day tending the wounded soldiers with Lady An. The following day, under the direction of Princess Yangxin, she helped pack chests of food, silks, and wine that the Duke was sending to the Xiong Nu as a gift of thanks.

Two days after the attack, Beibai Palace had returned to its usual calm rhythms. Except for the banging of hammers and the smell of damp, burnt wood in the air, it was as if nothing had happened. Ping spent the day in the Hall of True Delight, the Princess's private recreation room, where the Princess and her ladies were busy weaving, embroidering, and spinning silk thread. Despite more than a year of daily encouragement from the Princess, Ping had developed no interest in these pastimes. The only time she sat to sew with the other women was if there was a hole in one of her socks or a tear in an undergarment. She preferred to spend her spare time reading.

All of the Princess's ladies wore fine silk gowns with embroidered edges. Since Ping wouldn't embroider a gown of her own, the Princess had insisted on giving her some that the other ladies had discarded. They had deep sleeves and were made of dyed silk. A long sash was tied in a bow around the waist. Ping thought they were far too impractical, but she didn't want to be impolite.

Kai hadn't returned to the well after the attack. He'd started playing a game of hide-and-seek with the children. He had grown so much during his hibernation that it was now difficult for him to find a hiding place. The Princess's chair and the wood box no longer concealed him.

Today Ping was neither reading nor sewing. The recent events had jolted her out of her winter idleness. She sat on a rug staring at a silk square spread out on a cushion. It was a small piece of undyed, unhemmed fabric just a few inches across.

Ping examined the silk square for the first time in many months. On one side it was marked with faded, scratchy lines and squiggles drawn in what Ping believed was blood. It was a rough map of the Empire drawn by Kai's father, Danzi. A solid line represented the Great Wall, the northern boundary of the Empire, built to keep out the barbarians. To the east was Ocean. To the west was a number of jagged points, like arrowheads. These represented the Kun-lun Mountains. A winding line indicated the course of the Yellow River as it snaked across the whole Empire from its source in the western mountains, northward to almost touch the Great Wall before it turned south and then meandered eastward to Ocean. The southern border of the Empire must have been beyond Danzi's knowledge, because it wasn't marked.

There had been other characters on the map marking rivers and mountains, but those had faded completely. Only nine characters remained. Ping was sure this was what Danzi had intended. These were the only characters she needed to follow the map. They were the names of three places: Long Dao Xi, Qu Long Xiang, Ye Long Gu—Dragon's Lament Creek, Quiet Dragon Ridge, and Blazing Dragon Valley. But there was no route to follow, no clue as to what she might find if she went to any of these places. Ping had asked the Duke and his advisers if they knew of the three places, but no one had heard of them.

At first Ping hadn't noticed that there was anything on the other side of the square, but when she had been examining it in bright sunlight one day, she'd discovered several faint intersecting lines and small characters arranged as if they had been thrown down on the silk like dice. The jumble of characters made no sense.

She called Kai over from where he was unsuccessfully hiding behind a pot plant.

"Are you sure you don't know what Danzi's map means?" she asked.

She had started to teach Kai to read some characters before he had begun his hibernation.

"No. Kai has told Ping many times."

"I know, but I thought after your sleep it might . . . look different."

The silk square had been delivered to Ping by her pet rat a year and a half ago. Hua had been badly injured in an attack by the dragon hunter Diao on the sacred mountain Tai Shan. Danzi had been injured as well. He had taken the rat with him to the Isle of the Blest so that they could both be healed by the water of life that flowed there. Ping had never seen Danzi again, but the rat had returned unexpectedly one day, carried on the back of a red phoenix.

Ping could now read as well as an imperial scholar, but even though she understood the characters, the map was still a mystery to her. When she had been with Danzi she'd often been unable to understand his pronouncements. Nothing had changed. His message made no sense at all.

Ping hadn't thought of the old, green dragon for weeks. They had met on Huangling Mountain, where he had spent more than forty years in captivity. Ping shivered as she remembered her childhood in that cold, lonely place. She had been an ignorant slave girl without even a name. She had expected her future to be nothing more than an endless repetition of her past, spent serving the lazy Master Lan and feeding the creatures in the run-down imperial palace on that bleak mountain. Lan was supposed to care for the imperial dragons, but his neglect had led to them dying one by one, until only Danzi had remained. One day Ping and the old dragon had escaped together. She smiled to herself. That wasn't really true.

Ping, frightened of the world beyond Huangling Mountain, had been reluctant to leave. Danzi had kidnapped her, snatching her up in his talons as he took wing. He was the one who had revealed her name to her.

She touched the bamboo square hanging from a silk cord around her neck. It had been given to her by her parents when she was a small child. There was a single character written on it in faded ink—Ping.

A gong sounded to announce that the midday meal was about to be served. As the dining hall was still being repaired after the fire, the servants brought the food to Princess Yangxin and her ladies-in-waiting in the Hall of True Delight.

Kai sat on embroidered silk cushions next to Ping. A servant brought in a low table set with a bowl, spoon, and chopsticks for Ping and a large dish for Kai.

The first course was golden-thread mushroom soup. Kai's meal was different. His dish was piled with fifteen stuffed quails and thirty turtle eggs. While everyone else was quietly sipping their soup, Kai hungrily stuffed

the birds and eggs into his mouth, eating everything—
including the bones and the eggshells. Ping didn't eat
much.

"Doesn't Ping want her soup?" Kai asked.

Ping shook her head, so Kai drank her soup.
Servants brought in the second course—baked deer in
hot sauce. For Kai there was a large bowl of warm
ewe's milk sweetened with honey, which he slurped up
happily. Since Ping didn't seem to be interested in the
baked deer, Kai helped himself to that as well. The
serving girl returned, and Kai looked at her expec-
tantly. His spines drooped when he realized that the
meal was over and she was only clearing away the
dishes.

"Any worms?" he asked Ping.

"I thought you would've grown out of eating worms
and insects by now," Ping said. "I'll mention it to the
cook."

After the tables and dishes had been removed, Ping
studied the silk square again.

"Those shapes look like Lady An's game of Seven
Cunning Pieces," Kai said.

Ping traced a fingertip over the faint intersecting
lines. They formed four triangles, a square, and a misshapen diamond.

"May I borrow your Seven Cunning Pieces?" Ping
asked Lady An, who was sitting nearby marking a
design on a piece of dark blue silk.

"Of course," she said. "They're in the box with the chessboard and other games."

Ping went over to the box and pulled out a little bag. She brought it back to the rug and emptied out the contents. There were seven shapes made of ebony wood, carved with patterns of plum blossom and bamboo. The shapes were the same triangles, square, and diamond that were marked on the silk.

Ping had seen Lady An play this game. It involved rearranging the pieces to make shapes—a rabbit, a running man, a bird in flight. Ping didn't mind playing chess, which improved the player's skills at strategy, but she had never seen the point of playing Seven Cunning Pieces.

"Can I borrow your chalk, please?" she asked.

Lady An handed her the piece of chalky rock that she'd been using to mark lines on her sewing.

Ping formed the seven pieces into a square, as they were arranged on the back of the silk square. She marked the characters on the black pieces, exactly as they were on the silk.

Ping turned the shapes this way and that on the rug. She arranged them to make patterns and shapes—a jug, a boat, a dish. It was amusing for a few minutes, but she soon grew bored. The characters were still a senseless jumble. She studied the silk square again. There was no clue as to what she should do with the pieces.

Lady An came over to see how Ping was doing. "Which shape do you want to make?" she asked.

"I don't know, that's the problem. Danzi didn't say."

"A dragon," said Kai.

"You're right, of course! It has to be a dragon." Ping was the only one who could understand Kai. His metallic dragon sounds translated into words in her mind. She could also speak to him in her mind, but she had gotten into the habit of speaking aloud to Kai whenever they were in company. It seemed polite.

Ping rearranged the pieces.

She made a passable fox and a rabbit. She created a dog, a goose, and a bat.

She sighed impatiently. "It's impossible. There aren't enough pieces. Do you know how to make a dragon, Lady An?"

"I have never heard of a dragon shape," Lady An said, "but there is a dragon's head shape."

"I don't know how to make that."

"That's the whole point of the game, Ping," Lady An laughed, "to work out how to make the shapes."

"Can you show me?" Ping said.

Lady An rearranged the pieces. With a few moves she made a dragon's head.

"There," she said.

Four of the characters now lined up in a vertical row. Ping read them out from top to bottom.

*Hui dao mi jia.* Ping frowned. "Return to the

secret home. I don't understand what that means."

"Perhaps Father means Ping's family home," Kai suggested.

"No, there's nothing secret about where my family lives."

"Must mean Father's home."

"But he never mentioned any home to me. When he spoke to you in your dreams, did he say anything to you about his home?"

Kai shook his head.

Ping looked at the silk square again. She read out the names of the places Danzi had marked on the map— Dragon's Lament Creek, Quiet Dragon Ridge, Blazing Dragon Valley.

"All these places have dragon names," Kai said.

Danzi's meaning was suddenly clear to Ping.

"He means a secret *dragon* home. He wants me to take you to a place where you could live safely. A secret place where no one who means you harm can ever find you. A place where you can be free, just as Danzi was when he was a young dragon. A dragon haven."

"Father didn't want anyone else to read the message," Kai said.

Ping nodded. The square might have fallen into other hands, so Danzi had written a coded message, just for her.

"There are three places marked on the map," she said. "How do I know which one we should go to?"

"Perhaps you can choose any one of the three," Lady An suggested.

"Yes!" Ping exclaimed. "There's a choice. There were once many dragons in the world. There would be more than one place where they sought refuge. Danzi didn't know where I would be when I discovered the silk square."

Dragon's Lament Creek was closest to Yan. It was difficult to tell from the rough map, but it looked like it couldn't be more than three hundred *li* to the west.

"It sounds like a rather sad place," Lady An said.

"I know," Ping replied. "But I have to trust Danzi."

Ping honestly didn't know what she would find at Dragon's Lament Creek, but she knew she must follow the old dragon's advice. He had lived in the wild for over a thousand years before he was captured for the Emperor. Who else would know better where Kai would be safe?

Lady An went off to arrange the menu for the evening meal.

"It's time for us to start our journey," Ping said to Kai. She suddenly felt like leaping up and leaving immediately.

Kai's eyes sparkled. "Yes," he said. "Time to follow Father's silk."

Ping smiled at him. Over the winter months, he hadn't only grown in size, he had matured as well. His speech had improved, though no one knew that but her. Other people could hear the metallic sounds he made, but in her mind these sounds were translated into words. His eyes had changed from the green of an infant to the brown of a mature dragon. He wasn't a dragonling anymore. He was aware that they had to leave the comfort of the palace. He knew from experience that the world of men wasn't a safe place for dragons.

Ping had only meant to stay at Beibai Palace until the weather had improved, but somehow more than a year had slipped by. After Ping and Kai had escaped from the Emperor with the help of Princess Yangxin, it had taken the Duke less than a month to discover that there was a dragon hidden in his palace. Ping knew the Duke could be brutal to those who offended him, and she was afraid that he would punish the Princess for her concealment. But though he could be stern and short-tempered, he would defend anyone staying at his palace with his life. He also understood how privileged he was to have a dragon under his roof.

The Duke wasn't a greedy man. He didn't want to sell Kai's body parts or harvest his blood, as others had. He knew that a dragon could bring him good luck. He thanked Yangxin for bringing Kai to his palace, and he treated the dragon well. The Duke issued bronze weapons to his soldiers once he learned that iron hurt dragons. He made sure none of the palace women wore gowns made of five-colored thread, as dragons didn't like that type of cloth. He arranged for the cooks to provide Kai with special meals.

The Duke had experienced unusual good fortune since Kai had been a part of his household. Spring had brought good rains to Yan, though the rest of the Empire had suffered a drought. The summer crops grew well, and autumn had brought a plentiful harvest of wheat, millet, and green vegetables. The people of Yan ate well, while many inhabitants of the Empire were hungry.

The Duke's negotiations with the Xiong Nu had gone smoothly, and all bloodshed had ceased. But the best luck of all had happened the previous spring just when Ping had been preparing to leave. Princess Yangxin had discovered that she was going to have a child. Still homesick and missing her mother, the Princess had begged Ping to stay until the birth. After all the kindness she'd been shown, Ping couldn't refuse. And it had seemed sensible to give Kai time to grow bigger and stronger before they started their journey.

The Duke was delighted when he heard the news. Though he had six other wives, between them they had only produced two daughters. There had been many miscarriages and stillbirths, and the Duke was worried that he would never have a son to inherit his lands.

Ping had stayed with the Princess through the summer and an entire winter. A healthy boy had been born three months earlier. The Duke named his son Yong Hu, which meant brave tiger. He was convinced that Kai was responsible for this blessing and pampered the little dragon even more. The other wives were so relieved that the Duke finally had an heir, none of them minded when the Princess was elevated to the position of first wife.

Motherhood had changed Princess Yangxin. Her face was a little fuller than it had been when Ping first met her, her cheeks had more color, she laughed a lot. The weeping girl Ping had encountered at Ming Yang Lodge had become a cheerful woman who was happy with her life as wife and mother.

In other parts of the Empire, northern winters were spoken of with dread. It was a common threat that misbehaving servants and argumentative wives would be sent to the north for winter. Terrible tales were told of children being snatched by starving tigers and villages discovered in spring with their entire populations frozen to death. Soldiers didn't want to be sent to garrisons in the north, so they were manned by convicts—thieves and murderers who had been conscripted into the imperial army.

Yet Ping had spent a whole winter at Beibai Palace on the northernmost edge of the Empire—and she had enjoyed every minute.

"In the south of the Empire," Princess Yangxin had told her, "when winter arrives, people put on thin coats and tell each other it isn't really cold." The northerners were different. They knew how to prepare well for the cold. They wore winter gowns and coats lined with silk floss. Torches burned in every room of the palace day and night. The stone floors were covered with thick felt rugs purchased from the Xiong Nu. Animal skins kept people warm at night.

No one could leave the palace because of the snow piled a *chang* or more high outside the gates. No farming was possible during winter. The goats, sheep, and oxen were housed inside the palace walls. In the past it had often been a time of hunger, but since Kai's arrival, food had been plentiful. For the inhabitants of the palace, winter became a holiday from their usual chores. They kept warm by dancing to music performed by the palace musicians, or running races and playing ball games organized by the kitchen staff. The soldiers were unable to go out on maneuvers, so they learned acrobatic skills to keep themselves fit. They also held archery contests to improve their bow skills. The whole palace enjoyed watching these activities.

Winter had been a holiday for Ping as well. Her dragon-keeping duties were few, as Kai spent most of the winter hibernating. He woke two or three times a month, ate enormous amounts of food, and then climbed back into the well. At first she thought that people might object to having a dragon sleeping in their drinking water, but it was just the opposite. They believed that Kai gave the water healing powers and were eager to drink it. As soon as the snow had begun to thaw, people with all sorts of ailments had started arriving from far and wide to drink the "dragon water."

Though dragons could bring good fortune to those who cared for them, Ping knew that the rain had nothing to do with Kai. Rain was more likely to fall near the coast, so she suspected that it was the palace's proximity to Ocean that had been responsible for the rain. The Duke had had the foresight to have cisterns dug under the palace to store rainwater. So even if the rains hadn't been plentiful, there was enough water. Ping had tried to explain this to the inhabitants of the palace, but they didn't want to listen. They preferred to make a fuss over their dragon.

Despite the uneventful winter, Ping hadn't been idle at Beibai Palace. The Duke had an excellent library. While the other palace women had spent the winter months embroidering, Ping had passed the dark days reading books. She had learned a great deal about the Empire.

She had spent time with the palace herbalist as well, learning the uses of many herbs. He had taught her which seeds and berries could turn a simple meal into a tasty dish, which flowers and roots could cure illness, and which bark could heal wounds. He had shown her how to combine different herbal ingredients to make medicines and tonics. She gathered piles of petals, fruits, and leaves, and boiled them together until they became a foul-smelling brew.

Ping had also improved her control over her *qi*

power. Danzi had taught her how to strengthen the spiritual energy within herself by focusing her mind, controlling her breath, and performing slow physical exercises in the golden *qi*-rich light of the morning sun. Once her body was full of *qi*, she had to control it—to concentrate it and send bolts of *qi* power shooting from her fingertips. She had once used her *qi* power against a dragon hunter, and he had fallen to his death. She had also used it to free herself when she was trapped beneath a huge boulder.

Through the winter, the Duke had allowed her to practice with his soldiers, and she had become quite skilled. She could now summon enough power to defend herself against several armed attackers. She could knock spears and crossbow bolts aside before they wounded her.

Her second sight, however, was still something she couldn't control. She could not summon it at will. Instead it came upon her, unannounced, when her dragon was at risk. She hadn't experienced a single feeling of foreboding in all the months she'd been at Beibai Palace—even when the palace was under attack. But her second sight hadn't let her down—Kai hadn't been in any danger.

All the time Ping had been at Beibai Palace, the high walls had made her feel protected and safe. But now she felt confined, like a bird in a cage. It was time to leave Yan.

· CHAPTER THREE ·

# THE BOOK OF CHANGE

Ping waited a day before she spoke to Princess Yangxin. She found her playing with Yong Hu, who was lying on a tiger skin trying to grab the jade fish that his mother dangled above him.

"I must leave the palace soon," Ping said.

The Princess's smile faded. "I don't see why you need to go anywhere," she said. There was a sharp edge to her voice. "You and Kai are safe here. Even when the palace was under attack, Kai didn't come to any harm. My husband will look after you both."

"I know," Ping replied. "But Danzi went to a lot of trouble to get this message to me. I can't ignore it any longer."

She had ignored her duty before, choosing the easy path. She couldn't do that again. If there was one thing Ping knew with certainty, it was that a place of safety could quickly transform into a place of threat and suffering. She didn't share these thoughts with the Princess, however.

"The Empress will be arriving soon," Ping said. "You won't need me."

Immediately after the battle, the Duke had sent a squad of men to Chang'an to escort Yangxin's mother, the Dowager Empress, to visit her new grandson. After his defeat, he didn't believe the Emperor would object.

"I will always value your friendship," the Princess said. "No matter how many other people I have around me."

"We can wait a month or so for the weather to improve," Ping said. "But then we must depart."

The morning was only halfway through when Ping received a summons from the Duke. She went to the Peony Hall, where the Duke was waiting for her, standing with his arms folded. There were strands of gray in his neatly knotted hair. He was much older than the Princess. When Ping had first seen him, he had seemed stern and humorless, but during her stay at Beibai Palace, she had come to know him as a man who smiled often.

The Duke wasn't smiling now. Ping made a polite bow. She didn't sink to her knees with her forehead to the floor, as she had been required to do in the presence of the Emperor. She bent just from the waist.

"Yangxin tells me that you plan to leave us," he said.

"That's what I always intended to do, Your Grace."

"Didn't you believe me when I promised to protect Kai?"

"I know that you will guard Kai with your life."

"But you think that I will succumb to temptation and sell him."

"No, Your Grace. I have complete faith in you. I would love to stay here, but I can't. Danzi has instructed me to take Kai away." She made it sound like the old dragon had left her detailed instructions instead of a perplexing message. "I am a Dragon Keeper, I have a duty." Ping hesitated. "Kai will live for hundreds of years beyond your lifespan, beyond mine. I have to find a safe place for him to live."

"Where is it you intend to go?" the Duke asked.

"To a secret place."

The Duke was silent, his mouth clamped shut and his eyes hard. Ping wondered if she was about to experience his more brutal side.

"Will you stop me from leaving, Your Grace?" Ping asked.

The Duke still said nothing. Ping knew she had to stand up to him.

"Your luck will fail if you keep us here against our will, I'm sure of it," she said bluntly.

The servants moving around the hall stopped what they were doing. The guards stiffened and gripped their weapons, waiting for an order. Her sharp words hung in the air. Everyone's eyes were on Ping. Had she gone too far? There was a long, uneasy silence until the Duke spoke.

"Do you think you know Heaven's will?" he asked quietly.

"I know it's my destiny to make this journey," Ping replied.

"There is one sure way to discover what Heaven has in store for us," the Duke said. He motioned to one of his captains and whispered something that Ping couldn't hear. The captain hurried from the hall.

A few minutes later, a man entered. He wore the black robes edged with blue and gold that all of the Duke's advisers wore. In one hand he held a bundle of dried plant stalks all cut to the same length. In the other hand was a bamboo book, its canes dark and shiny from use. He bowed to the Duke. Under his arm were writing implements—calfskin, ink stone, and brush.

"This is my seer," the Duke said.

Ping sighed with relief, but she still regarded the man in black robes with a curious look.

"What is the nature of your enquiry, Your Grace?" the seer asked.

"I want to know if it will be favorable for Ping and the dragon to leave Yan."

"Then it is Ping who must pose the question and divide the stalks," the seer said, bowing again.

The Duke nodded his consent.

The seer knelt at a low table and beckoned Ping to kneel opposite him. The Princess had spoken of this method of divination before, but Ping had never actually seen the process.

"What is your query?" the seer asked.

Ping glanced at the Duke. "Is it favorable for me to take Kai away from Yan?"

The seer laid the bundle of stalks on the table. "These are fifty stalks from the yarrow plant."

Ping knew the plant. It was a common, unlovely herb also known as staunchweed, because it was good for stopping bleeding.

"Select one stalk, and set it aside," the seer said.

Ping did as he asked.

"Now pick up the forty-nine remaining stalks, and divide them into two bundles," the seer said. "Use your left hand."

That was easy for Ping, as she was left-handed. She picked up about half the stalks and separated them from the rest with her thumb.

"Place the two bundles on the table, take a single stalk from the bundle on the right, and place it between the little finger and the second finger of your left hand."

Ping followed his instructions, thinking how silly it was to be planning her future with a bunch of weed stalks.

"Now pick up the left-hand bundle, and, with your right hand, remove them four at a time till four or less are left. Place the remaining stalks between the second and third fingers of your right hand."

Ping fumbled with the stalks, wishing her right hand wasn't so clumsy.

"Now count off the right-hand bundle in the same way, and place the remaining stalks between the third and fourth fingers of your left hand."

Ping concentrated, trying not to drop any. It was difficult to juggle the stalks. When she had finished, her hand resembled a worn-out broom with stalks bristling in all directions.

The seer took the stalks from between the fingers of her left hand and counted them. Then on a piece of calfskin he drew a line.

"The number of stalks determines whether the line I draw is solid or broken," he explained.

He gathered up the uncounted stalks.

"Now we must repeat the process five more times. The resulting lines form a simple diagram—six lines, one on top of the other. This diagram will indicate which of the sixty-four passages I will read from the Yi Jing—The Book of Change."

Ping divided the stalks again, and the seer drew another unbroken line. She divided the stalks for a third time, and he drew a third unbroken line. She divided the stalk three more times. The finished diagram on the calfskin consisted of six strong, unbroken lines.

The seer raised an eyebrow and glanced at the Duke.

"These six solid lines form the diagram known as

*Qian,*" he said. "They represent pure yang. The meaning of the diagram is intense activity."

He put the calfskin aside and opened the bamboo book. He rested his finger on the very first character of the book.

Ping could see the character he was pointing to. She had learned thousands of characters, but she had never seen this one before. Beneath the character were several sentences.

"This is the answer to your query," the seer said. He read the first line aloud. "'At the beginning, a hidden dragon. It is wise to be inactive.'" His finger moved to the second line. "'A dragon in the fields. It is advantageous to meet the great man.'" As he read, he pointed to each line of the diagram on the calfskin, moving from the bottom to the top. The reading was full of dragons. Every line except the third mentioned a dragon.

The seer looked up from the book. "It is a very auspicious divination," he whispered. "The most auspicious."

"But what does it mean?" Ping asked.

"The meaning of each line can only be interpreted by the one who divided the yarrow stalks," the seer said. "But the answer to your question is without doubt that it is favorable for you to leave Yan."

The Duke frowned, and his eyebrows met in the middle. Then he sighed. He couldn't argue with the reading.

"Kai has brought me nothing but good fortune," he said. "To go against such a reading would be folly."

The seer nodded. "You are most wise, Your Grace. Catastrophe would surely follow if you opposed the counsel of the *Yi Jing*."

The seer wrote out the six readings on the calfskin next to the six lines. Then he turned the calfskin over and wrote six more characters on the other side.

"This is the final reading. It is what the book has to say about the diagram as a whole." He folded the piece of calfskin and handed it to Ping. "It is for you only to read."

Ping took the calfskin and started to open it.

"Wait!" the seer said. "You should reread the six lines as your journey progresses. Each one will reveal its wisdom in turn. But I advise you not to look at the final reading now. Read it only when you are faced with your greatest difficulty."

Ping looked down at the folded calfskin. She had hoped their journey would be without difficulties.

"Now we must find out when is the most auspicious day for Ping to leave," the Duke said.

The seer bowed and left the room.

# CHAPTER FOUR

# LEAVING YAN

Ping didn't take part in the ceremony to choose the auspicious day. The seer did that in the privacy of the palace's inner shrine.

The repairs to the palace had been completed, and, later that day, Ping took Kai to the dining hall for the first time in months. Although the weather was still chilly, spring had reached Yan, and the sunny weather was reflected in the mood at Beibai Palace.

Everyone was delighted to have the dragon back among them. Servants brought Kai cushions; the cooks prepared him a special meal. The Duke's wives and sisters made a fuss over Kai. His daughters and the other palace children all wanted to play with the dragon. The women were one minute clucking over Yong Hu, watching him laugh as someone bounced him up and down, the next minute exclaiming over Kai and how much he'd grown. Kai loved being the center of attention and made lots of tinkling wind-chime sounds.

It was more like a party than an ordinary midday meal.

The palace carpenter brought a special back-scratcher that he'd carved over winter for Kai. The dragon often had an itch on his back that he couldn't reach and had knocked over several expensive ornaments and left grubby marks on walls while trying to scratch the spot. The children all took turns scratching the dragon's back with the new backscratcher. The Duke was quieter than the rest of his household as he ate his midday meal. Ping was quiet too.

Halfway through the third course, the seer entered.

"Must you interrupt my meal?" the Duke said, though he was only picking at his food.

"I must, Your Grace," the seer replied. "My message is urgent. There is only one auspicious day for Ping to leave. It is the day after tomorrow."

The mood of the meal soon changed once the news circulated and everyone realized that Kai was going to leave. The servants were complaining, the children were crying, the cook was wondering what he was going to do with all the snails and worms he'd collected for Kai to eat.

"He is going," the Duke said, "whether we like it or not."

Silence descended over the room, broken only by the sniffling of a small child.

The next day and a half passed in a bustle of preparation

as Princess Yangxin supervised the packing of Ping's baggage. Ping didn't object to the piles of clothing and cooking equipment, the boxes of animal furs and cushions, the large tent, and the great quantity of food that was being packed for her and Kai. It was better that the household was occupied. Ping collected more practical things—a jar of red-cloud herb ointment for healing, a good bronze knife, a pair of fire-making sticks.

The Princess gave Ping a roll of calfskin, brush, and ink so that she could write to her. Ping tried to refuse, but the Princess insisted. Yangxin also wanted her to take fine gowns and jewelry. This time Ping was firm.

"A simple gown is best for traveling," she said, selecting a dark green hemp gown with shallow sleeves and simple pale-green silk edging. "And my bamboo square is all the jewelry I need."

"Kai wants to take the backscratcher," the little dragon said. "And plenty of jujubes. And worms."

Ping was telling him they couldn't take any worms when an attendant arrived with a message that the Duke wished to see her in the Peony Hall.

"You will need money for your journey, Ping." The Duke signaled to his administrator, who gave Ping a purse.

"There are some gold pieces," he said. "But gold attracts attention like flies to a dead dog. I have also given you plenty of copper coins for making small purchases."

"That's very kind of you, Your Grace," Ping said.

The Duke smiled at her. "I will miss our poetry readings in the library," he said.

It was a tearful farewell. Ping had made many friends at the palace, and Kai had endeared himself to everyone—from the chief advisers to the kitchen boys. They were all sad to see the pair go. But there was another reason for their sadness, though nobody mentioned it. No one in the palace wanted to see the cause of all their good luck leave. The Duke had done his best to convince the palace's inhabitants that the dragon's departure was the only way to continue their good fortune, but they didn't believe him. Every single person in the palace wanted to touch the dragon one last time for luck.

The Princess was crying again.

"I know you are following your true path, Ping," she said as she hugged her friend. "I am being selfish. I will miss you, and I did so much want Yong Hu to grow up with a dragon."

Before long, their carriage, crammed with enough baggage for a dozen people, was passing through the western gateway of Beibai Palace. Though Ping had been eager to begin the journey, now that she was actually leaving, she was sad to say good-bye to her friends and the place that she had come to call home. She had a feeling she would never return.

The Duke had insisted that they travel with an

armed escort. He had wanted to send six men. Ping had managed to convince him that six soldiers would attract too much attention, and that two soldiers and a driver would be more than enough. She leaned out of the carriage and watched Beibai Palace shrink into the distance. It was unimpressive from the outside. Made of unadorned mud bricks, its blank walls gave no clue as to what lay inside.

Kai was hanging out of the carriage window, making sounds like a cracked bell ringing. But when the palace finally disappeared from sight, he pulled his head into the carriage and settled down quietly with his head in Ping's lap.

The regret Ping had felt was disappearing. She knew the time was right to leave. Her stomach was churning with excitement and anticipation. She remembered the first line of her *Yi Jing* reading. *At the beginning, a hidden dragon. It is wise to be inactive.* Ping had interpreted it to mean that while Kai was submerged in the well, it was all right to stay at the palace. Now that he was not hidden, it followed that it would be unwise to be inactive. To delay any longer would lead to misfortune.

The carriage headed west, passing through bare orchards and the drab, empty fields where plows pulled by oxen were preparing the ground for spring planting. Beyond that were the tussocky grasslands where the battle between the Xiong Nu and the imperial soldiers had taken place only a few weeks earlier.

The road was littered with weapons, boxes of food, and occasionally a dead body, dropped by soldiers in the imperial army to lighten their loads so they could gain more speed as they retreated. A group of the Duke's men was still busy with the grisly task of collecting the dead for burial, piling the broken and bloody bodies of imperial and Yan soldiers onto a wagon. A smashed war chariot lay on its side with one wheel in the air. A dead horse lay rigid, the fatal arrow still sticking out of its chest. Patches of dark dried blood stained the winter-pale grass. Ping wondered how many men had died because of this latest imperial folly.

After an hour, they left the signs of battle behind as the road wound its way through the bleak hills of Yan. The driver had been uneasy when they departed. There was no dot or cross on the map to indicate precisely where Dragon's Lament Creek was. He was used to knowing his exact destination. But Ping felt no fear of this journey. She was the Dragon Keeper, and she meant to do her job properly. With Danzi's map and the *Yi Jing* reading to guide her, she was sure she would find her way to wherever it was they had to go. She had her second sight to warn her of danger. She could summon her *qi* power to protect herself. Whatever difficulties they faced, she was confident that she would be able to overcome them.

Ping stared out the carriage window. The spring rains were overdue, and the hills were dry and yellow.

After so many months of seeing nothing but the inside of courtyards and halls, even these bleak hills seemed beautiful.

When Danzi had first told Ping that she was the true Dragon Keeper, she hadn't believed him. Even though she had all the characteristics—left-handedness, second sight, the ability to hear dragon speech in her head—it still hadn't seemed possible. She was such an insignificant person. How could she be so important? Others had also doubted that she was the true Dragon Keeper. She was, after all, a girl. No other Dragon Keeper in the hundreds of years of imperial history had been female.

Ping had initially been very hesitant and unsure about becoming a Dragon Keeper, but she had grown more confident over time and had finally come to accept that it was her true role.

At first the responsibility of being a Dragon Keeper had been a burden; now it was what Ping wanted to do more than anything in the world. It had been easier than she'd expected to leave behind friends and comfort. She had a job to do, a purpose, a destiny. No amount of fine clothes and good food could replace that.

The first task Danzi had given her as Dragon Keeper was to carry his precious dragon stone to Ocean. He wouldn't tell her why. Their journey across the Empire had been difficult and dangerous. They had been tracked by a dragon hunter who wanted to capture the old dragon for his body parts, which were worth a great deal of gold because of their medicinal and magical properties. Then a shape-changing necromancer had pursued them. Both of these powerful men had tried to take the dragon stone from her. Neither had succeeded. Ping had confronted the dragon hunter, and he had fallen to his death from a peak on Tai Shan.

When they reached Ocean, Ping had finally learned the secret of the purple stone after it cracked open and, to her amazement, a tiny purple dragon slipped out of it. By that time, Danzi was badly wounded, and weary of the world of men. Though his wings were in tatters, he flew off across Ocean to the Isle of the Blest to be healed, leaving her to care for the newborn dragon. Since then she'd had dreams of him, which had helped her find her destined path, but she had never seen Danzi again.

She pulled one of Danzi's scales from the pouch around her waist. She missed the old dragon. She'd discovered that if she held the moonlit dragon scale before she went to sleep, she would dream of him. In her dreams, he always had some words of guidance, though their meaning wasn't always clear. But during her stay at Beibai Palace, her dreams of Danzi had ceased. She had held the scale in the light of a full moon, but her sleep had been dreamless.

"Kai, do you still have dreams of Danzi?" she asked.

The dragon shook his head. "No, Father doesn't visit Kai in dreams anymore."

Ping knew in her heart that the old dragon had died. He had spent a year or so in peace and contentment on the Isle of the Blest, and now his soul had gone to Heaven. Heaven seemed like the proper place for Danzi.

They stopped for the night by what had once been a river. Because of the drought it was now not much more than a stream. The soldiers put up the tent, while the driver lit a fire and prepared a three-course meal served in red-and-black lacquerware bowls. There were two kinds of roasted meat, soup, and dried fruit.

"This is a good way to travel," Kai said as he ate his third roast pheasant.

Ping wasn't so sure. She would have preferred to slip through the landscape unnoticed like a leopard.

The Princess had given Ping a white nightgown. She felt silly changing into this delicate embroidered garment out in the wilderness, but she had to admit it was comfortable to sleep in. Kai slept in the tent with her, but where Ping slept under her warm bearskin, Kai curled up on top of his.

The next morning, it took more than an hour for the driver to prepare breakfast, and even longer for him to pack up the tent. The soldiers didn't travel inside the carriage. One sat up front with the driver, while the other stood on the back. Ping was left to pass the hours listening to Kai chatter on about anything that came into his scaly head.

Kai didn't need to be entertained as he had when they'd traveled in a carriage before. He didn't ask to play games. When he wasn't speaking, he seemed content to look out of the window. Ping was pleased they were making such good progress. After putting off the journey for such a long time, she was eager to find the dragon haven as soon as possible. At this rate they would reach the area where Long Dao Xi was marked on the map in a week or two. She hadn't wanted to travel in a carriage at first, but now she appreciated the speed with which the landscape was slipping past her window.

During the afternoon, the sun made Ping pleasantly warm. The motion of the carriage was soothing. She was dozing off when Kai jumped to his feet.

"Stop the carriage!" he shouted.

The driver couldn't understand the dragon, but the sound of crashing copper bowls that Kai made was so alarming that he stopped anyway. He reined in the horses so suddenly that Ping slipped off her cushion onto the carriage floor.

"What's the matter, Kai?" she said. "We're not due to stop to eat for hours yet. Do you need to pee?"

Kai pointed a talon into the distance. One of the

soldiers opened the carriage door. The dragon leaped
out and ran off across the plain.

"What's wrong with him, madam?" said one of the
soldiers. "Is he injured?"

"He's seen something." Ping scanned the landscape.
"Dragons can see much farther than we can."

Danzi had told her that dragons could see a mustard
seed from one hundred *li* away. She could see nothing
but tussocks of dry grass, but she got down from the
carriage and hurried after him. Kai stopped at a particular clump of grass about half a *li* away. It looked the
same as all the others.

"There'd better be a good reason for making us
stop," Ping said. She was out of breath. She'd done a lot
of things during her time at Beibai Palace, but none of
them involved running. "If I find out it's just a lizard or
a colored stone, I'll—"

Ping's words died in her mouth. There was something behind the tussock. It was a body, a twisted
corpse lying facedown in the dust. An arrow was sticking out of its thigh.

Kai made sounds like a cracked bell.

The soldiers came up behind them. "We've seen
quite a few bodies since we left the palace," one of
them said. "Why is he so concerned about this one?"

"Turn the body over," she said to the soldiers.

The soldiers looked at each other dubiously, but did
as Ping asked them. She knelt down next to the body.

The face was cut and swollen, caked in dust. There was an old scar that cut through the right eyebrow.

The soldiers stood staring at the dirty, blood-stained body.

"He's past help," one of them said. "The burial squad will find him eventually."

The man was wearing the red leather tunic and leg guards worn by all imperial guards. But Ping knew his chariot would have been marked with red bat and blue crane symbols. His horses would have had yellow plumes on their bridles. There should have been mounted soldiers surrounding him, carrying yellow banners proclaiming his rank, but they were nowhere to be seen. There was nothing to distinguish him from any common soldier.

"Don't you know who this is?" Ping said.

The soldiers shook their heads.

Kai squatted at her side.

"Lu-lu," the dragon said softly.

Ping nodded. "It's the Emperor."

# CHAPTER FIVE

# HEALING

"Poor Lu-lu," Kai said.

"How can you feel sorry for him?" Ping remembered the last time she'd seen the Emperor, and hatred seethed inside her like coiling snakes. He had ordered her execution. But worse than that, far worse, was his cruelty to Kai.

Ping touched Kai's shoulder. "Did you know it was the Emperor when you saw his body?"

"Didn't know. Kai saw what he was holding in his hand."

Ping knelt at the Emperor's side. His right hand was clasped around something. It was encrusted with dried blood and dust. She reached out and touched the Emperor's hand, but then pulled away again as if she'd been stung by nettles. After a few moments, she reached out again. This time, she uncurled the Emperor's fingers one by one so that she could take the object he was holding. It was thin and just a few inches long. It could have been the end of a spear or a fragment of clay pot, but when Ping wiped it with her sleeve, its true color was revealed. It was purple and as shiny as if it had been made from some sort of gemstone. It was a shard of dragon stone, a piece of the egg from which Kai had hatched.

She looked at the Emperor's dirty, bruised face. He had been her friend once, but he had betrayed their friendship. She could have easily walked away and left him for the burial squad. It was what he deserved. But she knew she'd regret it if she did.

Ping grasped the arrow sticking out of the Emperor's thigh and pulled with both hands. She could feel the flesh resisting. The soldiers watched in horror, wondering what sort of person would pull an arrow from a corpse. The barbed head of the arrow was designed to penetrate flesh, not to be pulled out. Ping took her bronze knife from her pouch and made an incision in the Emperor's leg. Dark blood oozed from the wound. As she drew out the arrow, a low groan escaped from the Emperor's mouth. Ping threw the bloody arrow aside, undid the Emperor's shoulder buckles, and pulled off his leather armor. She slit open his clothing, revealing his other wounds. The spear wound in his stomach was the worst. It was deep and ugly.

"Did Ping know Lu-lu was still alive?" Kai asked.

Ping nodded. "I knew when I took the shard from

him. His hand was warm." She turned to the dragon. "You didn't know?"

"No."

Ping looked up at the soldiers. "We must carry him back to the carriage." She instructed them to cut down a small, dead tree and make a stretcher. She was getting quite used to ordering soldiers around.

The driver was still staring at the gaping wound. He was young and had probably never seen a spear wound before.

"Find some staunchweed," Ping said. "Pick as much as you can."

"I . . . I don't know what it looks like," he stammered.

"Kai will show you."

The driver looked at the dragon doubtfully.

"Hurry," Ping shouted.

Kai ran off, and the soldier followed him. Ping was glad she had learned the uses of herbs from the Duke's herbalist and taught Kai to recognize some.

"Be gentle," Ping said as they lifted the Emperor onto the stretcher, then stumbled over the uneven ground. They put him down next to the carriage.

She turned to the soldiers. "Light a fire. Heat up some water."

The soldiers hurried off to collect firewood.

Ping filled a cup with wine, supported the Emperor's head, and dribbled the liquid into his mouth.

The soldiers built a small fire and placed a pot of water on top. As soon as the water was warm, Ping cleaned the Emperor's wounds. She found her jar of red-cloud herb ointment and smeared the sticky balm over the gashes on his face, arms, and legs. When Kai and the driver returned with the staunchweed, she packed the wounds with some of the leaves. The rest she threw into the pot of hot water—tea made from the herb would help keep fever at bay. Ping hadn't expected to need knowledge of healing herbs on the second day of their journey. She pulled the nightgown from her bag and tore it into strips, which she used to bandage the Emperor's wounds.

When the tent was erected, the soldiers gently moved the Emperor inside. Ping put one of Kai's cushions under his head and brought rugs from the carriage to cover him. Ping sent the soldiers off to hunt for food, and they soon returned with a rabbit and a pheasant. The driver made stew with the meat and flavored it with kitchen herbs that Kai had found. They ate the meal in silence.

A cough woke Ping during the night. She knew it was neither of the soldiers. Even though one of them was supposed to be on guard at all times, they were both snoring outside the tent. The driver was asleep in the carriage. Kai was sleeping as well. Ping threw off her bearskin and went over to the Emperor. He coughed again. She lifted his head and gave him some of the staunchweed tea sweetened with a little honey. He swallowed and opened his eyes. Ping wasn't sure whether she was pleased or disappointed that he had revived.

"Are you dead too, Ping?" he asked.

"No," she replied sharply. "Neither of us is dead."

He tried to turn his head to see where he was, but even such a small movement made him groan with pain.

Ping looked at his bruised and bloodied face. He would have other scars to go with the familiar one that cut through his right eyebrow. His hair was hanging on his shoulders in tangled clumps. He didn't look at all imperial. She could see conflicting emotions in his dark eyes—pain from his wounds, relief at being alive, confusion at finding himself with his head resting on her lap.

"Have you saved my life, Ping?"

"It wasn't me who found you. It was Kai."

"Kai," he whispered.

He drank more tea and sank into sleep again.

Ping stayed awake.

The first time she'd met the Emperor, on the banks of the Yellow River, he had been a cheerful boy of fifteen years. They had become good friends, and she was truly sorry when she had to escape with Danzi against the Emperor's wishes. The second time they met, circumstances were different. She was under arrest for stealing the imperial dragon. It was less than a year later, but the Emperor had changed. He'd become preoccupied by a desire to live a long life. That desire had gradually become an obsession to live forever, at whatever cost—even if the cost was Kai's life. All his energy had gone into working with scientists and shamans to achieve this. But their schemes and elixirs had produced the opposite effect. Beneath the grime of war, his hollowed cheeks and sunken eyes made him look much older than his seventeen years.

Later in the night, the Emperor woke again and slowly, haltingly, told Ping what had happened. After his defeat, the Xiong Nu had allowed him to retreat until he was far ahead of his troops. Then they had circled around him and his squad of personal guards. There were only six barbarians against his twenty soldiers, but his men were confused by the enemy's constant circling. They had been taught to shoot while on one knee. This technique wasn't very effective against a moving target. One by one the Xiong Nu had picked them off. The Emperor had been forced to flee with the only two guards who had survived.

"My driver was dead," he told Ping. "I drove the chariot myself. They shot me in the leg. I couldn't even stop to remove the arrow. I forced the horses to gallop for hours until I was sure I had left the barbarians behind."

He paused to catch his breath; just speaking about

his ordeal tired him. "But they followed me. They shot at my exhausted horses, killing one of them. The other horse kept running. The chariot overturned. I was tangled up in the wreckage and dragged along the ground. When the horse finally stopped, they speared me to finish me off."

"Didn't your men come to your aid?" Ping asked.

The Emperor made a small movement with his head.

"I watched them flee. At first I thought they had gone for help. After a while, I realized no one was coming back for me. They had left me to die. I found the strength to stand, and stumbled in a direction I hoped was away from my enemies. But I had lost too much of my life's blood. I don't remember falling."

He looked at Ping. "The next thing I knew, you were at my side."

Ping avoided his eyes. She didn't want to feel sorry for him. She scooped up a cup of broth from the stew, which was still warm over the dying embers of the fire. He couldn't sit up. She had to support his head and hold the cup to his mouth.

Kai turned over in his sleep.

"I'm sorry for what I did to Kai," the Emperor said. "And to you."

Ping finally looked into his eyes. "You're sorry now as you lie here in the darkness, far from your servants, close enough to death that it might still reach out and take you." Her bitterness spilled out. "You won't be so repentant when you return to your imperial life."

She waited for anger to flare in his eyes. It didn't. He winced as a salty tear ran into a gash on his face.

Ping remembered how he had bled Kai until the little dragon was too weak to stand, just so he could use the dragon blood in his elixir of immortality. She remembered his eyes as he blamed her for everything that he had brought upon himself.

"I don't believe you can change that much. You are the Son of Heaven, everyone bows to your will. You tax your subjects heavily to pay for your search for immortality, even though they're already struggling to feed their families because of the lack of rain. You think you have the right to use people as if they are tools, then you throw them away like broken arrows."

Most people were forbidden to speak directly to the Emperor. Speaking to him in this way could have resulted in a death sentence—if there had been anyone to hear. She waited for him to defend himself. He said nothing.

"The people of the Empire are your subjects, but to get the best out of them you must treat them well. Even the humblest gardener knows that he has to feed and water his plants to make them thrive. Give them any less than what they need and they'll yield less fruit. If you want your people to serve you well, you must nurture them—with food, and with thanks.

Punishment and ill-treatment will never make them achieve their best."

The Emperor licked his dry lips before he spoke. "Before I woke, I was dreaming of a golden dragon descending from the sky to take me to Heaven. I would be dead if it weren't for you, Ping. My search for immortality was pointless. Heaven decides the time to live and die—even for me. I am truly sorry for what I did to you and Kai."

Ping's raised voice had woken Kai. He got up to pee and then came over to see how the Emperor was.

"Lu-lu looks better," the dragon said, making happy tinkling sounds.

"Can you forgive him after what he did to you?" Ping asked.

The dragon nodded his head. The Emperor couldn't understand the dragon's sounds, but from Kai's soft tone and the look in his brown eyes, he knew that he had been forgiven. Kai yawned and went back to his bed.

Ping turned the dragon-stone shard over in her hands. She had washed it, and it shone in the lamplight. "Why were you carrying this?"

"I thought it would bring me luck," he said.

A mirthless smile twisted Ping's mouth. "It didn't."

She felt the sharp end of the shard with a fingertip.

"I don't expect you to forgive me, Ping," the Emperor said. "Not yet, anyway."

He reached out and took her hand in his. "The shard did bring me luck. I am alive, and I have changed. If Heaven grants me a safe return to Chang'an, I will abandon my quest to live forever. I already have. I am content with however many years of life Heaven chooses to give me. I will call back the expedition searching for the fungus of immortality. All my attention will be on ruling the Empire well, for the good of all my people."

Ping pulled her hand from his and checked the bandage on his leg wound.

"I hope that in time, when you see that I have truly changed, you will forgive me. Death has breathed in my face. I have learned the value of true friendship. It is precious. I won't discard it again. Not ever."

"You've given me your friendship before and then snatched it back."

"I'm offering you more than friendship, Ping."

She put fresh staunchweed on his stomach wound. "I don't want an imperial position, it's not my destiny."

The Emperor smiled. It made his lip crack and bleed. "I'm not offering you a job, either. I'm offering you my heart."

Ping looked at him in surprise.

"You are strong and good," the Emperor said. "The only true friend I've ever had. Will you come with me, to be at my side for life—however long that might be?"

Ping tried to hold on to her hatred, but she couldn't

stop images forming in her head—of the time she had spent with Liu Che at Ming Yang Lodge. He was just a boy then, with a beautiful smile and eyes that sparkled with the pleasure of life. They had walked together as the petals of spring blossom drifted in the breeze. He had given her unexpected friendship, something no other person had ever given her before then. For the first time, she admitted to herself that her feelings for the Emperor had been more than friendship. Now he was offering her a place at his side. Not as an Empress, of course—an ex-slave could never sit on the imperial throne—but he was offering her his love for his lifetime.

She gently squeezed his hand and smiled at him for the first time in a long while.

"Once I would have been filled with joy at such a proposal," she said softly. "I did love you once, Liu Che, but not anymore. I can never forget what you did to Kai. I am taking him away from the world of men. You might no longer wish him ill, but there will always be others who do."

"Isn't it time you did what you want to do, Ping? Haven't you served others long enough?"

"This *is* what I want to do."

"Are you refusing my offer?"

"Yes."

He didn't argue. He closed his eyes. The conversation had drained away the little strength that he had. He slept. Ping felt suddenly very tired, too. It was not long until dawn, but an hour or two of sleep would be better than none. Kai's scales were glowing faintly in a band of moonlight. She went to him, touched his scales gently, and he stirred.

"Is Lu-lu all right?"

"Yes, he'll be fine."

Kai turned over and went back to sleep. Ping pulled her bearskin around her, letting the sleep drag her into unconsciousness, like the powerful pull of the tide.

# CHAPTER SIX

# NEW HORIZONS

The next morning, Ping unloaded all the baggage from the carriage.

"What are you doing, Ping?" the Emperor asked.

He was still pale, still far too weak to stand, but his eyes were clear and bright.

"You need to be in the care of physicians. The soldiers must take you to Beibai Palace."

"I don't know if I will be welcome there," he said.

"Your sister will receive you with open arms."

"Won't you come with me?" he asked.

"There isn't enough room for us all. Kai and I will wait here until the soldiers return, then we will continue on our journey."

"Where are you going?"

"We're going to a place where no one can find us."

"Where is this place?"

"I don't know."

"You'll never trust me, will you?"

"It's not a matter of trust. I really don't know where we're going. Danzi sent me a map, but it isn't clear."

"Show me, I might be able to help."

"I can read now, Liu Che, I don't need your help."

Ping felt a slight tug at her waist. She turned and discovered Kai pulling the silk square from her pouch.

"Kai!" she exclaimed. "What are you doing?" She snatched the silk square back.

"Kai trusts me, even if you don't," the Emperor said. "Lu-lu might know where Dragon's Lament Creek is."

"He doesn't know every place in the Empire," Ping hissed at the dragon. "And I don't want him to know we're looking for Long Dao Xi." She stopped abruptly. She had been speaking aloud.

"What did you say?" Liu Che asked. "You're taking Kai to a robber's ravine?"

Ping was relieved he'd misheard. "No, I told you, I don't know where we're going exactly."

The Emperor sighed. The soldiers lifted him into the carriage.

"There's one more thing I have to ask you, Liu Che."

The Emperor turned his head toward her.

"What happened to Jun?"

"Who?"

"The boy who was pretending to be a Dragon Keeper. The one who you made Imperial Dragon Keeper when you imprisoned me." Ping waited for anger to bubble up inside her again, but it didn't.

The Emperor didn't answer straightaway. He swallowed. "I don't know."

"You didn't have him executed?"

"No, but I can't remember what happened to him. I'm sorry, Ping."

The horses were harnessed to the carriage. The driver took his seat.

"I owe my life to you," the Emperor said.

Kai bounded up to say good-bye.

"I wish you well on your journey, Kai, wherever it is you're going. I will issue a decree forbidding dragon hunting anywhere in the Empire."

Kai made his tinkling wind-chime sound.

"May Heaven protect you both," the Emperor said.

Under the cuts and bruises, Ping could see the handsome face of her friend again.

She leaned over and kissed him on the cheek. "I'm glad we met again," she said.

One of the soldiers shut the carriage door.

"Drive slowly," Ping said to the driver. "And take the smoothest way, not the quickest."

She waved good-bye.

"Bye-bye, Lu-lu," Kai said sadly.

Ping watched the carriage slowly trundle away until it disappeared from sight. Kai was busy chasing butterflies, jumping over rocks, and pouncing on tussocks of grass. She smiled. It was good to see him carefree and with space to play. She remembered the second line of her divination. *A dragon in the fields. It is advantageous to meet the great man.*

There was Kai chasing butterflies in the field. They had met a great man—the most powerful man in the Empire. It had certainly been an advantageous meeting for him. He would have died if Kai hadn't found him. If he did keep his promise and concentrated on ruling well, then it would be advantageous for the whole Empire. But the meeting had also been good for Ping. The anger and hatred had left her. Such bitter feelings could poison like dirt in a wound. It was good to be rid of them. A shard of dragon stone had been returned to her as well. It had proved useful before, strengthening her second sight. It might well be useful again. The soldiers had left, too. Perhaps that was also a good thing.

The pile of baggage and the colorful tent looked out of place on the bleak plain, as if they had dropped unexpectedly from the sky. There were six baskets of food, a chest of clothing, several large jars of wine, rugs, cushions, and cooking pots. It was a ridiculous mound of baggage for one girl and one small dragon. Ping started unpacking. From her clothing chest, she pulled out another pair of shoes, some socks, a jacket, and a pair of trousers. From the basket of cooking equipment, she retrieved a small pot, a pair of chopsticks, a cup, and two bowls. From the food supplies, she took bags of grain and lentils, some dried bean curd, a jar of plum sauce, dried fruit, nuts, and powdered ginger for flavoring hot water. She also pulled out two small bearskin rugs, a water bag, her knife, the jar of red-cloud herb ointment, and the fire-making sticks. Kai stopped to watch her.

"Ping isn't waiting for the carriage?" he asked.

"No," Ping replied. "We're going to go on by ourselves, just you and me."

"That's good," the dragon said.

Ping scratched him under the chin. "You don't mind?"

He shook his head. "Just Kai and Ping."

Ping packed their things into a leather saddlebag. She had always intended to dismiss the soldiers before they reached their destination, but hadn't suspected that it would be so soon. Kai looked wistfully at the things they were leaving behind.

"Not taking any cushions?" he asked.

Ping shook her head.

"No backscratcher?"

Ping laughed. "No."

She hoisted the saddlebag onto her shoulder. It was very heavy. She put it down again.

"I'll have to take something out," she said.

She pulled out the spare pair of shoes and a bag of jujubes.

"Must take the jujubes!" said Kai.

"But the bag's too heavy," Ping said.

"Kai will carry the bag."

Ping argued that he wouldn't be able to manage it,

but he insisted. She strapped the saddlebag just behind his shoulders. It fit surprisingly well. She repacked the shoes and jujubes.

It was a cold morning. A strong wind whipped up dust. Ping put on her cloak and pulled up the hood. They set off. Kai's ears drooped. He was nearly two now. He had changed a great deal in the time they had been at Beibai Palace, growing from a dragonling to the young dragon who was walking alongside her. He carried the bag without complaining and easily kept pace with her.

"It's good to finally start our journey," Ping said.

Kai made a tinkling sound. She was glad he agreed.

The hills that had looked soft and low through the carriage window seemed steeper now that they were climbing them on foot. Ping's leg muscles were aching before midday. Most of the time Kai walked at her side, but sometimes he scampered off, darting this way and that as he played some game or other. When he wandered too far away, she flashed her mirror and he came back to her side.

"What were you playing?" she asked.

"Looking for dragon stones," he replied.

Ping felt a stab of sorrow. Kai had never said so, but she guessed he'd be lonely when they reached the dragon haven. He'd had many human friends at the palace; he'd had dogs to chase, goats to annoy. She'd never considered that he might also yearn for the company of other young dragons. She pulled out the silk square and peered at it. Was that what they would find? Another dragon egg? Perhaps a cache of dragon stones? Now that she knew about raising a baby dragon, rearing a whole brood of them would be no trouble at all. In fact, she would enjoy it.

As she walked, Ping thought about Danzi and the long journey they had made together. They had traveled from the western border of the Empire to where it ended in the east on the shores of Ocean. The Empire was green and lush when she had traveled with Danzi. Now it was dusty and dry from lack of rain.

Danzi was a dragon of few words, but his son was a chatterbox. As they walked, Kai talked endlessly. He pointed out interesting things—a hill shaped like a sleeping animal, a snaking riverbed, a large bird's nest. Because of his exceptional eyesight, most of the things he indicated were too far away for Ping to see. He also enjoyed recounting his own adventures, most of which Ping already knew about, though she would occasionally discover some mischief that he had caused at Ming Yang Lodge or at Beibai Palace when her back had been turned. The only time he stopped talking was when someone approached them on the road and he had to shape-change. Ping was glad Kai had mastered this dragon skill. She didn't want to attract any attention.

Ping was also relieved Kai had grown out of the

stage where he constantly asked questions. Now he preferred to show her how clever he was—naming plants, birds, and animals—and telling her how brave he would be if they met a tiger or a dragon hunter. Ping grunted occasionally to show that she was listening, though much of the time her thoughts were elsewhere.

As Kai recounted the story of how he'd been stuck inside a vase at Ming Yang Lodge, more than half of Ping's attention was on what they would eat for their evening meal. She saw a slight movement out of the corner of her eye. It looked like something had fallen from the saddlebag. She stopped and looked back.

"Did you drop something, Kai?" she asked.

"No," the dragon replied.

"Are you sure?"

As she checked the ties on the bag, she noticed something lying on the road behind them. She went back to pick it up. It was one of Kai's purple scales.

"Are you feeling all right?" she asked anxiously, hurrying back to the dragon and feeling the tips of his ears. "Do you have a fever?"

"Kai is feeling well."

He scratched himself behind his left shoulder. Another scale fell off.

"Is it the bag? It must be rubbing your scales and making them fall out."

"No, Kai's scales are tough, like a soldier's armor."

Ping made the dragon sit down while she looked at

his tongue, felt his pulse at each ankle, and peered into his eyes. He seemed to be perfectly healthy. As she examined his scales, another one came off in her hand.

"What's happening to you, Kai?" exclaimed Ping, now very alarmed. "Why are your scales falling out?"

"Molting," Kai said calmly.

"Molting?"

"Like goats losing their winter coat. Like a snake changing its skin."

Ping looked closer at the part of the dragon's hide where this latest scale had fallen out. In the space between the hard, leathery purple scales there was a soft new one. It was pale green and shimmered when it caught the sun. There were more pale green patches where the other scales had fallen out.

"You're changing color," Ping said in amazement. "The purple scales must be your baby scales."

Kai twisted his neck and lifted his leg to try and see. He lost his balance and fell over. He rolled onto his back, but still couldn't get a glimpse of his new scales.

"What color are they?" he asked.

"Green," Ping said. "A beautiful, soft green like new spring grass."

Kai made tinkling sounds. "Same as Father," he said.

She smiled. "Yes. The same as Danzi."

He dug a hole and scooped the purple scales into it, then covered them over with dirt.

"What are you doing?"

"Don't want people to find scales."

Ping set a fast pace, but their progress was much slower than when they had been in the carriage. At the palace she'd grown used to getting whatever she wanted as soon as she spoke it aloud. Now she would have to learn to be patient all over again.

Late in the afternoon, they were walking through a sparsely-wooded area. Buds, already turning brown at their tips, were struggling to open on the spindly trees. There was no spring grass to cushion their steps. Last year's dry yellow grass crunched beneath their feet. Flowers should have been opening, but there were none. Kai suddenly stopped and sniffed the air. He looked into the empty wilderness, peering at a particular tree.

"What?" asked Ping anxiously. "Do you see danger? Can you smell something?"

The sound of tinkling wind chimes rang out. "Swallows!" he said, and ran off.

Kai's favorite food was also the same as his father's. His hunting techniques, however, needed improvement. His lumbering approach gave the swallows plenty of warning. There was no tasty bird for dinner that night. Ping was disappointed. She had developed quite a taste for roasted swallow herself. They ate a decent meal of bean curd and grain, but they were both used to the palace banquets. The meal didn't fill Kai up. He managed to catch some moths, but he was much too big to be satisfied by a few insects. He poked his head into the saddlebag.

"Any baked quails?" he asked hopefully.

Ping shook her head.

"Honey cakes?"

"No."

The spines along the dragon's back drooped. Another scale fell out.

"You can have a jujube," Ping said. "Just one."

She handed him the dried fruit and took one for herself.

Lumps of dirt suddenly flew in her direction, striking her on the face and collecting in her lap. Ping had never seen Kai make a nest before. First he dug a hole with his strong front talons—taking great care that it was just the right size for his coiled body, but paying no attention to where the excavated soil went. Then he collected dried grass and leaves to fill the hole and laid his bearskin on top. Finally he jumped onto the bed and wriggled around until it was comfortable. He was soon asleep.

The sky was clear. It had been a long time since Ping had been out in the open at night. The black sky, studded with countless stars, was huge compared to the square of night sky she'd grown used to seeing above the courtyard at Beibai Palace. The vast blackness surrounded her. It made her feel as small as an ant, and sucked away her daytime confidence. What exactly was she doing? Wandering in unknown lands, following the puzzling directions of an absent and ancient dragon scribbled hastily on a scrap of fabric, guided by a riddle obtained by juggling plant stalks. It was as if she were looking for one particular star among the many thousands. In the darkening night, she wasn't so sure that she could find it.

Ping huddled into her bearskin. The clear sky also meant that it was a cold night. Though she didn't miss the spines sticking into her side, she did miss the dragon's warmth. She could hear snoring coming from Kai's nest. She considered digging her own hole to sleep in, but she was too weary. She pulled the bearskin around her. She would have to get used to sleeping out in the open all over again.

· CHAPTER SEVEN ·

## PRAYERS AND PLEAS

On the whole, Ping liked being out in the countryside again, with no one but herself and Kai deciding when they ate and slept. Palace life had been comfortable, but it was confined and unvaried, and she was often bored. She preferred a life that kept pace with the slow march of the sun across the sky. The constant search for the next meal, somewhere to fill the water bag, a comfortable place to sleep. She enjoyed the pleasure of discovery as she caught sight of a plant or a new species of bird she'd never seen before. Just the way the color of the earth gradually changed was a delight. Every day there was a new horizon.

Over the next few days, Ping estimated that they traveled about a hundred *li*. It was a good pace, but they were still at least two weeks from reaching Dragon's Lament Creek. They hadn't followed the main road. Ping wanted to avoid contact with people as much as possible, and she didn't want the Duke's

soldiers to find them again. The track they were traveling on skirted a small hill. A few goats were searching
for any remaining blades of grass on its brown slopes.

Ping heard voices ahead of them. The dragon, whose
hearing wasn't as sharp as hers, hadn't heard anything.

"Quick, Kai, shape-change!" she hissed. "Someone's
approaching."

The air around the dragon began to shimmer. Ping
looked away while the transformation took place.
Watching a dragon shape-change made her feel sick.
When she looked back, instead of a purple dragon,
there was a young boy aged about six. It was an image
of Ping's own brother. Kai had never met him. The
dragon had copied the memory she had of her brother
from the last time she had seen him. It was Kai's
favorite image when shape-changing.

Ping put her hand on the shoulder of the young boy
standing beside her. Though her fingers appeared to
rest on the smooth cloth of the boy's robe, she actually
felt the rough texture of dragon scales. Three people
appeared on the track in front of them. Ping got ready
to greet them politely and then quickly continue on her
way. When they caught sight of her and the boy, they
stopped and stared, whispering loudly to each other.
Then they turned and ran back the way they had come.

"Don't change back yet, Kai," Ping told the dragon.
"They might be coming back."

They rounded the hill and found a crowd of people

waiting for them. They seemed very pleased to see the strangers. The people were dressed in worn gowns, and the children were dirty. Their fields were just dusty, brown squares of earth. Their only crop consisted of some wilted winter greens, but they were smiling as they led Ping and Kai to their small village.

The village gates were open, and what looked like the entire population of the village was rushing out to meet them. They lined both sides of the track, cheering and waving colored silk scarves. Ping couldn't understand why they were making such a fuss.

The village elder, a wrinkled old man with a stooped back and a limp, stepped forward. His pale, watery eyes were fixed on the young boy at Ping's side. She pulled Kai toward her, but the old man's knobbly fingers reached out and touched the boy's shoulder. Ping knew he was feeling a rough, scaly hide instead of the robes of a young boy. She waited for him to collapse unconscious, which was the usual reaction when someone unexpectedly touched a shape-changed dragon. But the elder didn't pass out. His thin lips pulled apart in a smile, pushing aside the wrinkles on his face to make room for a set of stained teeth.

"It's the dragon!" he shouted. "He's come to answer our prayers!"

"How did you know he was a dragon?" Ping asked.

"News spreads even to our humble village," the elder said. "Word came from Beibai Palace to look out

71

for a young girl and a dragon in the shape of a boy."

Ping realized for the first time that if someone knew they were touching a shape-changed dragon, they would have no reaction.

People cheered and pushed forward, all wanting to touch the dragon for luck. Other hands grabbed Ping's sleeves and pulled her toward the village gates. There were still several hours of daylight left. She had planned on walking until nightfall.

"We have a long way to travel," Ping protested. "We can't stop."

"You must stay and eat with us. Bless our humble village with a visit."

The smell of something delicious wafted through the gates, and Ping's resolve melted away. Since they all knew who the boy at her side was, there didn't seem any point in Kai staying shape-changed. The villagers gasped and looked a little queasy as he transformed, but once he was in his dragon shape, they cheered even louder.

"Welcome, dragon! Welcome, dragon-girl!" they shouted.

It had been a week since anyone had made a fuss over Kai. He was quite happy to be the center of attention again.

They were taken to the elder's house and invited to sit in front of a blazing fire. A smiling woman gave Ping wine and Kai a bowl of goat's milk. Then they were given dishes of gruel followed by stewed melon sweetened with honey.

Ping learned that the villagers had been watching for them ever since word arrived that the dragon had left the palace. News of the dragon that lived at Beibai Palace had apparently spread throughout Yan. Ping guessed that the soldiers had something to do with that. Every village had to provide a certain number of soldiers to protect Yan, and when they returned home they were forbidden to talk of the dragon. But it seemed that few of them had obeyed this rule. The villagers knew all about Kai's antics at the palace. Everyone wanted a chance to touch the lucky dragon before he left Yan for good.

"We were rationing our food, preparing for another bad year, but now that the dragon has come to bring rain, we can celebrate," the elder said. "The Duke promised to send us grain so that we don't go hungry, but I will send a message to say we won't be needing it."

"You mustn't do that," Ping said, but no one took any notice.

The food was simple fare compared to what they had eaten at the palace, but it was tasty, and there was plenty of it.

"Kai can't make it rain," the dragon said to Ping.

"I know," said Ping. "But they think you can. Even if we tell them you can't, they probably won't believe us."

She felt guilty that the villagers believed Kai could bring rain, but nothing she said would convince them otherwise. Danzi had made it rain once. He had flown above a cloud, and, by spitting on it, he had made the rain fall. But Kai would need two things to achieve this—wings and clouds. He had neither. Dragons could make rain fall from existing clouds, but they couldn't conjure rain from nothing.

That evening, all the villagers, adults and children alike, gathered to hear Ping tell her story. Since they were feeding her and giving her the best accommodation in the village, Ping didn't feel she could refuse. Everyone sat spellbound as she told the story of her and Danzi's journey to Ocean. She described Kai's birth. The villagers gasped as she told them of her dealings with the necromancer.

Ping was exhausted, but no one seemed to notice. Kai was curled up asleep on the pile of animal skins that had been brought for him to sit on. Small children gradually gathered up the courage to tiptoe forward and touch his scales.

Ping showed the villagers Danzi's scale and her Dragon Keeper's mirror. They were passed from hand to hand, touched reverently. The village elder stepped forward.

"Could you tell us just one more tale?" he asked. "The tale of your flight from Huangling Palace, perhaps?"

A woman handed back the mirror. Ping fingered it. It was warm from so much handling.

"I really am tired," she said. She was almost asleep standing up.

As she rolled the mirror in her hands, it caught the firelight, and a beam of orange light reflected into the elder's eyes.

"She's too tired," the old man said. "We must let her rest."

Ping was surprised that he'd given in so quickly. There were groans of disappointment, but no one argued with the elder. A woman led her to a room. Ping sank gratefully onto a straw mattress.

This was the sort of reception they would get everywhere on their journey. Word would spread before them wherever they went, even if the villages were few and far between. The elder of this village had relatives that lived outside Yan. He had already let them know of the dragon's approach. Villages would be vying for the privilege of having the dragon visit them, so that he would bring them the gift of rain. But Ping knew that if the spring rains didn't arrive, their joy would soon turn to anger.

She took out the calfskin with the *Yi Jing* divination on it and read the third line in the lamplight. *Active and vigilant all day. In the evening alert. All will be well.* They should be traveling quietly, attracting as little attention as possible. No one should know that Kai was a dragon.

Instead, their journey would be like a festival. Though the villagers meant them no harm, there was always the chance that the news would reach someone who was not as honest and well-meaning. It would only take one person with visions of becoming rich by selling a dragon to a sorcerer, and then Kai would be in danger again. Ping tried to think how she could stop this from happening, but she fell into a deep sleep before she came up with even one strategy.

The next morning, the sun was high before they managed to get away. The whole village was out to wish them farewell. Ping gave the elder one of Kai's fallen scales to thank him for his hospitality. The old man held it in his hands as if it were made of gold.

"We will pray to the dragon," he said, "and he will bring us rain."

Ping waved good-bye.

In the comfort and safety of Beibai Palace, Ping had put her past adventures behind her and given them little thought. Time had softened the memories, making them less threatening. But as she recounted them, she was reminded of the powerful enemies she and Danzi had attracted. A dragon hunter, a necromancer, and the Emperor himself had all tried to strip Ping of her authority as Dragon Keeper. They had all attempted to capture her dragons—first Danzi and then Kai.

As she walked the bare hills on the edge of Yan,

she was glad that she no longer had to fear those enemies. It was as if a sack of grain she had been carrying for years had been lifted from her shoulders. She believed that Liu Che would keep his word and would not try to capture Kai again. The dragon hunter was long dead. She and her friends—Jun, Hua, Kai, and Dong Fang Suo, the Imperial Magician—had taken away all the necromancer's powers, and he had poisoned his body with his own spells. He would be dead now, as well.

She would still have to watch out for bandits and wild animals, but she was sure no one was searching for Kai. She didn't have to keep looking over her shoulder.

All she had to do was keep out of the way of villagers eager for rain. When they crossed the dry hills, they were visible for several *li*. There was nothing to hide them, and the villagers would be on the lookout for a young woman with a boy.

"Keep your dragon sight alert, Kai," Ping said. "If you see anyone, you must shape-change. We must try to travel in secret."

When Ping scanned the horizon she could see no one, but Kai was always spotting a farmer or a goatherd in the distance. His skills at shape-changing had improved. He could take the form of anything he chose—a basket, a boy, a bush—and stay that way for many hours if need be, though it did make him weary.

Ping tried to find other ways to travel without being

seen. They walked through the night and slept by day. They avoided villages and remote farms. But it didn't make any difference. Somehow news of their approach always went before them. A welcoming party would always track them down and lead them to another village, another simple banquet, another telling of their tales. Kai soon grew tired of all the attention as the villagers begged him to make it rain.

Although Ping was sure that no one was hunting Kai, her mind was still not at ease. One morning, after they had left a tiny village, Kai was recounting for the sixth time how he would overcome a python if one happened to cross their path, but Ping wasn't listening. She was searching for a sign of foreboding. There was no sense of dread in her stomach, not even a prickle on the back of her neck. She trusted her second sight, but she also remembered how the necromancer had been able to shield his presence from her by wearing a vest made of jade squares.

"Kai will be brave," the dragon was saying. "Kai can fight off bears and tigers. Many tigers. Take on five barbarians at once. Ping doesn't have to worry."

"I'm not worried," Ping said defensively.

Kai went back to practicing a new skill he'd discovered. Instead of shape-changing each time someone appeared on the horizon, he had learned how to create a different kind of illusion. It was a sort of mirage. His scales took on the color of his surroundings, so that he blended into the landscape completely. Creating this new illusion took much less effort, and he could maintain it all day long.

"What's that smell?" Ping asked.

Kai sniffed the air. "Deer?" he suggested hopefully.

"No, it's something else . . . nearby."

It was Ping's turn to sniff the air. She moved closer to the dragon.

"It's you!" She sniffed again and then held her nose. "You smell terrible." She started examining the dragon, peering into his ears, between his toes. "Have you been cleaning yourself properly?"

"Yes," said Kai indignantly.

"Is your stomach upset? What color are your droppings?"

"That's Kai's business, not Ping's!"

She touched his scales. More than a third of his old purple scales had fallen off now. The new scales had hardened and were a lovely deep shade of green like the leaves of the scholar tree in summer, but the old ones were dull and grayish. Ping was about to examine his teeth. She sniffed again.

"What have you got behind your reverse scales?" she asked.

"Nothing."

Like all dragons, Kai had five larger scales beneath his chin, which lay in the opposite direction to all the others. This made them useful for storing things. When he was little, the reverse scales were so small Ping couldn't fit a finger behind them. Now that they were bigger, she could just dig into them. She pulled something out and held her sleeve over her nose.

"What's this?" she exclaimed. "It smells disgusting!"

Kai didn't answer. Ping examined the thing between her fingers and then dropped it to the ground. It was a long-dead sparrow. She reached back behind Kai's scales and took out a dried fish and several large grubs of the sort that were found in rotting wood. Ping looked accusingly at the dragon.

"Sometimes Kai gets hungry during the night," he said.

They passed beyond the borders of Yan, and for two days didn't meet a single person on the track. Ping was beginning to hope that they had finally traveled beyond the reach of inter-village gossip. Then late in the afternoon, another welcoming party stopped them along the track. Anxious villagers begged them to stay for the night. The children were thin and didn't have enough energy to play. These villagers had planted seeds and watered them from a shrinking pond, which was their source of drinking water. A few pale seedlings had pushed their way through the hard earth. Ping didn't like their chances of survival.

There was no banquet at this village, but the people performed a rain ceremony for Kai. The children had made small statues of dragons from the mud around their pond. They held them up above their heads and sang a song.

"This is what we want you to do, dragon," they sang. "Awake from your winter sleep, and fly into the sky. Bring rain, so we won't be hungry anymore."

The next morning, the sky was still cloudless. There was no cheering when Ping and Kai departed, just unhappy muttering.

Kai was very quiet as they walked that day. Ping didn't pay much attention to his silence, but she stopped suddenly when she realized that he wasn't alongside her. She walked back and found the dragon crouched by the side of the path. White mist was curling from his nostrils.

"What's the matter, Kai?"

"Trying to make a cloud," he said.

The breath of humans would turn to vapor only when the weather was very cold, but Kai could produce misty breath whenever he felt like it. It usually meant that he was in a sulky mood. Kai was concentrating hard. The white mist surrounded him, but evaporated as it rose. Ping put her arm around his damp shoulders.

"You can't achieve the impossible, Kai," she said. "It's just a story that's told about dragons. It doesn't mean they really can make rain where there are no clouds."

They both watched the mist rise and evaporate. Kai made soft, sad sounds.

Every day they moved closer to the area on the map where Dragon's Lament Creek was marked. When it seemed they had finally reached areas where no one had heard of them, Ping decided it was safe to travel on roads again. Whenever they met travelers, Ping asked if they had heard of Dragon's Lament Creek. She spoke to many people—a merchant, an imperial messenger, a family moving south to find better land—but no one had heard of such a place.

One morning they met a shaman. He was an old, old man. He wore a short gown, and his bare legs were strong and brown. They sat down and shared a midday meal with him.

"Where are you going?" Ping asked him.

"My destination isn't a place in the world. It is more a peaceful state of mind that I am seeking."

He told them that he had spent his whole life walking the lands between the Yellow River and the Great Wall.

"Do you know of a place called Dragon's Lament Creek?" Ping asked.

The old shaman shook his head. "If there was such a place, I would have passed it."

Ping sighed as she watched the old man walk away. "We're never going to find it."

"Perhaps we can find the next place on the map," Kai said hopefully. "What was it called? Crooked Dragon Village?"

"It wasn't called Crooked Dragon Village," Ping said. "It was Quiet Dragon—"

She stopped and pulled out the silk square. She remembered how Liu Che had also misunderstood one of the place names. The language of the Empire was very economical with the sounds it used. Each written character meant something different, but many sounds were used again and again. This meant certain sounds could have different meanings.

Ping read out the name of the first destination. "Long Dao Xi." She found a stick and drew several characters in the dry earth. "These characters are all pronounced *long*."

Kai peered at them. "Kai only knows the one that means 'dragon.'"

Ping drew other characters that were pronounced *dao* and *xi*. Each of the three words had several other meanings. She repeated the words, trying not to picture the characters in her mind, instead just listening to the sounds.

Kai suddenly pointed to the west. "*Xi*," he said. "It also means 'west.'" He mimed walking. *Long dao xi* could also mean "seek westward."

The map transformed before Ping's eyes. An idea suddenly exploded in her mind.

"It's a puzzle!" she exclaimed. "These aren't place names at all. They're directions. Danzi is telling us how to find the dragon haven."

There wasn't a choice of three dragon places that they could go to. The name of the dragon haven wasn't even on the map. They had to find their destination by following Danzi's coded instructions.

She read out the next place name, Qu Long Xiang, and wrote other characters with the same sounds.

"*Qu!*" said Kai triumphantly, pointing to the character that meant "go."

Ping drew two characters that were pronounced *xiang*. One meant "box," the other "village." "Yes. 'Go to something village.'" She went back to the *long* characters that she had written. Rising Moon Village, Prosperous Village, Steep Village. There were many possibilities.

She read the last place name. Ye Long Gu. The characters told her that *long gu* meant "dragon valley." She looked at the other characters that were pronounced *long*. It could also mean "basket," "hazy," or "deaf."

"Perhaps there is a valley where baskets are made, or one that is often hidden in mist," Kai suggested.

Ping sighed. "It could mean many things. I'll have to think about it when I'm not so tired."

She couldn't believe she'd been so stupid. "The dragon haven is a secret place. I should have realized Danzi wouldn't write it on the map for anyone to see.

The silk square could have fallen into the hands of enemies."

"Trust Father," Kai said. "He will lead Ping and Kai to the secret dragon place."

"At least we know where we're heading. West."

Another group of villagers blocked their path. It was three weeks since they had left the palace. Ping and Kai looked at the villagers' unsmiling faces. The elder stepped forward.

"We need rain," he said, pointing to the withered seedlings in the fields. "We need it now, or our children will starve."

Kai, in the shape of a small boy, huddled close to Ping.

"I can't bring you rain," she said.

"*You* can't," the elder replied. He grasped Kai's shoulder. "But your dragon can."

Other village men, armed with rakes and spades, surrounded them.

Kai had been shape-changed for most of the day. He was tired and frightened. The small boy shimmered, faded, and Kai's true shape was revealed.

"My wife has just returned from her family in Yan. She passed through several villages that you had been to. They told her how the dragon was withholding the rain."

"He isn't withholding rain," Ping protested. "He

*can't* make rain. There are no clouds. He has no wings."

They wouldn't believe her. "You will stay here until we get rain," the elder said.

Some of the village children were ill. Kai gave them his bearskin, but it was food the villagers wanted, not warmth.

No one wanted Ping to tell them stories that evening. There was no banquet. Ping and Kai were led to a barn. Villagers took turns to guard them. Kai wasn't feeling well. He tossed and turned all night. When Ping got up to find out what was wrong with him, she discovered small pieces of iron hidden in his bedding straw.

"This is to punish you. They think you're withholding the rain on purpose." She hurled the iron pieces out the barn door. "It's only a matter of time before villagers start openly attacking us with weapons."

It was easy enough for them to escape from the barn. Kai made his scales seem as black as the night. Ping left a bag of grain in the barn and flashed her mirror in the eyes of the sleepy guards. Just as she suspected, they let her pass.

By dawn they were many *li* from the village. As soon as she was sure that no one was following them, Ping turned off the westward path and headed north.

"Wrong way," Kai said. "Father said we have to travel west."

"I know. But I have an idea."

# CHAPTER EIGHT

# THE WALL

Just before they had been taken to the last village, Ping had caught a glimpse of something on a distant mountain. It snaked across the peaks like one of Kai's pythons, like a line of embroidery on the billowing hem of a lady's gown. It was the Great Wall.

Ping had read about the Great Wall in the Duke's library. Hundreds of years ago, different warlords across the land had built high walls to keep out their enemies. When Emperor Qin conquered all the kingdoms, he decided to link the walls to form a single line of defense across the entire northern border of his new empire. It had taken many years and tens of thousands of workers to build it. Thousands had died from exhaustion. Others had been buried alive by rockfalls. Emperors had come and gone, and the task still wasn't complete. The wall was inching its way eastward and westward as the Empire expanded.

It took four days for Ping and Kai to reach the wall.

It had looked small from a distance, but when they finally stood in its shadow, it towered above them, at least three *chang* high. It was built from stone quarried from the surrounding mountains, cut roughly into squares and stacked one on top of the other. Beacon towers had been constructed along its length. Each tower was in sight of the next. Depending on the landscape, the next watchtower might be no more than a couple of *li* away, or, if it was on a high peak, there could be thirty *li* to the next one.

Ping didn't want to creep through the countryside, hiding like a criminal, nor did she want their path to be heralded near and far for all to see. She craned her neck and examined the Great Wall. What better way could there be of heading west? She changed into her trousers and jacket and packed away her gown. She tied her hair up in the style of a boy and put on a grass hat, like the ones farmers wore in the fields.

Kai wasn't convinced that Ping's plan would work. "The guards won't let us pass," he said.

"I'll say I'm a peddler," Ping replied. "We have grain and jujubes that we can sell to them."

They walked along the foot of the wall until they came to a beacon tower. It was set on top of the wall and built of the same rough stone blocks.

"They have iron weapons. Kai can feel them already."

"You must use your mirage skill so that the guards see only a patch of stonework. Get past the beacon tower as quickly as you can, and wait for me on the other side, where you can't feel the effects of the iron."

The two guards were busy trying to kill birds with a slingshot. They didn't even notice Ping approaching.

She called up to them. "Good morning!"

The guards scrabbled for their bows and spears. "Who approaches?"

"I'm just a peddler," Ping said in a gruff voice, hoping she sounded like a boy. "May I come up and show you what I have to sell?"

The Great Wall was built to keep out the hordes of barbarians who lived to the north. The guards had no reason to fear anyone coming from within the Empire.

"Come up," they called.

One of them went down to open a gate set in the wall and let in their unexpected visitor. Ping bowed respectfully. The guard looked behind her as if he saw some movement or a shadow, but soon convinced himself that the peddler was traveling alone. Ping and the invisible dragon followed the guard up a set of steps and emerged on top of the wall. Before they had a chance to peer under her hat, Ping pulled out a bag of grain and a handful of jujubes. She had guessed that a soldier's rations on the edge of the Empire would be meager and without variety. The two men were very interested in her wares. She let them haggle until they thought they had beaten her down to a very good price.

"There's been a truce between the Empire and the

nearest tribe of barbarians for half a year," one of the guards told Ping as he chewed a jujube. "Occasionally, a few of them will raid a storehouse—more for amusement than a need for food. But it's usually pretty quiet out here."

The guards stationed on the Great Wall were not the same as the disciplined men who Ping had seen guarding the Emperor. Only criminals and the sons of the poorest families were stationed on the Great Wall. The uniforms of these two guards weren't well kept. Their leather leg guards were cracked, they weren't wearing their regulation caps, and their spearheads were dull and covered with patches of rust. In addition to watching out for barbarians, they were also supposed to keep the wall in good order. If weeds were allowed to grow in the cracks, they would push the stones apart and make the wall weak. The guards had neglected their duty. There were weeds sprouting all along the wall.

"We can go for months without seeing anything more than a mountain goat or an eagle," the second guard said.

"May I travel along the wall to the next watchtower and sell my wares to the guards there?" Ping asked.

She gave them a few extra jujubes for free, ignoring a faint sound like a cracked bell that came from farther along the wall. Kai was finding it hard to create his mirage skill so close to iron. He had concealed himself in a cloud of mist instead. The wind carried away his mournful notes, so the guards didn't hear them. Ping hoped it didn't blow away the mist.

One of the guards shrugged. "We're here to stop barbarians getting into the Empire. No one said anything about stopping people using it as a footpath."

The other guard nodded. "Just to the next tower."

"Thank you," Ping said.

She bowed to the guards and set out walking westward along the top of the wall.

"Still hundreds of *li* to travel," Kai said when Ping caught up to him. "Ping will soon run out of grain to sell . . . and jujubes," he added sadly.

"I don't think I'll have to sell them anything."

"Why not?"

"You're not the only one with a new skill. I've discovered that the mirror Danzi gave me has another use, besides calling you."

"It shows Ping that her hair needs combing?" Kai suggested.

Ping smiled. "Another use besides that."

"What?"

"If I reflect a beam of light from the mirror into someone's eyes, I can suggest things to them with my thoughts."

Kai's brow creased.

"You don't believe me. We'll see if I'm right. I'll try it out at the next beacon tower."

The next tower was only a few *li* away. It wasn't built on top of the wall like the first one. An outcrop of rock rose up alongside the wall with a huge boulder balanced on top of it. The beacon tower was perched on top of that. Grass sprouted along the tops of the ramparts, and a small pine tree had taken root on the roof. The guards were playing a game of chess as Ping approached. They readied bolts to their crossbows and raised them, ready to fire. Ping held up one hand, palm facing out in a sign of peace. The mirror was nestled in her other hand. Kai hung back, making his scales look like a patch of stonework, keeping as far away from their iron weapons as he could.

"I mean you no harm," Ping said. "I have permission to travel along the wall."

She held out her mirror as if it were some sort of pass, and angled it so that it caught the sunlight. As she did, she formed a simple thought in her head. *You can let me pass.*

"We aren't allowed . . ." the second guard said, but when she flashed the mirror in his eyes, his sentence trailed off.

"I think that will be all right," the first guard said.

The guards wouldn't let her go until she had given them news from the east. They wanted to know if the drought was as bad in other places; if Wang, who was posted three towers away, was still sick; and if Ping had seen any signs of fresh supplies being transported in their direction.

Ping answered their questions, asked them about

their wives and children, admired their view. Then she bowed and walked on. The guards peered at a patch of stones that seemed to shift a little, then went back to their game of chess.

"Ping was right," Kai said as he caught up with her.

Ping was pleased that her plan was working. The top of the Great Wall was like an imperial road. It was more than two *chang* wide, and the surface was smooth and even, so that imperial guards could march along it. It was often so steep that the path along the top turned into steps, but it was much easier than clambering up mountainsides, stumbling over rocks, and trying to find tracks where none existed. Ping soon became very skilled at tricking the guards, and it was only when they came to a garrison where troops were housed that she had to sell some of their food supply.

The sky was kingfisher blue, and though the mountain air was cold, it was good weather for traveling. Each morning, they started out as soon as the first rays of light were visible on the horizon.

The wall wound along the crest of mountains and swept down into valleys. It snaked high above treetops, gliding over hills that would have taken them many hours to negotiate. Once or twice the wall marched across a river, the water channeled beneath it. The crumpled peaks of the mountain range stretched in all directions.

Ping felt as if she were striding across the sky and could see as far as Kai. They glimpsed deer and squirrels below, busy with their daily life. Sometimes they saw bears, still sleepy from hibernation, which Kai watched with great interest. Occasionally they met messengers or porters carrying supplies, but most of the time it was as if they had a road just for their own use.

They walked all day, pausing only to eat. Kai's hunting skills improved, and he caught birds to add to their dwindling supplies. Each evening they stopped after dark and made their camp on the wall, rising again before dawn to greet the next lot of guards. Ping's second sight gave her no warning of any danger. She felt as if she could march to the ends of the Empire.

"We're active and vigilant all day," she said to Kai as they walked. "In the evenings we're alert. We're obeying the third reading of the *Yi Jing*. At last."

Kai was lagging behind, staring back the way they had come.

"Kai, what are you doing? Can you see something?"

"No."

"Are you sure? I have this feeling there's someone behind us."

"No, there's no one there."

"Why don't you keep up?"

"Busy."

"Busy doing what?"

"Nothing."

Ping sighed with exasperation. Tendrils of mist streamed from the dragon's mouth. Ping knew he'd been trying to make rain clouds again and his failure had put him in a bad mood.

"We'll have some food when we get to the top of the next hill."

"Kai's sick of lentils."

"There's bean curd."

"Sick of that, too."

Kai spent the next hour recounting all the delicious meals they'd eaten at Beibai Palace—baked duck with ginger sauce, braised fish and lotus roots, bear paw soup.

Then he suddenly stopped. "Kai could go hunting and catch a bear!"

"No, we'd only be able to eat a little bit of it and have to leave the rest behind," Ping argued, though she didn't really believe that Kai was capable of killing a bear. "It would be a terrible waste."

"Kai can smell deer."

"No, Kai. You can't hunt deer, either. I don't want to lose sight of you."

The dragon muttered and mumbled to himself and fell even farther behind.

Each time they approached a beacon tower, they found the guards trying to amuse themselves by playing chess on a board carved into the stone of the wall itself, or wagering who could throw a stone the farthest. They were all bored and homesick. None of them had seen an attack from the Xiong Nu for months. Once Ping had convinced them that she was no threat, they were happy to be diverted by an unexpected traveler for a few minutes of their uneventful day. She did some sleight-of-hand tricks that she had learned from one of the Duke's soldiers over the winter months, or told them stories that she had read in the Beibai library.

They explained to Ping that if there was a barbarian attack, they had to light the beacon to alert the guards at the next tower. If it happened during the day, they would light a pile of straw and wolf dung, which produced thick black smoke. One column of smoke indicated that there were up to fifty attackers. Two columns meant that there were anything up to three thousand attackers. Four columns meant an invasion force of ten thousand. If there was an attack at night, they lit bright, flaming wood fires instead. Word of the attack would pass swiftly along the wall from tower to tower to the nearest garrison. It was quicker than sending a messenger on horseback.

Ping was enjoying walking along a relatively level section of the wall. She wasn't expecting to see anyone until they reached the next tower, which was at least ten *li* away. She was startled when she saw three men up ahead. She glanced behind and saw the dragon looking out over the edge of the wall.

"Quick, you must hide!" she said.

"Kai wants to catch a bear."

"You should be keeping a lookout on the wall, not looking for bears."

Ping was too close to the guards to argue further with the dragon.

"Hello there," she said cheerily as she approached them.

The men, who were half-heartedly pulling out the weeds that were growing in the cracks in the wall, jumped when they heard her voice. They were the first guards she'd come across who were doing their duty and maintaining the wall. They reached for their weapons. Ping was too far away to flash the mirror in their eyes, so she posed as a peddler again.

"I have some food to sell, if you're interested," she called out.

None of the men moved. They continued to stare at Ping.

"Fresh grain with no weevils," Ping said. Her forced cheerfulness was wearing thin. "Jujubes? Calfskin to write to your loved ones?"

Then Ping realized they weren't staring at her, they were staring over her shoulder. She whipped around. There, sitting in the middle of the wall, was a large ceramic vase.

"Or perhaps a lovely vase, a present for your mother or wife when you return home," she added.

The vase turned into a goat, and then a potted chrysanthemum.

The men were staring openmouthed at the changing shape. Ping moved closer to them.

"I also have this lovely mirror," she said.

She held her Dragon Keeper's mirror in her palm and angled it so that it reflected sunlight into each of the men's eyes.

"You can't see a vase, a goat, or a potted plant," she said. Kai popped back into his own shape. "Or a dragon, for that matter. What you see is . . ." Kai disappeared behind a cloud of mist. ". . . a small patch of morning mist that hasn't cleared yet."

The three men nodded their heads. "Good journey," one of them said.

"That wasn't funny, Kai," Ping said when they were out of earshot.

The sound of jingling bells told her that the dragon thought otherwise. His little joke had cheered him up.

They continued to march along the wall.

Kai's cheerfulness didn't last long. "Bored," he said before they'd reached the next beacon tower.

"I'm glad I had the idea of walking along the Great Wall," Ping said, making an effort to remain positive. "We have saved so much time, even if we've gone out of our way. Another week or so and we should be able to head south again, into lands where no one will know who we are, where we're from, or what our business is."

Kai sighed a heavy, moist sigh.

"Do you want to play Spot the Swallow?" Ping asked.

"Kai always wins. Ping can hardly see in front of her own nose."

"I could make a ball and you could chase it."

Kai looked sideways at her. "Ping can't throw."

"Just try to concentrate on our quest."

"Boring."

"What do you think the dragon haven will be like?" Ping asked, trying to distract him.

The dragon thought for a moment. "A place high on a mountain, where only someone with wings can go."

Ping didn't want to point out that neither of them had wings, so it might be difficult for them to find such a place. She tried to imagine the dragon haven herself. She pictured a lush green valley hidden high in the peaks of a mountain. It would be cold up so high, but the valley walls would protect it from the worst winds. After her experience at Beibai Palace, she knew that living in a cold place didn't have to be uncomfortable. She would build a sturdy cottage and collect a lot of wood for winter fires. She and Kai would be warm and cozy. She would carve a chessboard and Seven Cunning Pieces so that they would have games to play.

They walked on in silence for another half hour. The wall sloped down steeply, and the path turned into steps. Kai started jumping down two steps at a time, then three, then four. He suddenly sprang onto the top of the rampart along the edge of the wall.

"What are you doing? You'll fall."

"Kai won't fall. Kai's going to jump!"

The muscles in his back legs flexed as if he was ready to launch himself into the air.

"No!" Ping shouted, grabbing hold of his tail.

"Kai can leap like a deer, soar through the air like a squirrel, and land on his feet like a wildcat."

"You'll fall like a stone and break your neck."

Ping looked at Kai. He had lost almost all of his purple baby scales, and whiskers were just starting to sprout on either side of his mouth. She had been able to amuse a dragonling, but a bored juvenile dragon was a different thing.

"Kai is sick of the Great Wall."

"How can you say that?" Ping replied, sweeping her arm to take in the mountains that surrounded them. "Look at that magnificent view."

"Boring."

"We can't argue now, Kai. I can see the next beacon tower. You have to shape-change."

"Not going to shape-change."

The next tower was in a valley only a couple of *li* away.

"Come on, Kai, please."

"Kai is not a dragonling anymore and can find the dragon haven alone."

"Don't be silly."

The dragon fell behind. Ping glanced around. All she could see was a slight shifting in the stones. Then she couldn't even see that. "Come back here!" she called.

She was now close enough to see that it wasn't a simple beacon tower ahead, but a larger building. There were more than the usual two guards. A huddle of at least twelve men, all with weapons, were glaring in her direction. Their crossbows were trained on her. Other guards were climbing up from the barracks below. She raised her hands to show that she had no weapons.

"Kai, this is no time to sulk. It's a garrison. We have to be extra careful. At least five-times-ten men will be housed there."

There was no answer.

"Where are you, Kai?" Ping shouted, peering over the side of the wall looking for a distortion among the trees or a cloud of mist.

A shiver of fear passed through her. Had Kai really run away? She couldn't stop and look for him; there were too many crossbows trained on her. If she did anything suspicious, the guards would shoot her. She had to keep walking.

The wall around the garrison was just as unkempt as it had been near the beacon towers. Stones were missing from the ramparts, weeds grew in cracks. There was a bank of sand below the outer face of the wall, which was supposed to be raked daily. If barbarians had been creeping around during the night, their footsteps would be seen in the morning. The sand bank looked as if it hadn't been raked for months. It was covered with animal prints and littered with discarded bones. Ping had expected guards stationed at a garrison to be more disciplined than those posted at the remote beacon towers. But they seemed to be even worse.

Ping had no choice. She walked toward the garrison, waving her hand and shouting a cheery greeting. The voice in her mind was silent. Something jabbed her in the back. She turned, thinking it was Kai. It wasn't. It was two imperial guards poking her with their spears. She had no idea how they had gotten behind her. She reached for her mirror, which was still in her pouch. A spear tip cut through her jacket and dug into her skin.

"Raise your hands!" one of the guards said.

She held up her arms with her hands spread wide, so they could see that she had no weapons.

"I'm a citizen of the Empire," she said.

"Be quiet!" said the other guard. "Save your explanation for the commander."

It was getting late. The sun was low on the horizon. Unless she could get close to a fire, her mirror would be useless until the sun rose again in the morning. She had no idea where Kai was. She searched her second sight for any sense of foreboding. There was none.

When they reached the garrison, Ping tried to explain that she was just a peddler and that she'd been welcomed by other guards. About thirty guards gathered around her. They were just as disheveled as the other guards she'd met along the wall. Some wore their hair hanging untidily on their shoulders. Many had the shaved heads of convicts. The commander strode toward her. He was a large man with a thick mustache. He had a black eye from a recent fight and wore a bearskin vest instead of his regulation red leather one.

"Welcome to Ji Liao Garrison," the commander said sarcastically.

Someone pulled off Ping's hat.

"It's just a young lad," one of the guards exclaimed.

"What will we do with him?" said another guard, with a malicious grin.

The rest of the guards gathered around, eager for any diversion from their boring life.

"Can he dance?"

Ping shook her head.

Several spears jabbed her in the ribs. "Go on, dance for us!"

Ping didn't move.

"What about acrobatics?" one suggested. "Do some handstands!"

The guards laughed, and pushed her, but Ping stood her ground.

"Make him walk along the rampart!"

They pushed Ping to the edge of the wall and made her climb up on the narrow rampart. She looked down. There was a drop of three *chang*. Another spear jabbed her in the back. She focused on the wall and walked along it easily.

"He's no fun," one of the guards complained.

"Put him to work," said the commander. "Make him clean out the stables."

Ping was dragged from the wall and down steps that led to the stables below. She didn't object. Eventually most of the guards would sleep and then she would make her escape.

The stables were as neglected as the rest of the garrison. She shoveled horse dung out of the stinking stables until it was too dark to see. Then she was taken into the quadrangle outside the guards' living quarters and her hands and feet were tied to a post meant for tethering horses. The guards ate their evening meal in the barracks. Ping could hear them complaining about the shortage of food and water.

"At least that means our wine ration has been increased," someone said.

They all laughed. No one offered Ping any food. She was glad. It smelled worse than the slop she'd fed the pigs at Huangling Palace. Then the men started to pass around jars of millet wine. Good, Ping thought, they'll soon fall asleep.

Ping had to think of a plan. She'd thought of plans before. Good plans, successful plans. She'd used whatever was at hand to come up with ingenious strategies. But her hands and feet were tied. She had no resources. Kai had taken the bag with everything in it.

Ping focused her *qi*. She had once overturned a huge

boulder with her *qi* power. Surely she could break a few leather thongs. She took some deep breaths and concentrated. It was late and she was tired, but she collected up all that was left of her *qi* power and focused it around her wrists and ankles. The leather thongs snapped like grass stalks. She had to learn not to underestimate her powers.

The guards were all drunk now but showing no sign of getting tired. Just as Ping was about to slip away, a few of the guards came out to taunt her. She kept her hands behind her back, her feet together as if they were still bound.

"Let's use him for target practice," one said.

He went to get his crossbow. He was very drunk. Loading a crossbow bolt took strength and coordination. The drunken guard staggered around trying to load his weapon. It would take him a while, but Ping knew that eventually he would succeed. And if he managed to hit her, she would die. She was furious with the guards for ruining her plans, for halting her progress, for shattering her peace. And where was Kai? She felt panic rise in her throat. He was wandering around in the dark alone. He was young and overconfident. He might try and rescue her. The guards would kill him.

"You should keep better discipline among your men," Ping shouted to the commander, who had gone to get more wine. "When I get free, I'm going to send a message to the Emperor. He's a friend of mine. When he hears what you've done, he'll have you beheaded."

The commander laughed. "Of course you will."

"You're as stupid as your men!" she shouted.

The commander walked over to her and grabbed her by the hair. "What did you say?"

The other guards came out to see what was happening. The guard with the crossbow had finally managed to load a bolt and was waving the crossbow in Ping's direction. She had to calm down, control her anger. She couldn't take on fifty men.

The man with the crossbow came closer and aimed. His hands were shaking, but he was so close, there was every chance he would hit her. The others stood back, egging him on. It was dark now; another guard held up a lamp so that the marksman could see what he was doing. The guard with the lamp moved closer and shined it in Ping's face.

"I know who this is, sir," the guard said. "It's not a boy, it's a girl. She's a sorceress. It's because of her I was sent from an easy post at Ming Yang Lodge to this miserable place."

Ping didn't recognize the guard, but all the men were glaring at her as if she were responsible for them being stationed at the edge of the Empire.

"Good," the commander replied with a malicious smile. He put up his hand to stop the guard with the crossbow. "I've always wanted a slave."

Anger swelled inside Ping's chest. She was prepared

to put up with many discomforts. She would sleep in a barn, she would wear worn-out clothes, eat nuts and berries, but she would never again be anyone's slave. Her *qi* power focused without her having to think about it. She flung out her arm and sent out a strong bolt of *qi* that flattened ten men, including the commander. Ping knocked the crossbow out of the hands of the man from Ming Yang Lodge with another well-aimed *qi* bolt. She looked around for a way of escape. The men recovered from their surprise, picked up their spears, and confronted her again. Her third *qi* bolt was much weaker; it hit just one guard and only made him stumble. She'd used up all her resources on the first two bolts. Before she could summon more *qi*, six guards grabbed her arms.

"She's a sorceress, all right."

The guards muttered in agreement.

"I'm not a sorceress!"

She knew that her display of *qi* power had helped reinforce the idea, but what else was she supposed to do to protect herself?

"She *was* friendly with the Emperor," the Ming Yang Lodge guard told the commander. "She might have some influence with him."

"Then kill her," the commander said, as casually as if he were ordering the death of a goat.

The flame of Ping's anger was smothered by fear. She'd let her temper get the better of her. Now her life was in real danger. And Kai's. She had no idea where he was.

The man from Ming Yang Lodge drew his knife. His hand was steady; he wasn't as drunk as the other men. The blade glinted in the lamplight. He'd had plenty of idle time to keep it sharp.

"Kai!" she called in her mind. "Where are you? Help me."

The man leaned closer. He had an ugly pimple on his chin. He took a firm grip on his knife. Terror spread through Ping. Belatedly she realized that her second sight only warned her of danger to Kai. Not herself. Kai wasn't with her. He wasn't in danger—but she was.

The man with the knife drew his hand back, ready to plunge the blade into her heart. There was a piece of goat's meat stuck between his teeth. Ping closed her eyes.

Voices suddenly rang out, piercing the night. The hands holding her loosened. Ping opened her eyes. The guards were ignoring her completely.

To the east, two yellow fires blossomed like chrysanthemums.

"Two beacons!" someone shouted. "An attack! Three thousand barbarians!"

The commander yelled out orders, but no one listened to him. Each man ran to get his weapons, concerned only with his own survival. The ragtag imperial guards clambered up onto the wall facing north, their crossbows aimed into the darkness. Several men were still trying to get the long-neglected beacons alight to alert the next tower. The commander was attempting to organize a squad of men to go out and attack the barbarians. He wasn't having much luck. No one wanted to face the invisible enemy. Scuffles broke out among the men.

Ping took advantage of this disorder and crept toward the inner gate. She slipped out the bolt that held it shut and wrenched the gate open. The guards had finally managed to light the beacon. The light from the flames illuminated her escape.

"Get the girl!" someone shouted. "Send *her* out. If there are barbarians outside, they'll go after her!"

The guards had found something they could all agree on. Ping was soon captive yet again. Only this time instead of tying her up, they thrust a sword in her hands and pushed her through the outer gate and out of the Empire.

She ran headlong into the night. It was her only hope of freedom. With the sword pointed straight ahead, she screamed as if she had the force of a thousand courageous imperial guards behind her. She ran down the bank of sand, tripped and fell, got up and ran again. She lashed out at the barbarians who stood in her way, slashing the sword in all directions, not flinching when it met with resistance.

It was several minutes before she realized that the

things in her way weren't barbarians, but trees. She was lopping off branches, not arms and legs. She stopped, breathing hard, both hands grasping the sword hilt. No one attacked her. She turned a full circle. She was surrounded by nothing more than the dark shapes of trees and rocks. She listened for the sounds of barbarian attack that she had heard at Beibai Palace—the thunder of horses' hooves, the strange gurgling cries, the shouts in a foreign language. There were none.

Behind her, she could hear the muffled uproar of fighting and voices raised in anger as the imperial guards still argued about who should face the barbarians. She held the sword ready for barbarians to pounce on her. Nothing happened.

She turned another full circle. Suddenly the rocks around her came to life. They reared up and turned into cloaked men. For the second time that day, Ping's hands were grabbed and tied behind her. She couldn't believe the garrison men had been so quick and stealthy. She twisted around. The men holding her weren't imperial guards. They were barbarians.

# CHAPTER NINE

# INTO THE TIGER'S MOUTH

Ping struggled to free herself, but the hands that gripped her were strong and determined. They pulled her through the undergrowth. Branches slapped her in the face. She lost her footing and fell. Someone dragged her back to her feet by the armpits, lifting her effortlessly, and threw her over the back of a horse. Rough hands tied her behind the horse's saddle as another cloaked figure mounted the horse. Before she could raise her head to look at her captors, the horse began moving, building up to a gallop. Each time the horse's hooves hit the ground Ping felt the breath knocked out of her. She wondered if barbarians had captured Kai, as well. She knew what they were capable of. She'd heard about what they did to their captives—cutting off their fingers, blinding them with burning sticks, putting them in holes filled with venomous snakes. There were three more horses galloping behind, but she couldn't see if one of them carried Kai.

She listened for his voice, but it wasn't there. She had no choice but to allow herself to be bounced around on the back of the horse like a side of beef.

There was a saying that Lao Ma, the old woman at Huangling Palace, had been very fond of repeating. *Out of the wolf's den, into the tiger's mouth.* Just a few weeks earlier, Ping's only concern had been that the entire population of the Empire had seemed to want to be her friend. She'd had no enemies. Now people on both sides of the Great Wall wanted to harm her.

She tried to make sense of what had happened. Only a handful of barbarians had attacked the garrison. They had captured her, but ignored the imperial guards, leaving them cowering inside their barracks. She wondered if the barbarians had been tracking her. Perhaps that's why she'd had the feeling someone was following them. She had heard stories of how the Xiong Nu sacrificed white horses and drank their blood. She couldn't bear to think what they might do if they got their hands on a dragon. On the other hand, there were also tales of the barbarians making human sacrifices to their gods. Perhaps it wasn't Kai they wanted at all— but her. She called to Kai in her mind, but there was still no reply. Perhaps they had left him behind.

The horses galloped through the darkness for a long time. The ropes tying her arms and legs rubbed her skin until it felt like they were burning her. Ping couldn't tell whether she was awake and bouncing on the back of a horse or just dreaming that she was.

They stopped as the sky was turning gray. Ping was untied and pulled from the horse. Her legs were numb, and she couldn't stand. One of the barbarians carried her, putting her down outside a low hut. The sky grew lighter. It was above her and all around her. It stretched to the horizon on all sides. They had left the mountains and the Great Wall far behind. There wasn't a tree or a rock in sight, just an endless plain, bare except for tufts of yellow grass. She could see now that it wasn't a hut she'd been brought to, it was a tent—a large, black tent made from thick felt. A group of about twenty smaller tents was huddled around the central tent, like sleeping animals. There was also a corral made of branches that secured a herd of several hundred horses. Steam rose from the horses' backs as the sunlight warmed them. They were handsome beasts, tall and slender, with flowing manes— nothing like the short, stocky imperial horses. Several of the nearest horses studied her with interest. They looked powerful and intelligent.

It was only after she'd finished admiring the horses that she looked at her captors. They were dark men with their hair tied in braids. They wore sleeveless jackets made of animal skins, and leather belts with shiny gold buckles. Their felt breeches were tucked into high boots. Each man wore a fur-lined leather hat. They glanced at her and muttered to each other, making harsh sounds that Ping couldn't understand.

They smelled different from the people of the Empire. They had a sharp odor that reminded her of the goats she'd taken care of when she was a slave.

The tent flap opened, and a man came out. Ping was sitting on the ground because her legs wouldn't work. The man towered over her. His clothing was like the other men's except that he wore a silk shirt beneath his jacket. She had a closer view of his gold buckle. It was fashioned into the shape of two animals locked in a fight. It was hard to believe that such simple people could make such an elegant ornament.

The riders fell silent. The man spoke to them in their coarse-sounding language. Ping realized she had no way of communicating with these people. She couldn't explain anything to them. She couldn't even beg for her life. The riders turned and left. Someone had rekindled the embers of a fire. The man gestured for her to sit next to it. As the darkness melted away, more details of the camp were revealed. A smaller pen contained a flock of sheep. Several camels were grazing on the sparse grass. There was somebody on the other side of the fire. Ping's heart thudded. It wasn't a person. It was a dragon. He was slumped in a heap. She struggled to her feet and rushed over to him.

"Kai!" she shouted. "What have the barbarians done to you?"

She fell to her knees next to him. He opened his eyes and yawned.

"Nothing."

"Are their weapons causing you pain?"

"No. Swords and spears are made of bronze."

"You're not hurt?"

"No."

"Were you on one of the horses?"

"Yes."

"But I spoke to you with my mind. You didn't reply."

"Sleeping."

"It was so uncomfortable! How could you possibly sleep?"

"Kai can sleep anywhere."

The man was watching Kai with interest. Ping hadn't realized that she had spoken aloud.

"I was told that you could read the dragon's mind," the man said. Though he was speaking to Ping, he didn't take his eyes off Kai.

She turned to the man in surprise. He was speaking the language of the Empire. A woman walked over and handed Ping a wooden bowl. She put one on the ground for Kai but wouldn't go near him.

Ping looked at the contents of the bowl. Steam rose from a grayish liquid. It smelled worse than the barbarians.

"Drink," the barbarian said. "Renew your strength. I apologize for the rough journey on horseback, but my men do not speak your language. They had no words to tell you they meant you no harm. If they had lingered, the guards of the wall would have fired arrows at them . . . and you."

Kai slurped his hot drink hungrily.

"Tastes good," he said to Ping.

Ping was cold and hungry. She sipped the gray liquid and made a face. It tasted like rancid milk.

"It is *kumiss*, a drink made from mare's milk," the man said. "It might not be to your taste, but drink it anyway. It will do you good."

Ping held her breath and swallowed a mouthful of the sour drink. The taste made her shudder, but it did warm her.

"We are wandering people who live by drawing the bow. We don't grow grains and vegetables like the people of the Empire. All our food comes from our animals or the hunt."

Ping looked at the strange man.

"My name is Hou-yi," he said. "I am chief of this tribe. I see many questions in your eyes."

"How do you come to know the language of the Empire?" Ping asked.

"I learned it from my father."

That didn't explain anything.

"A generation ago, our Great King made a truce with the Emperor of the southern lands," Hou-yi continued. "To prove that he meant to keep the truce, the Emperor sent one of his daughters to be the consort of our Great King."

"A sister of the old Emperor?"

Hou-yi nodded. "Our Great King learned from fighting the soldiers of the Empire. He united all the tribes who live by drawing the bow. Together the tribes defeated the Empire, and your old Emperor was forced to make a treaty agreeing to give us silk and wine every year. His sister was included in the deal. She came with her servants and a learned man who was her tutor. He became my father's friend and taught him how to speak the language of the Empire."

Princess Yangxin wasn't the only imperial woman to be sent away as a peace offering. Growing up as a slave, Ping had imagined that anyone who was rich and royal could do whatever they pleased. Now she knew that wasn't so. A rich woman could be given away in the barter for peace, traded like a prize horse. At least Princess Yangxin still lived within the Empire. Liu Che's father, the old Emperor, had sent his sister beyond the Great Wall to live among the barbarians.

"So why did you capture Kai and me?"

"For your protection. News of your journey had reached us. A message arrived asking us to look out for you if you came within our territory. The men of the Ji Liao Garrison are ignorant and cruel. When we found out that you had been taken by them, I sent men to rescue you. They could have been more gentle, but you are safe now. You can continue your journey."

"We aren't prisoners?"

"You are free to go whenever you choose."

Ping had many more questions to ask, but Hou-yi stopped them by raising his hand. He went over to where his people were gathered. Together they knelt, facing the rising sun, and prayed. Ping particularly wanted to know who had sent the message to look out for them. It must have been the Duke. She was glad that she had left him on good terms. If it hadn't been for his message, she would have been killed at the hands of the guard from Ming Yang Lodge.

Ping turned to Kai. "You didn't leave," she said quietly.

"Did leave."

Ping's heart felt as it someone were squeezing it.

"But Kai changed mind, thought Ping might get lost on her own."

Ping had a sudden thought. She remembered the fourth line of the *Yi Jing* reading. *A dragon about to leap hesitates. There will be no mistake.* "I suppose you could say that you were about to leap, but you hesitated?"

"Like in the book."

"Yes. And there was no mistake, just as it said. Here we are outside the Empire at the mercy of the barbarians, but we're safe, safer than we were within the Empire."

Once the prayers were over, everyone ate the morning meal that had been prepared by the Xiong Nu women. The women were as dark-skinned as the men.

They wore long skirts and felt shoes. Beneath their jackets they wore blouses made of colored silk. One of them came over with bowls of food for Ping and Kai. She wouldn't come close to the dragon and left the bowls on the ground at a distance. She wore a gold necklace suspended from jade earrings that swung beneath her chin as she bent down. Ping picked up the bowls. They contained lumps of milk curd and strips of cooked meat.

Kai speared one of the curds with a talon and inspected it suspiciously before tasting it with the tip of his red tongue. Then he put it in his mouth and chewed.

"Kai likes the solid milk lumps," he said between chews.

The meal smelled strange, but Ping was hungry. Though she had chopsticks in her bag, she ate with her fingers, like the barbarians.

"Barbarians are nice," said Kai as he gnawed on a bone.

Ping had to agree with him. Though the Xiong Nu were wary of the girl who had been brought to their camp, and frightened of the strange creature with her, Ping and Kai were being treated well.

"Perhaps we shouldn't call them barbarians," Ping said. "Or Xiong Nu either." Xiong Nu meant "fierce slaves."

"Should call them Ma Ren," Kai said.

"Horse People. That's a good name for them."

Ping picked at her food, trying to tell herself that it would give her strength, even though it had the taste of sour milk and smelly socks. She felt safe with the Ma Ren. She hoped they were traveling west and that she and Kai could go with them. Ping chewed another piece of meat. She would have to get used to their strange food.

"Thank you for your hospitality," she said when Hou-yi came back.

"It is strange for a young girl to be traveling alone," he said.

"I'm not alone," Ping said, indicating the dragon.

Hou-yi smiled. "Stranger still to be traveling with a dragon."

Ping expected him to ask how she came to be in the company of a dragon, and where they were going, but he didn't.

"You are a wanderer, like we are," he said.

Ping nodded. "I am, but from need, not from choice. One day I hope to be able to stay in one place and call it my home. Don't you?"

"No," Hou-yi replied. "I will wander until I die."

After they had eaten, the women and girls set about their daily tasks—caring for the animals, preparing the next meal, mending the tents. The young boys practiced firing arrows with small bows. They also improved their riding skills—the older ones on young horses, the littlest on sheep. Ping couldn't help laughing at the sight of the toddlers careering around on the startled animals.

The Ma Ren were generous and courteous, but they kept their distance from Kai. They didn't want to touch him. If they had to pass him, they turned their eyes away. The children wouldn't go near him. Hou-yi was the only one who wasn't uneasy in the dragon's presence. He wasn't afraid to look at Kai, and even touched his scales and spines.

A tent was put up for Ping. It was very comfortable, carpeted with felt and furnished with silk cushions and fur rugs. Ping enjoyed spending the day resting and mending her jacket. Hou-yi didn't sit with her, but with the other men. Kai tried to play with the children, but they ran away and hid behind their mothers' skirts.

At dusk Ping was given a plate of mutton gruel and more *kumiss*.

"Thank you," she said.

The woman who had brought the food nodded and left.

"May we travel with you and your people for a way?" Ping asked Hou-yi.

"We are not riding in your direction," Hou-yi said. "The grass is sparse this spring. We must travel east to find better pasture. Perhaps we will have to breach the Great Wall and look for grass in the Empire."

"When are you leaving?"

"Tomorrow."

Ping couldn't hide her disappointment.

"I am sorry, but my people come first."

"They don't like Kai, do they?" Ping asked. She suspected that the search for grass wasn't the only reason they were leaving so soon.

Hou-yi pointed to his gold buckle, which gleamed in the firelight. Ping looked closely at the design. She could now see the animals that were fighting—a bear and a dragon.

"Such creatures are in our stories," he said. "Our tales tell of cruel creatures."

The dragon on the buckle had its teeth buried in the bear's neck. Its claws raked terrible wounds in the bear's belly.

"They are strong and vicious—not of this world."

The Ma Ren took down their tents early the next morning. What looked like a substantial village had, with the removal of a few poles, collapsed into a heap of cloth. Their entire homes were soon packed into baskets and loaded onto camels.

"I have something for you," Hou-yi said.

He was holding the reins of a horse. Ping had assumed it was his, but he handed the reins to her.

"This will speed your journey," he said.

She didn't know how much such a horse was worth, but she knew it would be many gold *jin*. "I can give you the gold I have, but it won't be enough to pay for such a fine horse."

Hou-yi smiled. "It is a gift."

"But I can't accept it," Ping said.

"You have a friend who is concerned about your safety. I promised him I would help you."

Ping wondered if the Duke had sent gold to Hou-yi.

The chief fondled Kai's ears. "And meeting a dragon has been a rare privilege."

"Thank you," Ping said. "It is very kind of you. But I don't know how to ride a horse."

"Nothing is easier," Hou-yi replied. "All you have to do is sit."

The Ma Ren learned to ride horses when they were children. For them, riding was as easy as walking. Hou-yi bent down and laced the fingers of his hands together so that Ping could step up onto the horse.

"What about Kai?"

Hou-yi looked at the dragon doubtfully. "I don't think the horse would let him mount."

"Kai doesn't want to ride the horse," the dragon said. He was as wary of the horse as it was of him.

"You have to," Ping said.

The dragon shook his head. "Kai can walk."

"But a horse travels fast, many *li* each day."

"If the horse carries the bag, Kai will be able to keep pace."

Kai was less than half the size of a horse, but Ping

didn't argue with him. Hou-yi took the saddlebag from Kai's shoulders and fit it onto the horse. He gave Ping some meat and a sheepskin bag full of *kumiss*. The Ma Ren were shifting in their saddles, children pulling at their mothers' skirts, camels making restless noises.

"Have you heard of a place called Long Xiang?" Ping asked.

Hou-yi shook his head. "There are no villages in the lands of those who draw the bow."

"Then we will return to the Empire."

"If you want to cross over the wall without the guards seeing you," Hou-yi said, "I can tell you of a place where the watchtowers are far apart and there is a hidden hole that leads beneath the wall."

Ping didn't ask if the Ma Ren had excavated it themselves, but she listened closely to his directions for finding this hole in the wall.

"You have been very kind to us," Ping said.

Hou-yi leaped gracefully onto his own horse and raised his hand. The riders dug their heels into their horses' flanks; those on foot flicked the camels' rumps with leather thongs. The Ma Ren set off, heading east. Ping watched their departure. Men on horseback herded the horses. Women on foot, with the smallest children strapped to their backs, urged on the flock of sheep. Swaying camels lumbered off, piled high with folded tents and baskets of cooking utensils. Only Hou-yi turned to wave good-bye.

Ping's horse snorted impatiently. Ping dug her heels into the horse's flank, as she had seen the Ma Ren do. It refused to move.

"Come on, you stupid beast!" she said, kicking the horse with her heels as hard as she could.

The horse didn't move an inch. Even though there was no more grass to eat, it examined the ground, snorting and snuffling at stones. She kicked the horse as hard as she could and flicked it with a leather thong Hou-yi had given her. It still wouldn't shift. Then as it turned to look for more grass, it caught sight of its horse friends disappearing into the distance. It suddenly cantered off—in the wrong direction. Ping was concentrating too hard on clinging—to the reins with her hands and the horse with her thighs—to try and stop it. They had almost caught up with the Ma Ren, when Hou-yi saw her.

He rode back and took the reins from her.

"You have to be firm when you command the horse," he said. "It has to know that you are its master."

He turned the horse around, gave the reins back to Ping, and flicked the horse gently on the rump. It trotted off as meekly as a tame dog.

"I think I'd prefer to walk," Ping muttered to herself.

# CHAPTER TEN

# YELLOW EARTH

The horse trotted obediently for the rest of the morning. Ping considered eating as she rode so that she wouldn't have to get the horse moving again after she'd stopped. But she knew eventually she'd have to stop to pee, and her bottom was getting sore. She reined the horse in and slid awkwardly to the ground.

Ping was glad to be able to stretch her legs, and she was surprisingly hungry considering she'd done nothing but sit all morning. She and Kai ate the strips of dried meat and drank *kumiss* from the sheepskin that Hou-yi had given them. All too soon it was time to get back onto the horse.

"You hold the reins, Kai," Ping said, "while I get on."

As soon as Kai took hold of the reins, the horse started rearing and whinnying. It didn't like the dragon any more than the Ma Ren had. Ping took the reins again and tried to calm the horse. Its back was as high as her shoulder. She grabbed hold of the felt saddlecloth, but she couldn't mount it. It was too tall. She looked around. They were surrounded by a flat plain. There wasn't a tree she could climb or a rock she could stand on to mount the horse.

"You can stand on Kai's back," the dragon suggested.

The horse was calmly pulling up a tuft of yellow grass, but when Kai approached, it cantered away.

"Try shape-changing," Ping suggested.

Kai took on the shape of a rock. The horse went back to chewing the dry grass. Kai inched closer, until he was next to the horse. Ping carefully stood on Kai's rock-shaped back and then flung her leg over the horse. She was glad she was still wearing trousers. The horse skittered around for a while but then settled. Ping thought she'd won, but now the horse wouldn't move. She kicked it, called it names, flicked it with the leather thong, but it wouldn't budge.

Without warning, Kai came up behind the horse and made a sound like someone banging a gong. The horse took off at a gallop. Ping lost her grip on the reins, so she clung onto the horse's mane. It kept galloping. She gripped the horse with her thighs, but she couldn't stay on. She fell, hitting the hard earth with a jarring thud.

"Is Ping all right?" Kai asked when he ran up to where she was lying in the dust.

Ping half hoped that the horse had run away for good, but when she sat up, she could see it quietly cropping a clump of grass a few paces away.

"I'm okay," she said.

"Perhaps it would be easier to leave the horse behind," Kai said.

Ping got to her feet. "No, it's not going to get the better of me. We need to find the dragon haven as soon as possible. Riding will speed our journey."

With Kai's help, she got back on the horse.

"Kai could roar again."

"No, don't do that."

Eventually, the horse decided it was time to move again. It walked a little faster than Ping would have liked, but she hung on tight. Kai walked alongside them, keeping pace as he said he would.

As Ping bounced along, it felt as if the horse beneath her was made of stone. They rode until it was dark. She had thought that her bottom hurt as they rode, but when she got down from the horse it was worse. It was so painful, tears streamed down her face.

"Ping sad?" Kai asked.

"Not sad, Kai. Sore. Very sore."

"Poor Ping."

"I can't walk," Ping said. "I've never been in so much pain before. Never. If feels like someone's ripped the skin from my legs, set it on fire, and stuck it back on again."

"Kai's legs ache, too. What's for dinner?"

There were no trees, so there was no wood for a fire, but Ping managed to light a small, smoky flame from animal dung that Kai collected. She made gruel from grain and the rest of the sheep meat that Hou-yi had given them.

When he had finished eating, Kai made himself a nest and was soon asleep. Ping wrapped herself in her bearskin and lay down. She couldn't sleep. The burning pain in her bottom and thighs was too strong.

They stayed outside the Empire on the northern side of the Great Wall, and no one interfered with their passage. The days passed in silent torture for Ping. She spent her time in a battle of wills with the horse, trying to get it to walk at a comfortable speed and not to wander from the road. She tried being nice to it. She tried being unpleasant to it. It made no difference. It started when it was ready, and once it had decided to stop, there was no shifting it. Ping tried to befriend the horse by giving it jujubes. The beast ate the dried fruit, but still tried to throw her off whenever the mood took it. She would have been happy to leave it behind, but it was too late for that. She was too sore to walk.

Each morning, Ping climbed painfully onto the horse and bounced uncomfortably as it trotted along. Her bones felt as if they were jangling out of their sockets, and her teeth rattled in her head. She thought that she would hurt forever.

She would have been grateful to listen to Kai's chatter to take her mind off her aches and pains, but the dragon didn't speak much as he loped along just behind her. He needed all his energy to keep up with the horse.

"I like most animals," she told Kai. "I liked the goats and the pigs at Huangling, but there's nothing about this horse that I like. I don't like its horsy smell. I don't like its hard hooves that step on my feet every time I mount it. I don't like its big teeth that have bitten me more than once. And I don't like the way it rears up whenever it sees you. Which is often."

"Perhaps if Ping gave it a name, it would be more friendly," Kai suggested.

"I can think of some good names for it," Ping said. "How about Stupid, or Stubborn, or Big Nose."

The horse suddenly sped up. Ping clung on, determined not to let it win their battle of wills.

On the fifth day, the agony began to lessen. Ping finally worked out how to move with the rhythm of the horse's gait, so that her bones didn't jar. Her body still ached, but it wasn't as painful. Kai must have been sore as well, trotting alongside the horse all day, but he never complained.

They were making good progress, but Ping still didn't know where they were going. She didn't even know the name of the place they were seeking in the west. Was it Rising Moon Village, or Prosperous Village? She hoped that it lay somewhere near where

Danzi had written the name on the map. That was the only clue she had.

Ping decided to continue following the Great Wall west, keeping it just on the horizon so that they didn't attract the attention of any imperial guards. When the wall turned sharply south, they followed it.

They passed very few people. Kai was quieter than he had been. The muscles on his legs had doubled in size, so his thighs were like those of a tiger. The pads on the bottom of his paws were calloused from walking faster and farther than he was used to.

The landscape changed. They were crossing a dusty, yellow plain. To the west was a stark range of pointy, brown mountains. To the east, beyond the line of the Great Wall, and hidden behind low hills, was the Yellow River. At certain times of the year, the wind blew the fine, yellow soil beneath their feet into the great river, giving it its name and color.

Kai kept glancing over to the low hills in the east.

"Can you see something?" Ping asked.

"No," he replied.

One night Ping woke to see Kai sitting, staring at the full moon. His green scales were luminous in the moonlight, as if they were made from jade.

"What are you doing, Kai?" she asked.

"Nothing," Kai replied, but he continued to stare at the pale yellow sphere, as if he expected to find some meaning there.

Each morning brought another uncomfortable, dusty day identical to the last. The sun was getting hotter, too. Every day it shone down from a cloudless sky. The yellow earth was very fertile, but even the best soil is useless without rain. There was nothing growing anywhere. Ping's mouth was constantly full of dust, which the horse kicked up in clouds as it walked.

They passed only one person—a merchant traveling in the opposite direction. His head was wrapped in a piece of cloth, leaving just a slit through which his eyes were visible. He led two camels piled high with goods that he was no doubt going to trade with the Ma Ren. He didn't acknowledge Ping as he passed, but his eyes lingered on the horse.

After two weeks, a thin, straight line appeared on the southern horizon, as if it had been drawn there with a brush and straight edge. It was the Great Wall. It had stopped clinging to the Yellow River and turned west to march across the yellow plain.

"Are we going to return to the Empire?" Kai asked.

"Hou-yi said he had never heard of Long Xiang. I'm sure the place we're seeking is within the Empire. Can you see the features that Hou-yi described—a small hill shaped like a resting camel, a dry riverbed, a dead tree with five branches?"

Kai peered toward the wall. "I can see the camel-shaped hill." He pointed to the southeast.

"Good. Then it's time to leave the road, head toward the wall, and look for the hidden tunnel Hou-yi told us about."

Later that afternoon, the wind picked up, whining like a miserable dog. It peppered Ping's hands and face with sharp grains of sand. When she wasn't fighting with the horse, she was fighting against the wind. She was losing both struggles. The horse took no notice of her commands, and the wind blew gritty earth into her eyes. Ping pulled out the remains of her nightgown. Dust had seeped into the bag, and the cloth was dusty brown instead of white. Following the merchant's example, she wrapped the cloth around her head. It protected her face, but she was still constantly blinking away dust and grit. Now she had sore eyes to add to her list of discomforts. Kai kept his head down. His bright green scales made him stand out in the yellow landscape, but they protected him from the sand.

Once or twice Ping looked over her shoulder, half expecting to glimpse someone ducking behind a rock.

"Can you see anyone following us?" Ping asked Kai.

"No, but even for a dragon it is hard to see through this dust."

The mountains to the west had disappeared behind a curtain of windblown sand. Ping relied on the sun, which glowed an eerie orange through the dust, to guide her. The wind grew worse. Soon the dust completely blotted out the sun and Ping could see nothing.

The horse refused to move, but Ping didn't want to stop. She was afraid that they would disappear beneath the sand. She got off and led the frightened beast.

The wind didn't die down that night. They kept walking until they were too exhausted to stand. They stopped and slept under the shelter of Ping's bearskin and the saddlecloth. When Ping woke during the night, they were almost covered by a deep drift of sand.

By the morning, the wind had stopped blowing. The air was clear again. And the Great Wall was towering over them. If they had walked another two or three *chang* in the dark, they would have walked right into it.

Kai stirred under his bearskin. "Don't come out until you've shape-changed, Kai! We're practically under the wall."

The dragon emerged in the shape of Ping's little brother. Everything looked bright and unfamiliar after being shrouded in dust for a day and a half. The wall wasn't made of stone, as it had been in the mountains. The builders had constructed it out of the earth itself, packing it down until it was as hard as rock. The surface of the wall was smoothed flat with clay so that it was impossible to climb. An arched gateway had been cut through the wall. Its name was carved in the mud bricks that formed the arch—Shabian Pass.

Ping looked around. "Can you see the camel-shaped hill?"

Kai scanned the horizon in all directions. "No."

Ping peered up at the sun. "We must have strayed farther west in the dust storm."

There were three watchtowers within the space of a couple of *li*. It was nothing like the deserted stretch of wall that Hou-yi had told them to head for. Even though it was very early, imperial guards were already patrolling the walls, scanning the land—and staring down at the strangers with the horse.

"The guards have seen us. We can't look for the hidden tunnel," Ping said. "We'll have to go through the gateway. If they get too inquisitive, I'll bribe them with gold."

The guards at Shabian Pass looked more disciplined than the ones they'd seen elsewhere along the wall. They were wearing their correct uniforms, their weapons shone in the sunlight, and they were pacing along the ramparts. Ping thought it was strange that these guards, who were even farther away from the capital, Chang'an, were more orderly, more conscientious in carrying out their duties.

Ping led the horse to the gateway. A guard grabbed her arm as she was walking through. "Where's your permit?"

The boy next to her moved closer protectively.

"No! Don't change back into your own shape," Ping told the dragon in her mind. "No matter what happens."

Kai could only attack in his own shape.

Other people entering the gate were showing pieces of calfskin with red seal imprints on them. The guard looked at the horse. It was dusty after their journey, but it was still a handsome beast, towering over a donkey pulling a cart out of the gateway.

"I was separated from my family during the dust storm," Ping said. "My father has the permit."

"No one can enter the Empire without a permit," the guard insisted.

"I don't have one, but I do have this." Ping pulled a gold piece from her pouch. It was worth more than the guard would earn in a year.

He glanced around, snatched the gold from her hand, hid it under his tunic, and then waved them through. Ping and Kai passed through the gateway and found themselves back in the Empire again.

A small town had clustered around the gateway. The houses were shapeless lumps made of packed earth, like the wall. Everything was the same dirty yellow color. There was a smell of dog urine and rotten meat in the air.

It was still early, but a few people were stirring, setting up market stalls and stocking them with wrinkled vegetables and fly-blown meat. Their clothes were nearly as dusty as Ping's; they looked as if they'd been fashioned from the sandy earth.

Merchants and traders from other parts of the Empire were wandering through the market, but they weren't interested in the poor-quality food. They inspected other stalls that displayed gold buckles and felt saddlecloths, which the townspeople must have bought from the Ma Ren. Imperial guards looked down from the wall, spears in their hands, crossbows slung on their backs, watching every move the townspeople made, as well as looking out for barbarian attackers.

Being back in her own land should have given Ping comfort, but instead she felt afraid. She didn't like towns. In villages, everyone knew each other. There was always an elder to speak to, and she only had to convince him that she had no plan to rob the villagers. In a town, people were less friendly—to each other as well as to travelers. There was no single person to speak to, and she had to persuade everyone she met that she meant no harm. And though townspeople almost always had more money than villagers, they were less generous. No one invited them into their home to spend the night.

"Not stopping for breakfast?" Kai asked. His nose had sniffed out the one stall that sold roasted meat.

"No. I don't like this place. I want to leave as soon as possible."

The horse didn't seem to like towns either. It was pulling at the reins and whinnying.

Ping looked over her shoulder. No sooner had she passed through the gateway than the feeling that she was being followed returned. Just as she turned, she was sure she glimpsed someone ducking out of sight. Ping put her arm around Kai's shoulder. She could feel his scales. It reassured her.

Ping saw a hat through the crowd that looked out of place among the dusty caps and headscarves of the townspeople. It was jet black, square, with beads hanging from each corner. Somehow the wearer had managed to keep it free of dust. Ping realized why the guards at Shabian Pass were so alert and well-presented—the hat belonged to a visiting government official. The official climbed the steps to inspect the guards on the wall. He had red ribbons hanging from his waist, so Ping knew that he was a very important minister. The guards stood at attention.

At the bottom of the steps there was a carriage. It was well made and painted with a pattern of bamboo stems and leaves. A woman wearing a blue gown stepped down from the carriage. She looked just as out of place as the minister. She held a sprig of dried jasmine flowers to her nose, and a servant held an umbrella over her head to protect her from the sun.

"Pretty lady," Kai said. "Like Princess."

As Ping got closer, she could see that the woman, though older than Princess Yangxin, was beautiful. But she wore an expression of distaste and impatience that Ping had never seen on the Princess's face. Another servant was clearing a way for the minister's wife, moving the people aside so that his mistress didn't have to touch them. Ping was intrigued. Why was this woman so determined to walk through the market, when she could have been up on the wall with her husband, above the dust and the smell and the grimy people? Though Ping knew she should be heading straight out of the town as quickly as possible, she found herself following the woman, pulling the horse behind her.

The servant led his mistress to a stall at the back of the market. Several merchants were crowded around the stall, but they stepped back to allow the lady to see. It was a stall displaying the most delicately carved jade jewelry Ping had ever seen. She remembered the Princess's earrings and the jade hair decoration she had worn the first time she saw her at Ming Yang Lodge. How did such beautiful work find its way to this distant, dusty town? The stallholder had hung his wares on a length of string, so that his stall was festooned with jade earrings and necklaces. The breeze caught them, and they gently brushed against each other. They made a lovely tinkling noise that sounded like Kai when he was happy. The minister's wife quickly purchased three pairs of earrings, two necklaces, and a bracelet. Then she hurried back toward her carriage.

"Where does this beautiful work come from?" Ping asked the stallholder.

He looked Ping up and down, from the torn and grimy cloth wrapped around her head to the worn and misshapen shoes on her feet. Ping realized that she must have looked even shabbier than the inhabitants of Shabian Pass. The stallholder ignored her—until she pulled some copper coins from her pouch.

"The jewelry is made at Long Xiang," he said. "Tinkling Village."

Ping's heart beat faster. She held out a handful of coins.

"Where is that village?" she asked as the man took several of the coins from her hand.

"It's at the foot of the mountains," he said, pointing west.

Since she hadn't objected to the number of coins he'd taken, the stallholder took another. "I've never been there myself, but it's near Xining. That's where I buy my wares."

Ping thanked him. "Did you hear that, Kai?"

Kai nodded. "Tinkling Village. That's where Father wants us to go."

Ping saw a movement out of the corner of her eye and whipped around. She was positive she saw someone crouch down behind a market stall when she turned to look. The feeling that someone was following her was stronger than ever. The guards were striding back and forth on top of the wall, watching her. The town felt stifling. The horse didn't like being enclosed in the street. It tried to pull away from Ping.

"Hey, watch out for that horse," the jade seller shouted anxiously. "If it kicks my stall, you'll have to pay for anything that gets broken."

Just as Ping was turning away from the jade stall, she saw the minister making his way through the crowd toward them.

"That's a very handsome horse," he said.

Ping would have quite happily given the man the horse, but she didn't want to attract any more attention. She bowed politely.

"It belongs to my master, sir," she said. "He asked me to fetch it from the stables, but it got away from me. My brother and I had to chase it."

"Perhaps you could take me to your master," the minister said, "so that I can check that he has a permit to import a horse from outside the Empire."

"Oh, I'm sure he does, sir," Ping said. "He's very particular about such things."

"Not so particular about the way he dresses his servants," the stallholder observed.

Ping smoothed down her jacket. A cloud of dust rose from it. The minister signaled the guards on the wall. They started down the steps.

"Time to leave the horse," Kai said.

The boy next to Ping let out a roar that sounded like someone banging a gong. People looked around to see where the noise was coming from. The horse reared up, beating the air with its hard hooves. It backed into a vegetable stall, sending melons and onions rolling in all directions. Ping grabbed the saddlebag and then flicked the horse's rump with the leather thong. People shrank away from the rearing horse, giving it a clear path down the street. The horse galloped off. Ping and Kai ran in the opposite direction.

Ping couldn't move fast because she was carrying the heavy bag. Kai led the way. He turned into an alleyway, even narrower than the street. People watched from their doorways as Ping and Kai ran past, dodging people and dogs and rubbish.

"Kai," Ping said, "I keep getting this feeling that someone is following us."

Kai turned. "Someone *is* following—imperial guards."

"Not them. Can you see anyone else?"

Kai dodged around a stray dog and then peered over his shoulder again. "No."

"Actually, now my second sight is telling me that whoever was behind us is now in front of us."

"How can someone follow if they are in front?" Kai asked.

"I don't know."

The guards were gaining on them. They were keen to impress the visiting minister with their efficiency.

There was a crowd of people ahead, gathered around a dumpling stall. Pushing past the crowd slowed them down. Ping scanned the roofs. The buildings were low. She was considering climbing up and escaping that way when she collided with someone. It wasn't an imperial guard. It was a man dressed in clothes as dusty as hers. He grabbed her. She tried to fight him off, but she was weary. She didn't think she had the strength to summon a *qi* bolt, so she kicked him in the shin and flicked his face with the leather thong, which was still in her hand. He yelped with pain and let go of her.

She turned to face the guards. Two of them already had Kai backed against a wall, their iron spear tips trained on him. She could hear the tearing metal sound of a dragon in pain. His boy-shape was shimmering. Ping knew he couldn't stay shape-changed for long in the presence of iron. The man grabbed her again from behind. Anger focused her *qi* without her even having to think about it. She turned and hit the man with a *qi* bolt, sending him flying into a nearby pile of bricks. The guards turned away from Kai.

Before Ping could refocus her *qi*, more guards had surrounded her with their crossbows loaded and pointed in her direction. The dusty man got up.

"Don't harm them," he said. "They're my slaves."

"I am no one's slave!" Ping shouted.

The crossbows moved closer.

"You should ask for your money back," one of the guards said. "No point in paying good money for a troublesome slave."

"I'll calm her down, don't worry. And you don't have to poke your spears at the boy," the man continued. "You won't do anything silly, will you, Kai?"

The little boy shook his head solemnly.

Ping looked at the man again. How did he know Kai's name?

"You'd better catch that horse of yours," the guard said, "before someone steals it."

"I'll give you a reward if you can catch it for me," the man said, pulling a gold coin from his sleeve.

The guards lowered their spears and turned to pursue the horse.

"Are you sure you can handle this one?" a guard asked, jerking his head toward Ping. "She's a savage. You can't trust a barbarian."

Ping let the insult pass. She'd met more savages on this side of the wall than the other. The guards hurried back down the alley, keen to earn the reward. The crowd that had gathered went back to their business. Ping examined the man. He was young, no more than sixteen years old.

"Why did you say I was your slave?" she asked.

"I wanted to get rid of the guards." He was smiling.

Ping heard a sound like small bells jingling. It was Kai laughing.

"Don't you recognize me, Ping?" As he said this, the young man looked down shyly, as if he didn't really want her to look at him at all.

Ping stared at him again. He held something out in his hand.

"You said I should keep this as a souvenir, but I think

it holds better memories for you than it does for me."

In his hand was the Imperial Dragon Keeper's seal. He glanced at her.

"Jun?"

He nodded.

Ping moved closer. The young man looked nothing like the boy who had tried to steal her job as Imperial Dragon Keeper the previous year. He no longer had a fringe to hide behind.

"Your hair's grown," Ping blurted out.

Jun smiled. "You'd expect it to in a year or more."

The rest of him had grown as well. He was more than a head taller than Ping. His face was fuller, his arms stronger, his voice deeper.

"What are you doing here?" Ping asked.

Jun took her arm. "I'll explain later, but right now I think we need to get away from Shabian Pass. You've already drawn enough attention to yourself."

# CHAPTER ELEVEN

# TRUST

Ping was exhausted, and Kai was weak from being near iron, but neither of them argued with Jun. They walked as fast as they could away from the Great Wall and the dusty town. Ping was glad to be traveling on her own two feet again.

She still found it hard to believe that the young man striding ahead of her was the skinny boy who had pretended to be a Dragon Keeper. Ping and the Imperial Magician, Dong Fang Suo, had found him living in poverty with his family on an unsuccessful silkworm farm. Although Jun's grandfather had been a Dragon Keeper, neither Jun nor his father had the characteristics. But that hadn't stopped his parents from trying to end their poverty by passing their son off as one.

No one spoke until Shabian Pass was far behind and they were sure that no one was following them. Jun slackened his pace, and Ping caught up with him.

146

"Tell me what has happened to you since I saw you last," she said.

Jun didn't answer straightaway. Their time together was not something either of them took pleasure in remembering. The Emperor had blamed all his failures on Ping and made Jun the Imperial Dragon Keeper. Jun, however, eventually decided that he couldn't go on pretending to be a Dragon Keeper. So he had helped Ping and the Imperial Magician defeat the necromancer, who wanted to use Kai's blood in his spells to give the Emperor eternal life. During that confrontation, Dong Fang Suo had been killed and Jun had volunteered to take his body back to the Emperor.

"The Emperor was very angry," Jun said. "Not about Dong's death, but about the defeat of the necromancer."

"Did he punish you?" Ping asked.

"He locked me belowdecks on the imperial barge, but he was soon obsessed with sending an expedition to the Kun-lun Mountains to find the fungus of immortality that's supposed to grow there. He sailed back to Chang'an, leaving behind anyone who'd had anything to do with his failed plan to make an elixir of eternal life. There was me, and the kitchen boy who mixed the potions, and the remaining members of the Longevity Council. Do you remember them, Ping?"

"Those three strange men?"

Jun nodded.

"I told them I was going home and that the silkworms

weren't producing silk. The Longevity Council members knew exactly what was wrong. It wasn't the worms that were sick, it was the mulberry leaves that they fed on. They knew how to cure the sickness."

The council members told Jun that the fallen leaves had to be burned during winter, and the new buds painted with a copper solution in spring. They made the solution from melted copper bowls that they found in the charred remains of Ming Yang Lodge.

"I walked home," Jun continued, "and arrived just in time to burn the leaves before the spring growth emerged. Then I painted the buds with the copper solution. The silk crop was the best we've had for years. This year's crop promises to be even better. My parents are convinced this change in our fortunes was because of the dragon's luck."

Ping was pleased to hear that Jun's family was experiencing better times, but there was another question she wanted to ask.

"So it wasn't just chance that made our paths cross again?"

Jun shook his head.

"For weeks, I've had a feeling that someone was behind us, always just out of sight." Ping looked at Jun. "Was it you?"

Jun lowered his eyes and nodded.

"I couldn't understand it," Ping said. "I've only ever been followed by people who wanted to harm Kai. I had no foreboding, because you didn't want to hurt Kai. I thought my second sight wasn't working, but it hasn't let me down."

"It wasn't working very well this morning," Jun said. "Why did you go wandering off to look at jewelry when the town was bristling with guards trying to impress the minister?"

"I think it *was* my second sight that drew me to the stall," Ping said.

"Your second sight told you that you needed earrings?"

Ping smiled. "No, it told me that I would learn something important there."

"And did you?"

"Yes."

Jun waited for Ping to tell him what she'd learned, but she was silent. "I only want to help you, Ping. Where are you going?"

"I don't know."

"You've wandered across the Empire without knowing where you're going?"

Ping nodded. "I know where I'm going next, but not my final destination." She looked around. "Where's Kai?" She couldn't see the dragon anywhere.

"Has he shape-changed into something else?" Jun asked.

Ping peered at a nearby bush, then poked at a rock. "Kai, where are you?"

There was no answer.

"It's because we've been ignoring him. He's gone off in a huff. He could get lost."

"He can't be far away. We were dawdling. Are you sure he hasn't gone ahead?"

"I don't know."

They hurried along the road. Suddenly something jumped out from behind a rock.

"Boo!" said a voice in Ping's head. To Jun it sounded like someone crashing a gong.

"Kai," Ping said sternly. "That wasn't very funny."

Kai was making a sound like small bells ringing. "Yes, it was!"

They walked on in silence. They had left the dusty yellow plain behind at last. To the south were the first thriving fields Ping had seen all spring. Farmers had channeled water from the Yellow River to irrigate their fields. The sight of green leaves was a balm for the eyes after so many days in the desert. Ping picked some berries from a bush near the road.

"I'd like to continue to help you," Jun said.

"We don't need an escort," Ping said. "We can look after ourselves."

"If Jun hadn't been there to rescue us," Kai pointed out, "Ping would be in prison in Shabian Pass."

Ping didn't tell Jun what Kai had said.

They stopped before it got dark, next to an irriga-tion stream. Ping had drunk nothing but sour milk for a long time. The water tasted fresh and sweet. Jun and

Kai went hunting while Ping lit a fire. They returned with a partridge. While they waited for it to cook, Jun continued his story.

"I was selling silk," Jun replied. "The women in my village wove many *chang* of silk cloth last season. Most villages in our area sell their cloth straight to the imperial stores. I didn't want to risk reminding the Emperor of my existence, in case he decided that I needed punishment after all. We'd heard that some silk growers in the north sold their cloth to the barbarians, who have developed a taste for silk, so we decided to give it a try. I wanted to reach the Xiong Nu before the other growers, so I left in spring. It was too early. I found myself in a snowstorm. I almost froze to death, but some of Hou-yi's men found me."

"Hou-yi! He rescued us as well," Ping said.

"They saved my life, and I sold them my silk," Jun continued. "Hou-yi also helped me meet other tribal chiefs who wanted silk. He thought I would get myself killed if I continued to wander around by myself. I liked him straight away."

"The bird is ready," the dragon interrupted. "Kai is hungry."

They shared the partridge between them, as well as some tubers that Ping had dug up and roasted in the coals. It was the tastiest meal Ping had eaten for some time. From the speed that Kai ate his, he obviously appreciated the food, too. He didn't stop when he'd eaten all the meat. He crunched up the bones and ate them as well.

They shared the berries that Ping had picked that afternoon and drank hot water flavored with ginger.

"It was brave of you to wander around the lands of the Ma Ren by yourself," Ping said.

"That's a good name for Hou-yi's people." Jun smiled. "Hou-yi didn't trust me to get home safely, so he sent one of his men with me as a guide. The guide picked up news of what was happening elsewhere. He heard of the Emperor's defeat and of the departure of the lucky dragon from Yan. I thought that with Danzi and Dong Fang Suo gone, someone should be keeping an eye on you. I picked up your trail when you started traveling along the wall."

"You don't think I can look after myself?"

"I didn't know why you'd set off to cross the country. I thought you might have new enemies who were after Kai. Or perhaps the Emperor was pursuing you again."

"The Emperor was badly wounded in the battle with the Ma Ren. I found him. I don't think he'll try to harm me again."

"I didn't know that. I wasn't sure if you would welcome my assistance, so I bribed two guards to give me their uniforms. My guide and I posed as imperial messengers. We followed from a distance, helping whenever we could."

"What sort of help?"

"When you were captured by the imperial guards at Ji Liao Garrison I knew there were too many for us to take on. I sent my guide back to Hou-yi for help, while I lit the beacons at the next garrison to throw the guards into a panic."

Ping looked at Jun in amazement.

"It was you who asked Hou-yi to help us! And then you stopped the guards at Shabian Pass from arresting me."

He smiled shyly. "I wasn't always successful in protecting you. I lost you in the dust storm. You could have become disoriented and died out there."

Ping turned to Kai. "How come you didn't see him, Kai? You're supposed to be able to see for many *li*."

"Kai did see Jun."

"So why didn't you tell me he was following us?"

"Ping needed another protector besides Kai." The dragon looked guilty. "Ping can be as stubborn as a horse. Kai thought Ping might send Jun away."

Because he had been so small and skinny when she'd first met him, Ping had always assumed that Jun was younger than she was—just a child. But now that he had eaten well for a year or more, he had grown to the right size for a young man of sixteen years.

Kai ate the last of the partridge bones, then he dug a hole, made a nest, and went to sleep.

"He's very tired," Ping said.

"He walked all the way from the Ma Ren camp to

Shabian Pass," Jun said. "He has every reason to be tired."

Though she said nothing, Ping had to admit to her-self that she did feel more secure with Jun there.

"Ping, are you sure you're doing the right thing?" Jun broke into her thoughts. "There must be many places where you and Kai can live peacefully without having to trek to the other side of the Empire."

"Yes, I'm sure. It's what Danzi wanted. If you'd known him, you wouldn't question his wisdom. He might have been an old dragon, but he was wise. At first I thought Kai needed more people, other Dragon Keepers to take over when I die. That's the reason we came to your village. But I was wrong. He doesn't need other people, just the opposite. He needs to find a home that's as far away from people as possible."

"But you don't even know where you're going. You're just wandering around hoping you'll come across this wondrous safe place."

"You're wasting your time if you think you can talk me out of it. I know I'm doing the right thing."

"I can see that Kai needs a safe place to live," Jun persisted. "But I don't understand why it has to be on the very edge of the Empire. You and Kai could live in my village. You could have your own house. Lu-lin is a prosperous place now, and the villagers are so grateful that I restored the mulberry trees to health, they would do anything I asked. They will keep Kai's presence a secret."

Ping sighed. "For how long? A year? Ten years? A hundred years?" She was tired of explaining it to people. "Kai has to be safe not only while he's young, but through his whole life, long after you and I are dead."

Jun was silent for a moment.

"So you're taking Kai to a place, but you don't know where it is. And when you find it, he's going to be safe but living in solitude for most of his life."

Ping had known that was the case, but now that someone had said it aloud, it did sound like a lonely life.

"It's a matter of trust," Ping continued. "Trusting Danzi, trusting myself. You don't always need to know your destination when you set out on a journey."

"Did you sell all your silk?" Ping asked Jun the next morning. "Are you going home to Lu-lin?"

"Yes, I've finished my business, but I'm not going home. If you will allow me, I'd like to travel with you. As a companion, if you're so sure you don't need help."

The sound of wind chimes filled the air.

"Yes!" Kai said. "Jun can come with us. Help us to find the dragon haven."

"Won't your family be worried about you?"

"I've sent a message along with the gold Hou-yi paid me for the first bolt of silk. My father will arrange the transport of the rest of the silk."

"You don't owe us anything, Jun. There is no need

for you to stay away from your family on our account."

"It's because of my family that I'm here, Ping," Jun explained. "They want me to make amends for their deception. I'm not a Dragon Keeper. I only pretended to be for a few weeks, but my ancestors were Dragon Keepers. They failed in their duty."

"It wasn't their fault. It was Lan and his father who took the job from them."

"Their job was to protect the dragons, and themselves, from devious people like the Lans. My parents think that their previous bad luck with the mulberry trees was because of their ancestors' failure. They told me that as soon as I had arranged to sell the silk, I should try to find you and help you in whatever way I could, so that they can continue to benefit from the dragon's luck."

Ping didn't say anything.

"It's all about trust, Ping, just as you said. Can you trust me?"

Her second sight wasn't giving her any warnings. She had few enough friends. "I can trust you."

Jun smiled. "Good."

"I'm not wandering around completely without a plan," Ping said.

She took out the silk square and showed it to Jun.

"I can see the Great Wall and the Yellow River," he said, peering at the map, "but where are you meant to go?"

"It doesn't say. Not directly, anyway. It's written in a secret code. See here." She pointed to the characters that said Dragon's Lament Creek. "That's not a real place. It's directions. You have to say it aloud to find its true meaning. It really means, 'Seek westward.'"

"And this one." He read out the words aloud. "'*Qu long xiang.*' What does that mean?"

"It means 'Go to the *long* village.' But until yesterday I didn't know which *long* it was supposed to be. It could have been Bright Village, Hazy Village, Basket Village, Rising Moon Village. All I knew was that it was somewhere in the west, probably in the mountains."

Jun still didn't understand.

"The jade jewelry was made in a place called Long Xiang," Ping explained. "*Long* also means the sound that jade pendants make when they clink together. Tinkling Village, that's where we're going now."

"Does that 'we' include me?"

"Kai wants you to come," Ping said. "And I still haven't fully deciphered Danzi's map. Two minds are better than one."

"Three," Kai said. "Three minds."

Ping laughed. "Three minds."

They soon left behind the irrigated fields that clung to the Yellow River. The countryside became dry again. Few people seemed to live in that remote part of the Empire, so Kai only occasionally had to use his mirage skill or create a cloud of mist to conceal himself. The narrow road was little more than a track that wound along a valley between meadows that should have been carpeted with green. Instead the fields were parched and brown. It was more than two months since Ping and Kai had left Yan. It was now early summer. The spring rains had failed again. There was no chance of rain for many months.

"Does Jun want to play?" Kai asked. "Remember how we played together before?"

Ping told Jun what he had said.

"I can't think of a game we can play while we're walking, Kai."

"Hide-and-seek?"

"What did he say?"

"He wants to play hide-and-seek."

"That would slow us down too much."

"Play ball?"

"We haven't got a ball, Kai," Ping said. "He loves to tell the story of our adventures. It's a pity he can't talk to you."

Jun blushed, and Ping wished she could have taken back her words. They had only reminded Jun of when he had pretended to understand Kai.

Straggling, dried-up melon vines were growing alongside the road. They were last year's crop. Since they hadn't been picked, Ping suspected they wouldn't be any good to eat, even if they weren't months old. Jun had in mind a different use for the melons.

"Perhaps one of these would do as a ball, Kai. We might be able to kick it to each other."

He pulled a melon from the vine and gently kicked it along the ground. Kai immediately raced after the ball and kicked it with his left front paw. They kicked the melon back and forth as they walked, until the melon hit a rock and smashed. The flesh inside was rotten and smelled terrible.

That night Ping cut a piece from the corner of her bearskin and, with the fur on the inside, fashioned it into the shape of a ball. She used dry grass to fill it and laced it together with a leather thong.

The next day Jun and Kai spent hours kicking and tossing the ball back and forth. Kai never tired of the game. Whenever Jun tried to stop, the dragon begged him to keep playing.

"Let Jun have a rest from the game, Kai," Ping said. "I'd like to talk to him occasionally."

Kai's spines drooped.

"Tell me more about your family, Jun," Ping said. "How are your sisters?"

Jun started to tell Ping how four of his seven sisters had received offers of marriage. As he talked, he absently tossed the ball up in the air and caught it with one hand. Suddenly, Kai launched himself at the ball, trying to grab it while it was in midair. In his enthusiasm, he crashed into Jun and knocked him over.

"Kai!" said Ping. "That's too rough."

"Sorry," said Kai.

Ping decided that since Jun was sitting down, it was a good time for a rest. She sat down, too. They drank some water and ate a handful of nuts.

"We must be getting close to Xining now," Ping said as she inspected the holes in her shoes. "I think it's time I got out my spare shoes."

Jun lay back in the sunlight, enjoying the rest.

"Look at that," he said, pointing up into the sky. "I've never seen a bird that size before."

Ping shaded her eyes. A white bird was circling above them. It had a huge wingspan. Kai, who had been snuffling through the bag looking for jujubes, leaped to his feet. He stared at the bird and made the strangest sound, as if he was happy and scared at the same time.

"What's wrong, Kai?" Ping said. "The bird can't hurt us."

"It's not a bird," the dragon told her.

"What's the matter with him?" Jun asked.

Kai made the same strange sound.

"What did he say?"

Ping's heart was racing as she peered up into the sky and translated Kai's words for Jun.

"He says it's not a bird . . . it's a dragon."

• CHAPTER TWELVE •

## THE TINKLING VILLAGE

"A dragon," Ping said. "Another dragon."

She hugged Kai.

"Are you sure, Kai?" Jun asked.

"He's sure," Ping whispered.

"Did you know there was another dragon?" Jun asked Ping.

"Not until now," Ping replied. "But now that I've seen it, I feel like I've always known."

It seemed so blindingly clear, she was amazed that she hadn't realized it before. Kai would live for more than a thousand years. He didn't need to spend the rest of his life alone after she died. He needed another dragon. One of his own kind to share his long life with.

While she was at Ming Yang Lodge, she had thought that Kai would need other Dragon Keepers to care for him, when she could no longer do the job.

She had searched for the Dragon Keeper families,

hoping to find a man with the three characteristics, and young enough to have sons who could take over when she grew too old for the task. Jun had turned out to be an imposter. She'd not found anyone.

Now she knew Kai wouldn't be living by himself in the centuries after she died. Her heart soared.

"Do you think the dragon saw us?" Jun asked.

"Of course it saw us," Ping replied. "It saw the holes in my shoes, it knows how many nuts we ate."

"So why did it fly away?"

"I don't know," Ping said. "It's probably wary of people. I hadn't dared to hope that we would find another dragon in the world. Now we know there is one!"

She took out the calfskin on which the seer had written the *Yi Jing* divination. She had been so focused on deciphering Danzi's map that she had almost forgotten about it. She read aloud the fifth reading. "A flying dragon in the heavens. See the great man."

Jun peered at the calfskin. "What does that mean?"

"It means everything is unfolding as it should. When I first read that line, I thought it referred to Kai. I didn't expect him to suddenly sprout wings, but I thought it was like one of Danzi's sayings—something that said one thing but meant another. I thought it was a way of saying that Kai would mature, that he would 'fly' in the sense of succeeding, achieving something. I didn't realize it meant there would be an actual dragon" —she laughed—"flying in the sky!"

"But who's 'the great man'?" Jun asked. He was not used to riddles and divination.

"I don't know," Ping said. "One step at a time. First we must find the Tinkling Village."

"Perhaps the great man will be there," Kai said.

Excitement radiated from Kai like heat from a brazier.

She nodded. "Yes, he'll know where this white dragon lives."

"It can teach Kai how to be a proper dragon."

Ping fondled his ears. "Yes."

They arrived at Xining the next day, stopped at an inn, and ate a good meal. The traders and travelers staying at the inn were all either on their way to or returning from the Tinkling Village. The jade was mined thousands of *li* away, on the other side of the Kun-lun Mountains, but for more than a century, this one small village had specialized in carving the finest, most beautiful jade jewelry in all the Empire.

Long Xiang was just half a day's walk from Xining.

Kai wanted to leave immediately and walk through the night.

"We'll wait till morning," Ping said. "You must be patient. There's no point in arriving in the middle of the night when everyone's asleep. Tonight we'll stay at this excellent inn."

But Ping was just as excited as Kai. Despite the fact

that she lay on a mattress for the first time in weeks, she barely slept.

In the morning, Ping tied up her hair and put on her traveling gown so that she looked like someone who could afford to buy jade jewelry.

Jun smiled when he saw her. "You look nice," he said, then stared at his shoes as he blushed.

"You take this." Ping handed her imperial seal to him. "We can pretend we are imperial officials inspecting the jade."

He took the seal and tied it around his waist.

They reached Long Xiang just after midday. It was a village of no more than twenty houses nestled comfortably into the slope of a hill. The village gates were thrown open, and traders from all over the Empire and beyond were visiting.

The sound of people carving jade could be heard from outside the walls. There were three streets in the Tinkling Village. Every household was involved with jade carving. Every person played a part in the village's industry. Each street had its specialty—in one, only hair decorations were made; the second, only necklaces; earrings were the specialty of the third. Three households specialized in wind chimes, which only the richest people in the Empire could afford. Stalls outside each house were hung with the household's wares, and they clinked in the breeze. That was what gave the village its name. Even the children had their own special task. They gathered dry grass for packing the jewelry so that it arrived unbroken when it was sent to all corners of the Empire.

There was no inn in the village. Traders usually arrived early, made their purchases, and returned to Xining in a single day. Kai was so excited he couldn't keep still, but in the shape of Ping's little brother, that didn't seem out of place.

"How do we know who the great man is?" Jun asked.

"The most important man is the village elder," Ping replied. "Once word spreads that there's an imperial official visiting, I'm sure we'll get his personal attention."

As they strolled around the village, Jun showed Ping's seal to the villagers, telling them they were there to buy jewelry for the imperial ladies in Chang'an. The villagers were very interested in the unusual white jade that the seal was made of, and no one noticed that the characters said it was the seal of an Imperial Dragon Keeper, not an imperial purchaser. Neither Ping nor Jun corrected them when they assumed that Jun was an important official and Ping was the Empress's head lady-in-waiting. News of the imperial visitors soon spread, and before long the village elder came and invited them to stay for the night in his home. Ping was sure that he was the great man.

The elder's name was Master Cai. He wasn't as old

as some of the village elders they had met, and he wore a silk gown as fine as those of the Duke of Yan. His house was a two-story building with many rooms. There were silk hangings and bronze ornaments more suited to the house of a lord than a village elder. That evening they were invited to eat with Master Cai's family. It was a lavish meal of four courses. Kai, in the shape of Ping's younger brother, was sent to bed early.

Ping hinted that they intended to buy many pieces of jewelry for the Emperor's sister and mother. Though the meal was excellent, Master Cai's wife found much to complain about to their three servants. After the meal, when Mistress Cai had gone to make sure that the servants cleaned the dishes properly, Ping tried to turn the conversation to dragons. But all Master Cai wanted to talk about was jade. Jun even said that he had been instructed in particular to find a jade dragon. Ping peered into the elder's eyes, looking for some understanding. There was none.

The next day, Master Cai had arranged a tour of Long Xiang for his guests. They visited many jade carvers. Jun bought a few pieces of jewelry, to keep up the charade. He said they were only buying samples on this journey, but the village elder was getting impatient. He had been expecting the imperial official to spend the Emperor's gold much more freely. Eventually, Ping decided that the only thing left was to be direct.

"I heard a story as we were traveling that there is a dragon living in the mountains around here," she remarked casually after they had finished the tour and returned to the elder's house.

"What nonsense!" Master Cai said. "I've never heard such a tale."

He left them to turn his attention to traders more interested in parting with their gold.

"I think we've just about worn out our welcome in the Tinkling Village," said Jun.

Kai was moping around miserably. "Look at Father's silk again," he said.

Ping took out the silk square.

"There is one more clue that you haven't deciphered," Jun said. "Just because you've made sense of one line of the *Yi Jing* reading, doesn't mean that you should ignore the map. Perhaps they work together." Jun read out the final place name. "Blazing Dragon Valley, Ye Long Gu. What else can that mean?"

Ping wrote down other characters pronounced *ye* that meant sickness, night, and liquid. She thought back to all the books she'd read at Beibai Palace, all the characters she'd learned.

"There's also this one." She wrote down the character that meant to visit someone who is revered. "Perhaps there's another 'great man' in the village besides the elder."

Ping and Jun went out to the courtyard and struck

up a conversation with Mistress Cai. Ping asked about the history of the village, how it came to specialize in jade carving. The woman didn't know.

"Is there someone else in the village who might know?"

"There is no one who knows more than my husband," she said proudly.

"But Master Cai is young for a man of such an important position," Ping said. "There must be men who are older."

The woman nodded. "My husband is wise for his years, everybody says so."

"Who is the oldest person in the village?" Ping persisted.

"Granny Wang is very old. So is Mr Chu. But I suppose the oldest person would be Lao Longzi. He's an old fool who doesn't know anything about jade carving. He's not from around here. He's not even a craftsman. He settled in Long Xiang and made a living as a merchant." She spoke the word as if it were an insult. "He used to take our goods to towns in the south to sell, until he got too old to travel. You won't get anything out of him. He's as deaf as a stone."

Ping looked over to Kai, who was sitting in his little-boy shape on the other side of the courtyard.

"Never mind. It's not important," Ping said to the woman. She stretched. "It's a nice day. I think we might go for a stroll around the village."

"But you have an appointment to see the head carver on Necklace Street," Mistress Cai exclaimed.

Ping looked at Jun, wondering how she could get away.

"I'll go and see the necklace carver," Jun said. "You and your brother go for a walk."

The woman called for a servant to bring her out-door shoes. Then she and Jun left the house.

"*Long gu,*" Kai said excitedly, after they had left.

Ping nodded. She wrote two characters in the earth. They read "deaf merchant." *Ye Long Gu* also meant "visit the deaf merchant."

It only took two inquiries to find the home of the deaf merchant. No one seemed to know his real name; he was just known as Lao Longzi—the old deaf one. Even though he had lived in the village for more than fifty years, he was still considered a stranger. He lived in the last house on Earring Street. The small house was so dilapidated, it was hard to believe it could still stand. Rain had washed away part of one mud-brick wall, lengths of wood propped up another. The wind or birds had carried away a good deal of the straw thatching from the roof.

"There doesn't seem much point in knocking on a deaf man's door," Ping said to Kai.

She pushed open the sagging door and entered a courtyard. A few herbs and vegetables were growing in a garden bed. Three skinny chickens pecked at the hard earth. A very old man was sitting on a bench in a patch of sunlight on the other side of the courtyard, with his chin resting on his chest. His gown was patched and darned. His hair was pure white and tied back loosely in a braid. A walking stick leaned against the bench at his side. He didn't notice them enter.

Ping went over to him and very gently touched his hand. The old man wasn't startled. He slowly raised his head and smiled at her as if he wasn't at all surprised to see a young woman standing before him. Ping took out the silk square and opened it up. She spread the map on the old man's lap. He peered at the markings for a long time.

"I don't think he understands the writing," Ping said to Kai. "His eyesight might be as bad as his hearing."

She took the mirror from her pouch and held it out to the old man. He reached for it with his left hand. His fingers were as stiff as twigs, but he managed to take hold of it. He ran a crooked finger over the dragon design and mouthed a word. Ping leaned closer. "What did you say?"

The faintest sound came out of the old man's mouth. "Danzi?" he whispered.

"Did you hear that?" she asked Kai.

"Didn't hear anything," Kai said. "Dragons don't have good hearing."

The old man's clawlike fingers reached out and

grabbed a fold of Ping's gown. "Danzi?" he repeated.

Ping shook her head. The old man thought she was a shape-changed dragon. "No," she said, though she knew he couldn't hear her. "I'm not Danzi, but I'm looking for the dragon haven."

The old man stared at his image in the mirror.

"How can we tell him what we want?" Ping said.

"Kai knows."

She saw something shimmering just out of the corner of her eye. Kai was turning back to his true dragon shape. The old man looked up from the mirror and gazed at the young dragon.

"Lao Longzi," said Kai. Ping could hear his words in her mind. "My father wants me to go to the dragon haven. Can you tell us where it is?"

The old man's lips were so thin they barely existed. He seemed unable to form a smile, but his cloudy eyes brightened. He reached out and touched Kai's scales. Tears filled his eyes.

"Dragon haven," he breathed.

He had heard Kai's unspoken words. He was a Dragon Keeper.

The old man was staring at Kai. "Who is your keeper?"

Ping could hear his words as well, but his voice was just a whisper.

"Ping is Kai's keeper."

Lao Longzi looked at Ping. "A girl?"

"I was Danzi's Dragon Keeper," Ping said.

"So was I," Lao Longzi said. "Is Danzi . . . ?"

Ping stared at the old man. Kai reached out and touched him with the pads of one paw.

"Danzi has gone to the Isle of the Blest," Ping replied. "He asked me to take Kai to the dragon haven. Can you tell me where it is?"

"Secret place," the old man said. "Must never be written down or spoken aloud."

Ping held her breath.

"Long Gao Yuan." The words echoed in Ping's mind. "Dragon Plateau."

"Where is it?" Ping's heart was beating fast.

"I've never heard of a female Dragon Keeper," he said.

Speaking those few words seemed to have taken all of the old man's energy. His head sagged onto his chest again. Ping and Kai waited, but he didn't stir. She took the silk square from his hands, then they left the courtyard.

They hurried back to the elder's house. Ping gabbled the news to Jun. Kai was making an excited gonging sound. Jun couldn't understand either of them.

"Slow down," he said.

"Lao Longzi told us the name of the dragon haven," she whispered. "It's called Long Gao Yuan."

"And where is it?"

Ping's excitement melted away like snow in spring.

"He didn't tell us that. I don't think he believed I was a true Dragon Keeper."

Kai wanted to pack their bag and run off to find Dragon Plateau immediately. Jun tried to calm them both down.

"We don't want to rouse the villagers' suspicions. As far as they're concerned, we're imperial officials buying jade jewelry. We'll leave tomorrow morning as planned and say we are returning to Xining."

"You're right," Ping said. "Lao Longzi has kept this secret for many years; we mustn't let anyone know our destination."

"That will be easy," Jun observed with a crooked smile. "Even we don't know where we're going!"

Ping did some *qi* exercises to calm herself, while Jun spread out his purchases. He had had to buy more jewelry to keep the jade carvers happy.

"You have nearly enough to start your own jade business," Ping observed.

"I might give them as gifts." He held up a lovely hair clip. "I think my mother would like this piece. My sisters will like the earrings." He picked out a pendant in the shape of a dragon hanging from a leather thong. "But this one is for you."

"I can't take that," she gasped. "It must be worth a fortune."

The dragon carved on it was nothing like a real dragon. It was delicate and curved. Its body was marked with spots, and its horns, talons, and knee hair were all carved as delicate curls. It was beautiful.

"I knew it was yours the moment I saw it," Jun said, reddening. "Please take it."

He slipped the leather thong over Ping's head. It was Ping's turn to blush. She studied a stain on the floor.

"Thank you."

Ping went back to Lao Longzi's house later that afternoon. The old man was sitting exactly where they had left him.

"Can you tell me where Long Gao Yuan is?" Ping asked him in her mind. "I have to take Kai there."

The old man opened his eyes but didn't reply.

"It's what Danzi wanted."

Lao Longzi slowly raised his head. "In the mountains." One of his twiggy fingers pointed toward the northwest.

Ping waited for him to say something else, but he didn't.

"Is there anything else you can tell me?"

Lao Longzi shook his head.

The evening was spent at a long and drawn-out meal with Master Cai, listening to him recount the special skills of his children. Then his wife entertained them by playing a zither and singing very badly. The night passed as slowly as water dripping through a crack in a bucket.

Ping was up before dawn, packed and ready to go.

She had changed back into her worn trousers and jacket. Kai was so excited he couldn't eat his breakfast. They set out before the sound of the jade workers' tools could be heard. The perplexed elder stood at the doorway yawning in his nightgown as they thanked him for his hospitality and promised to send a large order once they had shown their samples to the Emperor. They walked back the way they had come until they were sure they were well out of sight of the village. Then they stopped.

"So where are we going?" Jun asked.

"To the mountains," Ping replied.

Jun scanned the horizon. "There's a lot of them."

Ping sighed. "We'll have to hope that the white dragon finds us again."

"Look," said Kai. He pointed a talon into the morning mist.

Ping could make out what she thought was a large gray rock in a meadow. Then she saw the rock move. They edged closer. It wasn't a rock, or at least not all of it was. It was a person sitting on a rock. The person stood up. Ping couldn't believe her eyes. It was Lao Longzi. He leaned heavily on his walking stick as he shuffled toward them.

"I will take you to Long Gao Yuan," the old man whispered. "If Danzi chose you as his Dragon Keeper, that is all the recommendation I need."

Lao Longzi pointed his stick away from the road into

the hills to the northwest. The old man didn't look like he could take five steps on level ground, let alone walk many *li* over mountains.

He looked at Jun. "Is the young man accompanying us?" he asked.

Ping heard the question in her mind. "Yes," she replied.

"That is good," he said.

Lao Longzi lifted one foot an inch off the ground and moved it forward three inches. Then he lifted his other foot. It was going to be a long, slow journey.

# CHAPTER THIRTEEN

# THE SERPENT'S TAIL

Ping was convinced that Lao Longzi would collapse from exhaustion before he made it to the foot of the first hill, let alone to its top. But the old man had more strength than anyone expected. He moved slowly but steadily, like an ancient tortoise.

As he laboriously climbed the hill, he didn't speak. Kai ran ahead and back endlessly. Ping thought that she would burst with impatience.

Jun touched her arm gently. "Not much farther now," he said. "The journey will take its own time."

Ping had lost interest in the journey. The hills all looked the same. Even the fact that they were covered with mossy grass, dotted with small flowers, and watered by streams didn't please her. Reaching their destination was all that mattered now. Lao Longzi was silent during the day, as he needed all his energy for walking, but in the evening he spoke a little.

The next day was the same, and the next. Each

evening, they gleaned a little more information from the old man, word by whispered word. Lao Longzi preferred to speak aloud as a courtesy to Jun, even though it took more energy. His words were like rare gems. Ping turned each one of them over and over in her mind to make sure she hadn't missed any of its meaning. She had never expected to have the privilege of speaking to someone else who had been Danzi's Dragon Keeper.

"There were many dragon hunters in those distant days," the old man said. "They searched all over the Empire for dragons. That's why some dragons sought out a remote mountain hideout."

He paused for several minutes while he collected his thoughts and the breath for further speech. "I was Long Danzi's keeper for more than seventy years."

Ping looked at the old man. He must have been well over one hundred years old.

"Some of that time we spent on Dragon Plateau." The corners of his mouth turned up in the smallest of smiles. "But Danzi was an adventurous dragon. Life on the plateau didn't suit his wandering spirit. He left to explore the world. I was happy to go with him."

Kai sat close to Lao Longzi, barely breathing, listening intently.

"Tell me something about Father," Kai said.

The old man thought for a moment.

"He didn't like hibernating," Lao Longzi said. "He

would try to sleep, but he would wake often, get out of the pond, and talk to me and the other Dragon Keepers. He liked to walk in the snow, and sometimes he would make a mound of snow and then form it into a shape—a rabbit, a fish, an eagle."

Kai sat in silence. Ping knew that he was repeating the story in his head so that he would remember every word.

Ping realized that being the keeper of a wild dragon was very different from caring for the imperial dragons. Being an Imperial Dragon Keeper had been a bad experience for Ping, but in the old days it had been different. In an imperial palace, a Dragon Keeper could marry and have a family. In fact, marriage was encouraged, in the hope that more Dragon Keepers would be born. Dragons needed many keepers over their long lives. It was a safe and secure profession.

Caring for a dragon in the wild made for an exciting life, but it was a task for an unmarried man. It was a dangerous job. Often Dragon Keepers died while caring for their dragon charges—and not all of them died of old age. Some died in mountain accidents, others were the victims of dragon hunters.

One evening, Lao Longzi told them why he'd had to give up his treasured position as Danzi's keeper.

"My ears failed me," he said. Ping felt that his sadness had seeped into his bones. "Dragons cannot hear well. Hunters can creep up on them when they are sleeping. Keen hearing is essential for a Dragon Keeper in the wild. Danzi had to look for a younger man."

Ping remembered Wang Cao, the herbalist from Chang'an, and wondered if he had been Danzi's next Dragon Keeper.

Day after day they made their way at tortoise speed. As they climbed each hill, they saw before them endless, similar hills. Though they occasionally startled a herd of wild goats or a fox, they never saw another person.

"How many dragons were there on the plateau?" Kai asked.

"Many," the old man replied.

Ping could feel Kai's excitement.

"We saw one," the dragon said. "A white one. Do you think there will be more on Dragon Plateau?"

Lao Longzi nodded. "I expect to meet some old friends there."

"Are there any young ones?" Kai asked.

"When I was there, there were none, but two dragons had mated. There should be young by now."

"Kai can play with them." He ran ahead, his happy tinkling sounds filling the air. He could barely contain his excitement.

Ping hadn't dared to think that more than one dragon had survived in the wild. She had only ever dealt with dragons one at a time. Her feelings were confused. It was right that Kai should live with others of his kind, but she wasn't sure how she would fit into Kai's new life. If he had dragons to teach him, what would her role be?

Lao Longzi had questions too. He wanted to know what had happened to Danzi, and so Ping told him the story of their journey.

At midmorning the following day, they climbed another mossy rounded hill, identical to the many they had already climbed. But from the top of this one there was a different view. A huge lake lay before them. It stretched beyond the horizon like an inland sea. The hill sloped down toward the edge of the lake like a green carpet. More hills surrounded the lake to the north and south, but to the west, the tips of snowcapped mountains were visible on the horizon. Lao Longzi pointed a trembling finger toward the mountains.

"Long Gao Yuan," he breathed.

"The lake must be nearly 150 *li* wide," said Jun as he stared at the vast expanse of water.

"If we walk around the lake's shore it will be quicker," Kai said.

Lao Longzi shook his head. "Too open," he said. "We must stay in the hills."

Kai asked Lao Longzi endless questions about Danzi and the other dragons at Long Gao Yuan. Each of the old man's answers was long and slow.

Jun couldn't hear any of the conversations between the dragon and Lao Longzi.

"Now I know what it's like to be deaf," Jun said.

Ping tried to remember to speak aloud so that he knew what she was saying to the old man and Kai, but she sometimes forgot.

When Kai was questioning Lao Longzi, Ping talked to Jun. She enjoyed having a conversation with another person that wasn't constantly interrupted by dragon sounds. Jun told her about his childhood. His stories of how he had coped with seven sisters made her laugh.

Ping was as impatient as Kai to get to their destination. It had already taken them two weeks to travel a distance that they could have crossed in a few days without Lao Longzi. Creeping through the hills with him would take another week, at least.

"Does your second sight tell you anything about Dragon Plateau?" Ping asked. "Can you tell how many dragons are living there?"

A long ragged sigh escaped from the old man.

"Second sight usually only comes to a Dragon Keeper when he has a dragon in his care. When Danzi and I parted, my second sight vanished."

He turned his watery eyes to Ping. "Does your second sight tell you anything?"

Ping shook her head.

"This is a strange life you have chosen," Lao Longzi said.

"I didn't choose it," Ping replied. "It chose me."

He surveyed the bleak landscape. "Do you have any regrets?"

"None."

Ping had one more question for Lao Longzi, though she hesitated before asking it.

"Did you foresee that you would live a lonely life after Danzi left you?"

The old man nodded slowly. "Yes, but I wouldn't swap my years with Danzi for a more companionable old age."

He glanced over to where Jun was playing with Kai.

"I have never known a Dragon Keeper to have a companion," he said.

Ping didn't understand what he meant at first. "You mean Jun?"

The old man nodded.

"He isn't my companion," Ping said, feeling suddenly hot. "He insisted on coming. His family feels that they have to repay a debt. They sent him to assist me. It wasn't my idea."

"Kai likes him," the old man said. "There is no reason why a Dragon Keeper should be lonely."

"I've not been lonely," Ping protested. "I've had Danzi and Kai to keep me company."

Lao Longzi made no further comment.

The days were long, daylight lasting well into the evening. The old man knew that they were eager to reach the dragon haven. Though he couldn't increase his speed, he was willing to walk from sunrise until sunset.

Eventually they reached the foothills of the mountains to the west of the lake. Once again their eyes followed Lao Longzi's tremulous finger as it pointed to a cleft in the mountain range.

"We must pass between those two peaks," he told them.

Kai and Jun had managed to catch two hares during the day, and they were all able to eat their fill—even Kai.

"What is it like, Dragon Plateau?" Kai asked.

It was a question that Kai had asked many times, but Lao Longzi didn't seem to tire of answering it. And each time there was a little bit more information.

"I am one of only a few humans to have seen it," he said proudly. "It is a grassy plateau hidden high in the mountain peaks, protected from the icy winds. A mountain stream runs through it."

It sounded just as Ping had imagined Long Gao Yuan.

"It can only be reached by climbing the Serpent's Tail," Lao Longzi continued.

"What's that?" Kai asked.

"You will see."

"Were you welcome there?" Ping asked.

"Yes, all true Dragon Keepers are welcome at Long Gao Yuan. Dragons don't need keepers in the wild, but the bond between a Dragon Keeper and his dragon is strong. All those dragons who had keepers wanted them to stay."

"How many Dragon Keepers were there on the plateau?"

"Only four." The old man made a strange gurgling sound in his throat. It was a chuckle. "One dragon had a young Dragon Keeper—a carefree, adventurous young man, fond of jokes and pranks."

Ping wanted more information, but it was clear that the old man wasn't going to say anything else. Every word drained a little more of his precious energy.

The next morning, Ping was the first to wake. The sun hadn't yet warmed the earth, and the cold of the mountain night was still all around them. Something had woken her. Not a sound, not a movement. She tried to describe the sensation to herself as she snuggled into her bearskin, but she found it difficult. It was as if something that had been moving had stopped. She got up and relit their fire. Kai woke, and so did Jun. They walked off together to pee, as they did each morning. Lao Longzi didn't stir, and all of a sudden Ping knew what had stopped. It was Lao Longzi's heart.

She got up and went over to the old man's body. His wrinkled face looked as if it had been carved from gray rock. His skin was as cold as snow.

Ping felt a bond with the old man, as if she had known him for many years rather than just two weeks. He was the only other true Dragon Keeper she had met. And he had spent a long time at Danzi's side, much longer than she had.

When Kai and Jun came back and saw her standing over the old man's body, they guessed what had happened. Kai didn't say anything, but he made mournful sounds. Ping's eyes filled with tears. Lao Longzi had lived a long life, but since his happy time with Danzi, he had spent many years alone. Shunned by the people of the Tinkling Village, he had clung to life, waiting for news of his dragon. He had met Kai and knew that Danzi would live on in him. Now he could finally die in peace.

Ping had been looking forward to spending many long afternoons with Lao Longzi, learning about his life as a Dragon Keeper. But the old man had never spoken about what he would do when they got to Long Gao Yuan. She thought that he had known he would never reach it.

"If only he'd got as far as Dragon Plateau," Jun said, "we could have buried him there."

"He's in sight of Long Gao Yuan at least," Ping said.

She arranged his cold, twiggy hands on his chest and smoothed his white hair. Kai pulled out one of his scales, and Ping placed it inside the old man's robes. They gently covered his body with stones where he lay, and stood for a few moments in silence.

"Come," Jun said, taking Ping's arm. "We still have a long way to go."

Their progress was quicker now, and they reached the cleft the next day. It was no more than a narrow crack in the mountains. If Lao Longzi hadn't pointed it out to them, they would never have found it.

"I hope we can find the Serpent's Tail," Ping said.

"The dragons will be watching," Kai said. His voice was trembling.

They searched the sky and the mountain peaks, looking for dragons on the wing or perched on rocks.

"Can you see any, Kai?" Jun asked.

"No."

Jun didn't need Ping to translate for him. He knew what Kai's answer was by the sad sounds he made.

"Do you think your second sight would tell you if there were dragons close by?" Jun asked Ping.

"I don't know. I didn't feel anything when we saw the white one."

Ping held her breath and concentrated on her body. She searched for the smallest sensation—a twitch, a prickle, an itch—that might indicate that her second sight had detected the presence of a dragon. There was nothing.

They clambered through the cleft in the mountain. Ping felt instantly cold. The gap was so narrow they could barely squeeze through, so deep that the sky above them became a thin ribbon of blue. The ground continued to slope up. Loose stones under their feet made it difficult to climb without slipping over. Behind them the view of the lake grew thinner and thinner until it disappeared. The cleft became so narrow they had to squeeze through sideways. Just when it seemed that it was about to close up entirely, it started to widen again and opened out onto a narrow bank of grassy earth at the foot of a steep cliff. A thin waterfall dropped vertically down the cliff.

"This must be it," Ping said. "The Serpent's Tail."

"Yes," said Kai.

There was still no sign of any dragons.

"How will we climb up?" Jun looked up the sheer cliff. "That must be thirty *chang* high and as flat as a wall."

Ping smiled and pointed to something dangling down the cliff face. "We'll use that."

Jun went over to the rope and yanked it. It broke off halfway up and fell on his head. "However people get up and down, it certainly isn't by using this."

The frayed rope pulled apart in his hands.

They sat and rested while they considered this last obstacle, eating a little, though no one was hungry. The cliff curved away to the left and right, as steep and high as ever. Kai looked for footholds, but his sharp eyes could see none.

"If we follow the cliff around, perhaps there will be an easier way up."

"No," said Ping. "It will be a waste of time. The only way to get up to Long Gao Yuan is to fly up there. That's why the dragons chose this place. Lao Longzi said we had to climb the Serpent's Tail. If there had been an easier way, he would have told us."

"Why don't the dragons come down and carry us up there?" Kai asked.

"It's a test," Ping said. "Our final test. We have to work out how we can climb the cliff."

Jun gazed up at the waterfall again. He kicked at the rotten rope at his feet. "We could weave a strong cord from dried grass."

"It would take ages," Ping said. "And anyway, someone would have to climb up there first to tie it on to something."

Kai snuffled through the undergrowth at the base of the cliff, searching for hidden openings in the wall of rock. Ping tried to think of some way she could use her *qi* power.

It was late afternoon. There were still several hours of daylight, but Ping was beginning to think that they should wait and see if the morning brought new inspiration. Kai couldn't rest. He didn't take his eyes off the vertical rock face.

"We have to climb the falls," the dragon said. "That's what Lao Longzi said. Not the cliff, the falls."

"But the cliff behind the falls must be as sheer as the rest," said Ping.

"Maybe not," Kai replied. "There is a lip at the top. The water rushes over and falls away from the cliff, just a little way."

"Of course," said Ping. "That's why it's so straight."

"What did Kai say?" asked Jun. "I wish I didn't hear only half of the conversation."

"The waterfall doesn't touch the cliff on the way down," Ping explained. "There's a space behind it."

"So you have to climb behind the waterfall?"

"Yes."

The waterfall didn't collect in a pool, but hit the base of the cliff, spraying up and creating a mist. The smooth and slender waterfall was transformed into a noisy stream that crashed against rocks, churning this way and that in a wild cascade as if it were impatient to find another place to fall again. Then it swirled in a curve of rock, changed direction, and continued down the mountain.

"We should wait until morning," Ping said.

"No," said Kai. "Climb now."

Ping turned to Jun. "Kai wants to try to climb up now. I'm going with him." She took off the dragon pendant necklace that Jun had given her and slipped it into the saddlebag. She held out the bag.

"It's too dangerous," he said, refusing to take it. "You can't. Let me go instead. Please."

"This is the end of our journey. It's my destiny. You're not a Dragon Keeper, Jun. You would not be welcome." She placed the bag in his hands. "This is what I have to do."

He caught hold of her hand. "Be careful," he said. "Climb down if it gets too hard. Try again in the morning when you're fresh."

"I'll be okay," she said. "Thank you. I wouldn't have been able to get here without your help." She pulled her hand from his and turned toward the falls.

"Call down when you reach the top," Jun said. "I'll wait here. No matter what happens, I'll stay here until you let me know you're safe."

Ping walked toward the falls.

"What about your bag?" Jun had to shout to make himself heard above the roar of the water crashing onto the rocks. "How will you get it up there?"

"The dragons will have a way," she said.

"Good-bye."

Ping thought she heard a catch in Jun's voice.

She turned, went back, and hugged him. "I'll be okay." She felt his warm cheek against her face. "And so will you. Your family is depending on you."

Jun looked up at the cliff. "I hope you find what you are searching for."

"Ping, Ping. It's time."

Jun scratched the little dragon under the chin. "Good-bye, Kai. Take care of Ping."

Kai went to the base of the falls. Ping followed, the mist soaking her clothes long before she reached him.

The sound of water hitting the rock was deafening. If she had been with anyone else, they wouldn't have been able to speak to each other. But she wasn't with another person. She was with a dragon, and they could understand each other perfectly.

Ping looked up. The top of the cliff was a long way away. Kai slipped behind the waterfall and was hidden from Ping's view.

"There are footholds," he said. "Carved into the rock."

She followed him, flattening herself against the cliff. There was just enough space to keep out of the stream of water. Kai had begun to climb. The talons of all four paws were hooked onto narrow crevices. Ping could just make out the footholds he'd already used. They were man-made. She had hoped for deeply carved hollows with raised edges that she could grip firmly, but the footholds were rough clefts, chipped into the side of the cliff. She could only make out the two or three directly above her head. Slowly Kai inched his way up like a lizard. Ping watched with her heart in her mouth. She gripped hold of two of the narrow hollows above her head and placed a foot in another. She started to climb.

"Is Ping all right?" Kai asked.

Ping was glad she didn't have to find the energy to speak aloud. "Yes."

Ping soon discovered that if she let any of her body

protrude into the waterfall, the force of the icy water threatened to drag her from her precarious hold. The waterfall seemed eager to wash her down the cliff and smash her on the rocks below. It was difficult to move a foot to the next foothold while keeping herself squashed against the cliff.

The footholds grew farther apart as she climbed, and after a while, her arms and legs ached. Her fingertips were raw, her knees grazed. She was shivering. The deafening rush of the water made it difficult to concentrate. Each time she gripped a cleft, her fingers were stiffer than the time before. The muscles in her legs burned. Her movements slowed, and so did her mind.

The next cleft was almost out of her reach. She balanced on the toes of her left foot and reached for it. The fingers of her right hand slowly gripped it. She raised her right foot and felt for the next foothold. She couldn't reach it. Her legs weren't long enough. Her whole body was shaking with the exertion of supporting all her weight on the toes of one foot. Her fingers were frozen into unbending claws. Her clothes felt heavy, as if they had stones sewn into them.

"I can't move," she said. "I'm going to fall."

Even her voice in her mind sounded quavering and frightened.

"Kai will come back to help Ping."

A few moments later Ping felt something rub against her hand. It was one of Kai's hind paws.

"Grab hold," Kai said.

"Are you sure you can support me?"

"Kai can lift Ping to the next foothold," the dragon replied. "After so much walking, Kai's legs are very strong."

Ping unhooked her left hand and reached up. It closed slowly around Kai's ankle. If Kai had over-estimated his strength, they would both fall. She uncurled her right hand. She held her breath as she let go, trusting her whole weight to Kai. Her body started to rise, and her feet lifted off the footholds. She felt around with her raised foot until it found the next foothold. She found a cleft for her right hand and a place for her left foot.

"Okay," she said.

She let go of Kai's ankle. Her feet and hands took the weight of her body again. It felt as heavy as if she were made of bronze, threatening to drag her off the cliff.

"Kai is at the top," Kai said.

Ping looked up. She was less than half a *chang* from the top, but she couldn't move.

"Ping," Kai said anxiously. "Is Ping all right?"

She couldn't form any words in her mind to answer him. The strength was draining from her. Her fingers wouldn't move. They were hooked like claws around the lip of the cleft. She looked up to see if there was a ledge she could rest on for just a few minutes. But she found none. She closed her eyes. There was somewhere warm she could go. Sleep would take her there. Her fingers were slipping from the crevice, but she didn't care. She let go, ready to fall into oblivion.

Then she felt Kai's talons grip the back of her jacket, drag her through the water, and lift her up onto a grassy slope. She didn't dare look down. Her body was still shaking uncontrollably. She made her arms and legs work again, crawling inch by inch away from the edge of the cliff. She rested her cheek and her raw, bleeding fingers gratefully against the grass. She felt the pads of Kai's paw against her face.

"Ping is safe."

She reached up and touched his scaly skin. "Yes."

They'd passed the test. Their journey was over. They were up on Long Gao Yuan—Dragon Plateau. The sun was about to sink behind the mountains. Ping managed to sit up, the last rays of sunlight warming her.

She was perched on the lip of a wide circular plateau that dipped toward the center, where there were three clear pools. Everything was bathed in orange light. The breeze rippled the grass. There were bushes covered with yellow blossoms. The grass was speckled with purple bells and spikes of blue flowers. A stream cut its way across the plateau before it plunged over the edge and became the Serpent's Tail. Long Gao Yuan was just as Ping had imagined.

A sorrowful sound broke the silence. It was Kai. It made Ping's heart ache.

"Where are the dragons?"

The last curve of the sun disappeared. Kai was running across the plateau searching for places where dragons could hide. He found a cave, but it was empty. He dived into the pools. Ping waited as he searched the depths for sleeping dragons. Each time he surfaced, his cry was more pitiful.

"No dragons," he wailed. "No dragons."

The light was fading, but if there had been any sign of life, Kai's sharp eyes would have found it. The plateau was empty. There were no dragons living there.

There was something, though. Ping could see it in the center of the plateau. It looked like a pile of branches, like a bonfire ready to be lit. Kai stopped suddenly, staring at the pile. Tears filled Ping's eyes. Even though the light was almost gone, she knew what it was. It was something she'd seen before and had hoped and prayed she'd never see again. It wasn't a pile of branches; it was a pile of bones. Dragon bones.

# CHAPTER FOURTEEN

# DRAGON PLATEAU

Kai howled. Ping had heard a dragon mourn before. When Kai's mother had died, Danzi had made the same melancholy sound, and his wailing had echoed around Huangling Mountain. It sounded like copper bowls being crashed together. It had chilled Ping's heart. The sound of dragon grief was far worse than the sound of human sorrow.

Kai's distress was higher pitched. It was the saddest sound she'd ever heard. She wanted to crouch down, cover her head, and shut it out. Tears ran down her cheeks, but there were no tears on Kai's face. Dragons didn't weep.

There was nothing she could say that would console him. She held him tight, she whispered words of empty comfort, but she couldn't hide her own distress. For weeks Kai had talked of nothing but meeting another dragon. Ping felt she should have warned him not to get his hopes up. But she'd allowed herself to believe that they would find dragons at Long Gao Yuan.

As she held Kai, she looked at the dragon bones. The dragons hadn't died out gradually. Lao Longzi had told her that dragons buried their dead deep in the earth. These dragons hadn't died of old age. They had been slaughtered, butchered for their parts. If only her second sight allowed her to read the future, she could have had some warning of what they'd find.

Ping hadn't thought past this point. She had fulfilled Danzi's wishes. She had brought Kai to the dragon haven. She'd expected to find dragons on Long Gao Yuan. Instead they were alone on a cold mountain with night closing around them like a black cloak. They had no rugs, no food. Ping had imagined a joyous welcome from the dragons, with one of them flying down to get their belongings.

Ping went back to the edge of the cliff. She knew she couldn't climb back down the way they had come. Not now. Not ever. It was too dark to see the bottom of the falls. She called down to Jun, but the noise of the waterfall swallowed her voice. She hoped he wouldn't try to follow them up.

Night settled on the plateau, black and cold. They took shelter in the cave. It was too dark to see, but Ping could feel dried grass on the floor. And there was a smell. The smell of stale dragon urine. It wasn't much warmer in the cave, but it was dry. They huddled together in the darkness while the slow minutes of the night crawled by.

When morning came, Ping was stiff with cold. Kai had stopped wailing, but he wouldn't speak. Eventually the sun appeared over the rim of the plateau. It warmed them, but it also revealed the bones again. Ping looked around the cave. There were piles of dry grass, some dried meat. It was the den of wild animals. Kai was curled up. He wouldn't leave the cave.

Outside, the sunlight revealed that the dragon bones were bleached white. The dragons had been dead for many years. There was a rusty weapon among the bones. Ping hadn't needed proof that people had been responsible for the massacre, but there it was. She was glad that Lao Longzi wasn't there to witness it. He had died believing he was bringing Danzi's son to safety.

Ping searched the plateau inch by inch. She peered into the pools, where the water was crystal clear. She didn't need dragon sight to see that they were empty. She remembered that Danzi had lived on Long Gao Yuan for many years, and she was grateful that his restless spirit had led him away before the massacre. Her own life would have been very different if he had stayed.

During the morning, Ping half expected to see Jun clamber up over the lip of the waterfall. She went as close to the edge of the cliff as she dared and peered down, though it made her dizzy. She threw rocks down to get Jun's attention, but there was no sign of him.

"He must be looking for another way up," Ping said to Kai.

She hadn't eaten for more than a day. She found a few small mushrooms, some berries. The dried goat's meat in the cave was tough but still edible. She lit a fire and heated up some water in a gourd. Kai wouldn't eat.

"It's not the end of our journey, Kai," she said. "At least one dragon survived whatever happened here. We saw it. It has found somewhere else to live. It's wary of people, that's understandable. We have to find the white dragon, convince it that I'm a friend. We have to think of a new plan."

She began to wonder if Kai would ever recover.

"We could stay here," Ping said. "It's where Danzi wanted you to live. Whoever killed the dragons is long gone and will never return. You could hunt. There might be fish in the pools."

"No." Kai's answer was swift and firm. "This is a sad, bad place."

Ping didn't argue.

They spent the morning looking for a way down. She didn't dare suggest that Kai climb down the way they had come. In his misery, he might slip and fall. One thing was certain—she couldn't climb back down.

Kai still wouldn't eat, but Ping forced herself to chew the goat's meat. She sat in the sunlight, hoping that along with the warmth and food she would find new inspiration. She had slept very little through the cold night. The sun made her sleepy. She closed her eyes, just for a few moments.

A strange noise woke her, a sound like someone shaking out heavy blankets. She opened her eyes, and the glare of the sun blinded her. It was the wing-beat of a bird. A large bird. Kai called out. It was a strange cry—like wind chimes in a storm, but with a faint sound of knives being sharpened. A mixture of joy and fear. She shielded her eyes. A huge, winged creature was hovering above them, bigger than any bird.

Ping's eyes grew used to the bright light, and she saw talons and horns, wings, and scales. It was the dragon. High in the sky it had looked white, but close up, she saw that it was yellow. It reached down with its front paws and grabbed hold of Kai, digging its talons into his hide. She saw drops of purple blood surround each talon.

"Ping, Ping." The joyful sound of tinkling wind chimes disappeared from Kai's cry, replaced by the clashing of copper bowls.

"Ping!"

The dragon lifted Kai into the air. Ping reached up pointlessly. Circling above, the yellow dragon glared at her as if she were a spider or a snake. Then it flapped its wings and flew away, with Kai clutched in its talons. Ping called out useless threats and frantic pleas. But the dragon was gone. And so was Kai.

Ping sat staring at the bright sky for a long time. Her brain wouldn't work. She thought that the dragon might come back for her, but then she remembered its cold eyes.

She spent the rest of the day searching fruitlessly for a way down from the plateau. Night fell again. Ping crawled into the dragons' cave and lay down in the dried grass.

She remembered what the seer at Beibai Palace had said about the final reading of the *Yi Jing* divination. *Read it only when you are faced with your greatest difficulty.* This was it. She had lost Kai, nothing could be worse. She pulled the calfskin from her pouch and unfolded it. On one side were the six solid lines, each with its own reading. An auspicious reading, the seer had told her, the most auspicious. She turned it over. On the other side was the single line of characters. She read it for the first time. *A cluster of dragons without heads. Great good fortune.* Ping read the column of characters again. She must have made a mistake. She had seen dragons without heads, without hearts, without scales. They were nothing but a pile of bleached bones. How could that possibly mean good fortune? Tears of rage ran down her face as she screwed up the calfskin and threw it as far away as she could.

The next morning when Ping woke, she thought for a moment she was back on Tai Shan. Then she remembered. Kai was gone. Since she'd left Huangling Mountain, she'd cared for two dragons, she'd made many friends, kind strangers had helped her. But as quickly as they had entered her life, they had all left again. No one had stayed with her for long. She was alone. Totally alone. She had experienced loneliness and loss before, many times. She remembered the dreadful feeling when she had lost the dragon stone, but then she'd had Danzi at her side. Even in the lonely years on Huangling, she'd had the comfort of Hua's furry companionship.

She and Kai had trekked together across the Empire. Against all odds they had found the one place in all the Empire that Danzi had wanted them to find. Ping had reached the end of her journey. But all she had to show for it was another loss, more loneliness.

She went out into the crisp mountain air. There was no one to comfort her. No one to help her. She had never been so alone in her life. She felt as though there was a wound in her heart—the place where Kai had been ripped from her. She knew that it would never heal. She went back to the cave and didn't come out again that day. She made herself a nest in the dried grass, just as Kai would have. It was comfortable. She huddled there, curled in a ball through the night.

All through the next day she stayed in the same place, stirring only to go and pee in a corner. Her eyes had grown used to the dim light. She saw markings on

the cave wall. She moved closer. There were two characters scrawled in a shaky hand. The two characters
meant *betrayal*. Ping went back to her bed of grass. She
didn't eat. Another night passed. She no longer
expected Jun to rescue her. He might have tried to
climb the Serpent's Tail and fallen. She would just wait
until the world went away.

Ping felt a cold breeze on her cheek and shivered. She
was angry. The breeze had spoiled the only thing she
had left, the relative warmth and comfort of the dragon
cave. She turned away from it. Then she realized that it
wasn't coming from the cave mouth, it was coming
from somewhere in the dark depths of the cave. She got
up and felt her way toward the rush of cool air. The
back of the cave was solid rock. There was no way out.
She could no longer feel the breeze on her face. It was
now stirring hairs on the top of her head. She reached
up to the cave roof above her. There was a hole.

She had searched for an escape route that led down,
but instead she had found a tunnel that led up. It
wasn't built for dragons. It was human-size. She collected what food was left in the dragon cave and stuffed
it into her pouch. She dragged a large stone into the
cave so that she could reach into the overhead tunnel.
Handgrips had been carved just inside. She grabbed on
to them and, despite having eaten very little for two
days, she found the strength to lift herself up.

The tunnel led up almost vertically, but on one side she could feel narrow steps that had been carved into the rock. She clambered up them, feeling her way in the dark. The tunnel continued up for a short way and then turned at right angles and became horizontal. She crawled along the tunnel for several minutes, then, though it was difficult to tell in the dark, Ping thought that it began to slope down. The air was stale, but she found the dark strangely comforting. She crawled headfirst for a long time. Her hands were grazed as she tried not to slip forward too quickly. The slope was definitely becoming steeper. She felt the walls for places she could turn around in, but the tunnel was narrow everywhere she touched. She didn't think she'd be able to inch back again, so she kept going. Then she lost her hold on the tunnel floor and slipped. She couldn't stop herself. She slid headfirst, grazing her arms and knees and bashing her head as she tried to stop her fall. Then the tunnel ended and Ping landed hard. She was lying on a pile of grass that was probably meant to have broken the fall. It had become so dry and brittle that it wasn't much of a cushion.

She didn't get up at first. She couldn't. Her body hurt all over. She could feel blood running from her forehead. In front of her, light filtered through branches. A bush had grown over the entrance to the tunnel. Her arms were grazed and cut. Her trousers were ripped at the knees, and bloody skin was visible through the holes. She lay for a while and considered whether she wanted to get up or whether she would just lie there until she became food for the plants and small animals.

But she couldn't die without knowing what had happened to Kai. The yellow dragon could have been a kind female who wanted to care for him. He could be happily basking in the care of another dragon for the first time in his short life. Or it could have been an angry territorial male who didn't want another young male in his area. Whatever his fate, she had to find out. She broke off the branches covering the tunnel entrance and crawled out into the light.

From the angle of the sun, Ping knew it was midafternoon. She still had hours of daylight left. She got to her feet and walked around the base of Long Gao Yuan to the Serpent's Tail.

"Jun," she called. "Jun!"

There was no sign of Jun, or the saddlebag that contained her belongings. Ping kept walking and calling, stopping only to drink from a spring and eat some berries, until she had completed a full circuit of the base of Long Gao Yuan. The sun had sunk nearly to the horizon. She couldn't find Jun.

Ping sat and rested for a while. She had been confident Jun would wait for her. She would have staked her life on it. She called out again. Her voice echoed off the cliff face. She sighed heavily. He was just another person who had entered her life briefly and then left.

# CHAPTER FIFTEEN

# THE TOP OF THE WORLD

The *Yi Jing* had let Ping down. Danzi's map had led her to despair. There was only one thing left that she could do. She had to find Kai. She would search the Empire, search the world if she had to. If she couldn't find him, she would die trying.

It didn't matter that she'd lost her bag. She could do without spare clothes, cooking utensils, and gold coins. Her most precious things were in the pouch around her waist—her mirror, Danzi's scale, and the shard of dragon stone. It was late afternoon. Ping could stay where she was until morning—sleep in the mouth of the tunnel on the pile of straw. Or she could start straightaway, even though there were just a few hours of daylight left. The journey ahead promised no shelter, no dry straw to sleep on, and one night of relative comfort would be lost among many nights of discomfort in the open air.

She set out immediately. The yellow dragon had

flown southwest. That was the way she would go. Except she didn't have wings. All she could do was creep across the undulating landscape like a snail. When it got dark she kept walking, using the stars to guide her, until she couldn't walk any longer.

Ping walked from dawn till dark every day, for many days. She rarely bothered to light a fire. She had nothing to cook. Instead she ate raw mushrooms, berries, and the strips of dried goat meat that she'd brought from the dragons' cave. There were good days when the sun wasn't too hot and the hills offered her gentle slopes. She made fair progress then. There were also bad days when the wind blew and the mountainside was too steep to climb, forcing her to walk many *li* out of her way.

The weather grew hotter. She didn't have a water bag, so she could drink only when she chanced upon a stream or a shrinking pool. She ran out of dried meat. There were no mushrooms growing because the earth was too dry. Birds had stripped the bushes of the sparse crop of berries. Her face was sunburned, her lips blistered. She didn't have a hat or even the remains of her nightgown to shield her face and head from the sun. There were no trees to offer any shade. The sun felt as if it would burn a hole in her head.

Many blank days passed; she didn't bother to count them anymore. The sun was making it hard for her to think. She felt like her brain was melting. Every time she concentrated on a thought it would slip from her mind, like a weighted string slipping through her fingers, like a dream fading on waking.

Throughout the days, Ping thought of nothing. If she allowed her mind to wander, it only came back to her misery. And anyway, thinking took energy. She moved without thinking. As soon as night fell, she collapsed into an exhausted sleep wherever she happened to be, only to wake in the dark, shivering with cold and unable to get back to sleep. Then she would start walking before dawn, tripping over rocks and stumbling down slopes in the darkness.

She had been hungry before, but never like this. She remembered meager meals at Huangling—thin gruel and scraps of grisly meat left on Master Lan's plate. Her mouth watered at the thought of such feasts now. She rummaged in her pouch. Perhaps there was a scrap of food in there—a nut, a shriveled berry, a piece of moldy mushroom. All she found was a mirror, a purple shard, and a faded dragon scale.

She'd forgotten how long it was since she left Beibai Palace. She couldn't remember the name of the Emperor's sister. It would only be a matter of time before she forgot who she was and where she was going. She thought for a moment. Where was she going? She couldn't remember. She still had her name, though. She clutched at the silk cord around her neck. She could never forget her name. She looked at her bamboo square. It was blank. The sun had faded the single character that used to be written there. Too tired to stand, she sat down and closed her eyes. All her senses were shut down. She had become an empty shell.

Her fingers closed around the purple shard. It felt cool in her hands. She stroked its smooth surface and admired the pretty purple color. There was an itchy feeling in her chest. Her mind, empty of all other thoughts, focused on the itch. It wasn't so much an itch as an ache. Her mind couldn't make sense of it. All it understood was walking and sleeping. Anything else was confusing. She sat for a long time. The ache grew more painful, as if a branch were sticking into her, pressing harder and harder all the time. She opened her jacket and examined the patch of skin that hurt. There was no cut, no bruise, no insect bite, nothing that could have caused the discomfort. She knew that she had experienced this sensation before, but she couldn't remember when.

The bronze mirror lay in her lap. On one side there was a creature reaching out for the central knob as if it was something it wanted badly. It was a nice creature with four feet, a curving body, and horns on its head. What sort of a creature was it? She couldn't remember. She turned over the bronze disk. On the other side was a face. A human face—grimy, scratched, and red raw. Skin was peeling off the nose, and the eyes were vacant. She turned the disk a little, and the sunlight flashed in her eyes. She saw the face on the disk move, the eyes squint. It wasn't painted on or carved into the bronze, it was a reflection of a real face. Her face.

Memories trickled back into her mind. She remembered what the feeling in her chest was. It was the thread pulling her. She had this ability, part of her second sight. When she wanted something badly, more than anything else, it would lead her to it. She turned over the mirror again. She knew now what the creature was called. It was a dragon. Her name was Ping, and she was searching. For her dragon.

It was as if the thread were joining her to Kai. A thin strand like a single thread of silk spun by a silkworm. It was so fragile, so delicate, but it was unbroken. This thread had led her to things before. The shard of dragon stone had intensified the link. She grasped the shard with both hands. In some ways it was easier this time— her body and mind weren't distracted by anything else. She got to her feet and allowed herself to be pulled along. She wouldn't give up searching for Kai while she was still alive.

She found tubers and some tasteless wild melons to eat. She hollowed out one of the gourds so that she could carry water in it. The water tasted of rotten melon, but it quenched her thirst. When she came to a patch of long, coarse grass, she picked some of the grass blades and wove a misshapen hat. She caught a pigeon with a loop of cord. The cord was made of strands of hemp pulled from the fraying hem of her trousers and braided together. Ping made a fire that night and roasted the pigeon and the melon. She ate watercress leaves and berries. She found a sheltered place, made a bed of dried moss, and slept well for the first time in many nights.

Day after day she walked. Each day she grew stronger, her mind became clearer. The invisible thread felt less likely to break, more like string now than thread. She was getting closer, but she knew that Kai was still hundreds of *li* away.

Every day she was confronted by a new peak, the same as the previous one, only higher. It was as if she were endlessly climbing the same mountain, struggling to the top, scrabbling down the other side, only to find herself back at the bottom again. When she stopped to catch her breath, she looked around, and there were nothing but mountain peaks in all directions. She felt as though she were climbing to the top of the world. Although it was summer, she noticed patches of dirty snow still hiding in shadowy corners of rock.

The mountains were covered with small, mossy plants that had a reddish tinge to them. They looked rusty brown from a distance. She watched a white eagle glide high above her in search of food, and wished she had wings. If she could fly it would take no time to travel from peak to peak. But she had to crawl along the ground like an insect. Whether she chose to walk around a peak or clamber over it, she was always walking many times the distance that the eagle flew.

Some mornings, after a particularly steep climb the previous day, she found it difficult to wake. When she stood up, the mountains spun around her, and she had to sit down again. Her head throbbed, and she had no appetite. Every step took great effort. All she wanted to do was sleep, but when she lay down, sleep wouldn't come. She found that if she rested for a day, she felt better. She didn't want to rest, but she made more progress if she waited for the sickness to pass than if she stumbled on while she was feeling ill.

One day she struggled to the top of a slope and found a mountain plateau stretching perfectly flat in front of her. She hadn't walked along a flat surface for such a long time it seemed strange. It was effortless after so much climbing, she almost felt as if she were gliding a few inches above the earth. But on the other side of the plateau was another mountain range, soaring ever higher and topped by snowcapped peaks. Impatience overwhelmed her. She wanted to find Kai *now*.

And then there was the weather. How would she survive in the mountains once summer passed and winter approached? How would she stop herself from freezing? What would she eat? She inspected her food supply, which consisted of a few roots and some large snails that tasted quite good when roasted in ashes. She only had enough for one meal. She looked at the height of the sun in the sky and tried to work out how long it would be before winter came. But in the mountains, it would come earlier than she was used to. She remembered the freezing winters on Huangling Mountain. She was much higher now. She didn't know if she could survive the winter.

As she crossed the plateau she saw some people in the far distance. They were nomads, like the Ma Ren. They didn't have a permanent home. They followed the sun and the grass to feed their yaks. If those people could survive winter, then she could too. She would try to buy furs from them. She would find out what food they ate. If that was what she had to do, she would do it. But she no longer had any gold pieces. She had nothing else to offer them, so she watched the nomads disappear from sight.

A quiet, slow-moving stream meandered across the plateau, in no hurry to reach the other side, enjoying the flatlands, just as Ping was. She rested on the bank of the stream, sipping the icy water, wondering if there were any fish that she could catch.

A shadow fell over her. Ping hadn't seen a cloud for months. She looked up. Something hit her across the back of the head. She was knocked to the ground facedown, her head ringing. She didn't know who or what her attacker was. Was it a wild animal, a leopard, perhaps? Or was it one of the nomads she'd seen earlier? She tried to twist around to see who had hit her, but drops of liquid sprayed over her face. Some got into her eyes. It stung. She blinked and rubbed her burning eyes. She opened them again and found she couldn't see at all.

Her body was picked up and thrown on top of something hard and spiky. She felt rough rope criss-cross her back, binding her tight. She struggled, but it made no difference. Her hands were bound, her eyes were blind. She had no idea what was happening to her.

There was a smell that she recognized but couldn't place. It was a strong smell, fishy but with a hint of plums just about to rot. Then a cold wind started to whistle past her ears. The spiky thing beneath her rocked and swayed. That was familiar too. There was another sound above the rush and whistle of the wind. It sounded like dust being shaken from a large carpet. Suddenly Ping's mind put all these things together— the spiky shape, the sounds, the smell. The spikes beneath her were dorsal spines. The sound was the flap of large wings. The smell was that of a dragon. She was flying on the back of a dragon.

Ping felt the wind rush past. While she had been creeping along the ground, she had longed to skim above the world on a dragon. Her wish had come true. She could imagine the mountain peaks marching beneath her. And the thread was getting stronger by the moment. She could hear something in her mind—not words, not sounds, but an emotion—just as she had before Kai was born, when he was still inside the dragon stone. What she heard was a mixture of pleasure and fear. The dragon was taking her to Kai.

They flew for hours. The air grew colder, so she knew they were getting higher. At last the wing beats slowed, the wind stopped rushing by. They were hovering. Then they were descending.

The air suddenly became warmer and more moist. And there was a new smell, a bad smell, like when you break open an egg that's rotten inside. With a thud, they were on the ground again. Ping could hear the scratching of talons on stone. Her bonds were loosened, and she tumbled to the ground, landing on hard rock. She heard a wonderful sound in her head—the tinkling of wind chimes.

"Ping, Ping, Ping."

She held out her arms in the direction of the sound, but Kai didn't come to her.

"Are you all right?" She didn't speak the words aloud.

"Yes, yes. Kai is all right."

"I can't see," Ping said. "The dragon sprayed something in my face. I don't know what it was."

"Spit," Kai said. "Dragon saliva makes human eyes blind."

"The dragon spat in my eyes?" Ping exclaimed.

"It won't last. In a while Ping will be able to see again."

Indeed, her sight was already returning. She could make out dim shapes now. "Where are you?"

She peered at the blurred shapes. They were starting to take on a more solid form. She thought she was standing in the center of a circle of large, jagged, different-colored rocks.

"They are holding me," Kai said.

"They?"

Had she been captured by a tribe of people who had enslaved a dragon? Were the blurred shapes tall, cloaked men?

Something rushed toward her. It was Kai. He had broken away from whoever or whatever was holding him. He nearly knocked Ping over. She threw her arms around him, feeling his familiar scales and spines beneath her fingers. She touched his nose, fondled his ears.

"I thought I'd lost you."

"Kai is not lost."

The tears that began to flow soothed her sore eyes. She heard his happy wind-chime sounds. She could see him now, though he was blurred. He was safe.

Gradually, the jagged shapes around her came into focus. Ping turned in a slow circle. She wasn't surrounded by rocks or men.

She was surrounded by dragons.

· CHAPTER SIXTEEN ·

## HAVEN

There were seven dragons—two red, three white, two yellow. The white ones were the smallest, not much bigger than Kai, but two of them had fully developed wings. All three were females. Ping could tell because of their undulating noses and thicker tails. The yellow dragons were medium size. One was male, the other female. They were both winged.

Danzi had told Ping that a dragon's horns didn't start to grow until it reached five hundred years of age, which meant that even the youngest white dragon, whose horns hadn't finished growing, had to be older than that. The two red dragons were the biggest. They were bigger than Danzi, and both were female. The younger one had full-size horns, but no wings. A dragon's wings didn't form until it was a thousand years old. The other red one was huge and ancient. Her eyes were dim, and one wing hung unfurled at her side, ragged and crisscrossed with old scars.

Ping stared at the seven dragons, and they stared back, as if she were the uncommon creature. Their colors weren't bright like fruit or flowers. The yellow dragons were the color of sand, like the yellow of the Yellow River. The white dragons weren't bright white like snow, but a very pale gray. The reds were rusty orange, a similar color to a fox. The old one's scales had faded almost to brown. She was two or maybe even three thousand years old. Kai was the only green dragon. He was a baby compared to these dragons, not even two years old. His purple scales had all gone now, and his fresh, new ones were jade green. He looked like a polished jewel among them.

Ping finally dragged her eyes away from the dragons and looked at her surroundings. They were on a high plateau with the deep blue sky surrounding them on all sides. This plateau was very different from the one where she'd been seized. The earth was almost white. At first she thought it was snow, but then she realized it was white clay pocked with holes and craters, dotted with mounds, as if someone had dug holes all over the ground. Steam rose from the holes. Some of the craters were filled with water, but they weren't ordinary pools. They were all steaming, and the water within them was brightly colored. The largest pool was orange. There were two bright green ones, another was luminous pink, while others were white, yellow, and purple. Elsewhere there were pools, not of water, but of mud, which bubbled like boiling gruel.

There were caverns whose dark mouths were lined with small yellow crystals. They led deep into the earth. The sulphurous smell overwhelmed everything. Ping wanted to cover her nose, but thought it would be impolite. Water surged out of the earth in some places, only to disappear back into it again through other holes. There was little vegetation and not a single tree. Ping had never seen a landscape like it.

None of the dragons attempted to communicate with her. She had no idea what they thought about having a human in their midst.

Ping spoke to them in her mind.

"Hello," she said. "I am Kai's keeper. My name is Ping."

None of the dragons responded.

"Don't they understand me, Kai?" Ping asked. "Can I only speak to you?"

"Don't know."

"Do they speak to you?"

"Yes, but not like Ping. Only with dragon sounds."

The old red dragon leaned her huge head closer to Ping, as if she wanted to get a better look. Ping could feel the old dragon's warm breath on her face. She was a formidable beast. Her horns branched many times and were at least three feet long. She had a long shaggy beard beneath her chin, and the whiskers hanging on either side of her mouth were blue. Her eyes were cloudy, and Ping guessed that her dragon sight was fading.

The old dragon made a metallic sound that reminded Ping of someone chinking coins together in cupped hands. It wasn't like any of the sounds Kai or Danzi had made. Ping waited for words to form in her head, but none did.

"What did she say?" Ping asked Kai.

"She wants to know how long you have lived with dragons."

Kai replied to the ancient dragon with the same sounds.

The red dragon snorted through her nose. They were all so old; no doubt she was unimpressed by the fact that Ping had been a Dragon Keeper for less than three years. Ping reached into her pocket and pulled out her mirror. She was young, and her time as a Dragon Keeper may have been short, but she had cared for two dragons.

"My first dragon gave me this," she said, holding the mirror out to the old red dragon.

As the red dragon reached out to take the mirror, her stiff talons reminded Ping of Lao Longzi's fingers. The dragon held the mirror close to her eyes, peered at it, turned it over, and nodded.

"Did she know Danzi?" Ping asked.

"They all knew Father," Kai replied.

Ping would have danced for joy if her legs hadn't been so stiff. Danzi's wishes had been fulfilled. And Kai wasn't going to spend his life as a solitary dragon; he had other dragons to live with. She might not have brought him directly to them herself, but here he was in the dragon haven.

Ping looked around the plateau in the dying light. It wasn't the sort of place that would have attracted humans, nothing like the green pleasantness of Long Gao Yuan. But Ping remembered how Danzi had once bathed in a hot spring pool and enjoyed it immensely. It was a dragon's world. If Kai liked it, she would just have to learn to like it, too. With all the hot pools and boiling mud, at least she would never be cold. The smell would be the hardest thing to get used to. Beyond the pools and caverns, the plateau sloped down gradually before it ended in a sheer cliff on all sides. There was no way she could get down without the aid of a dragon. That didn't matter. She didn't want to leave anyway.

The sun had disappeared beneath the jagged mountains, leaving an orange stain on the horizon. The dragons stopped staring at Ping and moved away, returning to their dragon business.

Ping examined Kai from head to toe.

"Are you sure you're all right? Have the dragons been looking after you? Have you been eating well?"

"Kai was worried about Ping, but is very happy now."

"Is the water safe for me to drink?"

"Some of the pools are poisonous to humans."

Ping knew the white pool contained arsenic and would be poisonous to humans, although dragons loved to bathe in it and could even drink the white water.

Kai spoke to the other dragons and then showed her to a small pool that they had said was safe for her to drink from. Ping wasn't so sure. It was no bigger than a puddle, and it was cloudy and brown. She cupped some of the water in her hands and drank. It had an unpleasant sulphur taste, but Ping had drunk worse-tasting water from neglected wells. A warm bath would have been very pleasant. She longed to wash the sweat and grime from her body.

"Kai, ask if any of the colored pools are safe for me to bathe in."

Kai spoke to the old red dragon in the chinking voice that Ping couldn't understand.

"Gu Hong says the pools are only for dragons to bathe in."

"Is that her name, Ancient Red?"

"Yes," Kai replied.

"Did you ask them to look for me, Kai?"

"Yes. They refused at first, but the white dragons saw Ping when they were out scouting. Every day Ping got closer. They thought that Ping would eventually find the dragon haven and didn't want other humans led here."

"So they're not exactly pleased to see me."

Kai shook his head.

The dragons hadn't picked her up because they were worried about her well-being, not even because they were concerned that Kai was missing her. They had just been afraid that she would give away their hiding place.

It was almost dark. Ping wasn't sure if she was a prisoner or not. Her stomach was rumbling, but she didn't want to ask the dragons for food.

Without warning, a jet of steaming water spurted out of the ground nearby, high into the air. It startled Ping, but the dragons didn't seem at all surprised. They all walked toward the orange pool. The only male, the yellow dragon who had carried Ping, squatted on the rocks surrounding the pool, while the females waded in. The pool was wide and shallow. When the dragons sat down, the water came up to their haunches. They made low chinking sounds to each other.

"Are they having a bath?" Ping asked.

"Not a bath, a moon gathering," Kai replied. "When the moon is in the night sky, the dragons gather in the orange pool after the fire dragon has spurted."

"What fire dragon?"

"The one that lives beneath the earth. Every evening, he spurts water into the air."

Ping wanted to ask more questions, but Kai was moving toward the orange pool.

"Kai must go to the gathering and listen to the dragons."

Kai sat on the rocks next to the yellow male, listening to the females. In the light of a waning half moon, the dragons all glowed slightly. Kai's scales had the brightest glow.

The moon gathering didn't last long. The dragons soon made their way to the caverns to sleep, all except for one of the white dragons, who flew up to the highest point of the plateau to keep watch. The two yellow dragons had a cavern of their own. The others all slept together in the largest cavern. As she approached, Ping could see glints of color moving around inside. The dragons' scales retained their moon glow. It made the dark cavern look cheerful. The younger red dragon barred Ping's way when she tried to follow Kai inside.

"Tell them I have to be with you, Kai."

Ping watched from the mouth of the cavern as the little dragon went up to where Gu Hong was settling down for the night. He looked very small standing in front of the enormous red dragon, but he must have put his request well, because Gu Hong allowed Ping to enter the cave.

Once she was in the cavern, Ping wished she'd stayed outside.

The cavern stank. Judging by the smell, the dragons weren't housebroken. Their bedding straw was old and stained. There were half-chewed animal bones lying around. Ping had spent the night in some very unpleasant places before, but the dragon cavern had to be the worst. The ox shed at Huangling Palace, where she'd slept all through her childhood, seemed clean and tidy by comparison. It was cooler in the cavern than out near the steaming pools. The younger red dragon brought her an animal skin. Ping's heart started to thud. It was her bearskin, the one she'd left with Jun at the bottom of the Serpent's Tail. She knew it was hers because she could see where she'd cut a piece off to make the ball for Kai.

"Do they have our other things, Kai?" Ping asked.

Kai spoke to the dragons, and the young red dragon pulled the saddlebag from behind a rock. Ping opened it. Everything was as she had left it—the cooking things, the gold coins, her firesticks, the dragon pendant Jun had given her. Ping's stomach tightened. The last time she'd seen the bag, Jun had been holding it. She'd assumed that he'd taken it with him. Had Jun discarded the bag? Or had one of the dragons taken it from him?

"Kai," Ping said. "Where is Jun? Did the dragons hurt him? Is he still alive?"

"Don't know. Kai asked, but no one would answer."

Ping had convinced herself that Jun had given up waiting for them. She had pictured him sitting comfortably at home with his family. Now she wasn't so sure. She slipped the pendant around her neck.

The red dragon handed her something else—the crumpled piece of calfskin that she had thrown away on Long Gao Yuan.

The two red dragons slept at the back of the cave. The white dragons slept together, their bodies coiled around each other like a litter of enormous puppies. Kai slept between them. His nest straw was flattened and stale. Clearly, he'd stopped making a new nest each night.

Ping lay down in a pile of straw near the cave entrance. She had expected the dragons to welcome her, not treat her like an intruder. But after what she'd seen at Long Gao Yuan, she didn't blame them for being wary of people. She would have to be patient and win them over gradually.

Ping was tired, hungry, and very dirty. She shivered in the chilly cave and pulled the bearskin around her. The dragon haven wasn't the paradise she'd imagined.

# CHAPTER SEVENTEEN

# WILDLIFE

The next morning, when Ping woke, the dragons were still sleeping, even though it was hours past sunrise. The smell in the cavern was even worse. She decided that she had to find somewhere else to sleep. Kai was the only dragon awake. Ping found him outside squatting behind a large rock.

"Kai, what are you doing?"

"Poo," the little dragon said.

"I can see that, but why didn't you dig a hole and cover it over like I taught you?"

"Wild dragons don't do that," he said.

He had been living with the dragons for just a few weeks, but he was already changing his habits.

"We need somewhere to sleep that doesn't smell as bad as the dragons' cavern," she said. "Come and help me find a place."

They investigated several caverns that were little more than holes in the ground; they would fill up if it ever rained. Other caves offered more shelter, but their walls were encrusted with the yellow crystals, which had an unpleasant smell.

"Let's have a look over there," Ping said, pointing to the north of the plateau.

The ground rose in the center of the plateau so that the northern end was higher. There were fewer craters and some low bushes and tufts of grass. A cascade of pinkish water from a bubbling spring clattered down a rocky escarpment that separated the northern end of the plateau from the dragons' preferred pools and caverns. The water was hot.

This part of the plateau was more to Ping's liking. She preferred to be surrounded by bushes, rather than the smelly pools. But Ping didn't want to be unfriendly and live too far away from the other dragons. She found a small cave that burrowed horizontally halfway up the escarpment. It was dry, and there were no crystals on the walls. Though it was away from the pools, the slight elevation meant that she could still see the dragons. The cave was warmed by a steam vent near the entrance, and there were ferns and mosses growing around it. It was small, but big enough for two.

"What do you think, Kai? Will we be comfortable here?"

"It is a good cave for Ping," the dragon said. "But Kai will sleep with the rest of the cluster."

Cluster. It was a good word for a group of dragons.

Ping tried not to look disappointed. After all, that was why she'd brought Kai to the dragon haven, so that he could live with his own kind.

The dragons were gradually emerging from their caverns, yawning and scratching themselves. They had very different habits from Danzi, who hadn't slept much at all. They didn't take any notice of Ping. She fetched her few possessions and moved them into her new home. The dragons still didn't offer her any food, so she went out to investigate the northern part of the plateau to see if she could find anything to eat. There were burrows that offered the promise of rabbit. Snakes and lizards might be attracted by the warm rocks. She startled a pheasant as she walked through a clump of grass, but she would need a trap or a snare to catch rabbits and birds. She had hoped there would be a clear pool with fish, but there wasn't. She found a couple of mushrooms, but they were dry and withered because of the warm air.

The young red dragon came up to Kai and said something to him.

"The dragons say that Ping can bathe beneath the hot falls," he translated.

The cascade of pinkish water fell a few feet before it collected in a small pool and then ran into a crater and disappeared back into the earth again. Ping would have preferred a still pool, but she didn't complain.

To her surprise, most of the female dragons

gathered around to watch her bathe. Only Gu Hong stayed away. Ping was a little embarrassed to have an audience, but she couldn't remember the last time she'd had a proper wash. Her last hot bath was a distant memory, so she undressed and slipped into the steaming pool. The steam rising from the pool had the same unpleasant sulphurous smell as some of the other pools. It was so small that she only just fit into it, and there was nowhere she could avoid sitting under the falls. But she soon discovered that it was actually very pleasant to have warm water cascading over her.

The dragons grew bored with watching her bathe and wandered off. Ping felt her cares and concerns begin to wash away with the dirt. The dragon haven wasn't as comfortable as she'd imagined, the dragons weren't as friendly as she'd hoped, but Kai was safe and happy. She could allow both her body and her mind to relax at last.

Ping washed her clothes as well, and stayed in the pool while they dried on the rocks. Around noon, the yellow dragons dragged the remains of a deer carcass out of another cave. They cut off pieces, using their talons and a sharpened stone, and gave a piece to each of the dragons. The female glanced shyly at Ping and put a lump of the raw meat on a rock for her. Ping bowed her thanks as she took the piece of meat.

"Tell them that I can't eat raw meat, Kai. I'll need to light a fire so that I can cook it."

Kai made the sounds that didn't translate in Ping's head. The old red dragon made a sharp noise in reply.

"No fire," Kai said. "Gu Hong says smoke will show the world where the dragon haven is."

Ping didn't know how far she'd flown on the back of the dragon, but she was sure there was no one within a hundred *li* to see the smoke. But she didn't argue.

If she was going to stay in the dragon haven, she would have to find a way to cook her food. From the smell of the meat, Ping guessed that it was several days since the animal had been killed. The dragons were busy gnawing on deer bones. Ping looked around the plateau. The steaming pools reminded her of the kitchens at Beibai Palace. She inspected the smaller craters. Some were dark holes that went deep into the earth. Others were just depressions in the crumbly earth. One or two were basins of water so hot they were boiling. Ping selected one of these pools and dropped her piece of meat into the bubbling water. Kai came over to see what she was doing.

"Give me your meat, Kai, and I'll cook it for you. You shouldn't eat such old meat raw."

He glanced at the other dragons as he gave the meat to Ping. She scratched him under his chin while they waited for it to cook. Kai had spent a lot of his short life eating elegant banquets of tasty stews, braised meat, and fish with delicious sauces. He had a lot of adjustments to make if he was going to live as a wild dragon.

The meat took less than half an hour to cook. It wasn't as tasty as roasted meat, but at least it wasn't raw.

In the afternoon, most of the dragons dozed in the sun. Ping watched Kai playing with the male yellow dragon. Kai had told her his name was Tun, which meant Morning Sunlight. The game they played was something like hide-and-seek, but instead of hiding in one place, they kept moving until they could sneak up and jump on each other. The aim was to throw the other dragon to the ground. Kai called the game hide-and-hunt.

As she watched, Ping realized that it wasn't a game at all, but a way of training young dragons to hunt and to defend themselves. After a while, the young red dragon woke from her nap and joined in. Because he was small, Kai was at a complete disadvantage. He never won. He was good at hiding, but he could never get the better of the other dragons. That didn't stop him from leaping on their backs or trying to trip them up. Ping wasn't sure she liked seeing Kai play so aggressively. By the end of the game he had several small wounds. Ping had never really considered how much damage dragons could do with teeth, talons, and a swipe of their tails, if they chose to. But no matter how many times Kai was tripped, winded, or thrown on his back, he always went back for more.

Ping devised a routine to fill her days. She swept out her cave with a broom made of twigs. She explored the northern end of the plateau, looking for herbs and berries that she could add to her meals or dry, if they had healing properties. She carved a needle from a piece of bone so that she could mend her clothes. She also carved a set of Seven Cunning Pieces from the hip bone of a deer, to amuse herself in the afternoons.

Since she had no silk hangings to decorate the dull walls of her new home, she decided to create her own decorations. From around the edges of the pools she collected lumps of earth that had taken on the different colors of the water. She used them to draw pictures on the walls of her cave. She was no artist, but when she drew Danzi, Kai, and Hua, she was pleased with her work. She drew trees and flowers that she might never see again. She tried to draw her mother and brother, but they looked more like wooden dolls than real people.

The dragons led leisurely lives, spending many hours basking in the sun or wallowing in the pools. Ping sat at the mouth of her cave, watching her new neighbors and getting to know their ways.

The three white dragons were sisters. Their names were Bai Xue, Shuang, and Lian, which meant White Snow, Frost, and Lotus. Their mother had laid their three dragon stones at the same time, Kai told her, but each had been hatched hundreds of years apart. When dragons were more widespread, they had been able to rear more than one dragonling at once, but as their lives became endangered, it was only safe to rear one at a time. A dragon mother could choose to delay the hatching of her dragon stones. Kai didn't know how.

The white dragons were the smallest, but their wings were bigger in proportion to their body than the wings of other dragons. That made them the fastest and strongest flyers. They acted as scouts. It was Shuang who had been watching Ping as she had made her slow way across the mountains. She and Bai Xue also went out hunting, though Ping hadn't seen them bring back anything larger than a bird. Lian was the youngest of the wild dragons, too young to have wings.

The two yellow dragons, Tun and Sha, were mated. Tun had the strong straight nose of an adult male. Sha, whose name meant Sandy, was a shy creature who never came near Ping.

Gu Hong spent each morning sitting in the sun. Each afternoon she lumbered over to the white pool and stayed there for hours. Every evening, after the moon gathering, she dragged her huge, old body to the sleeping cavern. The younger red dragon was Jiang, which meant Ginger. She was Gu Hong's daughter and looked after her mother's needs, bringing her food and water in a gourd.

The dragons took little notice of Ping, though she sometimes caught them observing her when they thought she wasn't looking. They were, however, always talking to Kai, instructing him or playing with him. Ping was pleased that they were taking care of him. She wondered what they were saying, but whenever she asked Kai, he told her it was nothing important. She thought of Jun and how frustrated he'd been that he couldn't understand Kai. She now knew how exasperating that was. She tried to communicate with them by making signs with her hands, but they didn't seem to understand her.

The dragons found Kai's shape-changing skills very entertaining. And Kai liked nothing better than to be the center of attention. When he changed into a chicken or a pig, they made the same jingling bell sound that Kai did when he found something amusing. They gasped when he turned into a beautiful vase. He sometimes changed into an innocent-looking rock and waited until another dragon walked past him. Then he would suddenly change back into his normal shape with a roar to make them jump.

"I've never seen any of the other dragons shape-change," Ping said after Kai had startled Lian in this way.

"They're not very good at shape-changing. Not nearly as good as Kai," he added. "White dragons can only shape-change into one thing—a white eagle."

"I think I saw one when I was walking," Ping said.

"Yellow dragons can change size but not shape," Kai continued. "They can appear larger or very small. Red dragons only have the mirage skill."

"You can do all of those things," Ping said.

"Yes," said Kai proudly.

"What do the dragons speak about at the gatherings?" Ping asked Kai later that day as they walked together on the northern plateau looking for herbs.

"The dragons remember. They recall what has happened in their lives and in the history of all dragons in this land that is now known as the Empire."

Ping had never considered that there was a time before the Empire and that dragons would have existed then.

"Do they ever speak about . . . what happened at Long Gao Yuan?"

"They remember the Dead Ones at the moon gatherings, but they don't speak of what happened."

All of the dragons must have survived the massacre. Ping didn't blame them for not wanting to remember whatever had happened there.

"They also make decisions," Kai continued. "Such as whose turn it is to be on watch. They talk about whether they should bring the rains again, or whether they will let nature take its course without the help of dragons."

"But dragons can't really bring rain."

"Dragons can bring rain. Gu Hong said so," Kai insisted.

"It's just a story, a legend. Danzi could only make the rain fall if there were already clouds."

"Father was old and weary and had lost the ability."

"Well, if they can make it rain, why don't they?"

"They don't want to help humans. They have not brought rain since the massacre at Long Gao Yuan."

Ping had many more questions, but Tun called Kai over.

"Ping must stay away from the edge of the plateau," Kai said, before he ran off for a game of hide-and-hunt.

# CHAPTER EIGHTEEN

# BLACK THUNDER

Ping's days took on the slow, lazy rhythms of the dragons' lives. In the afternoons there was nothing to do but doze in the warm summer sun. One afternoon, her eyes had just closed when she felt something digging her in the ribs. It was Gu Hong. The old red dragon was poking her with a stick. Ping smiled and nodded, but wasn't sure what Gu Hong wanted. The old dragon scratched the earth in front of her with the stick and then poked Ping again, harder. Ping looked at the white soil. To her amazement she saw that the marks Gu Hong had made in the soil weren't random scratchings, but characters. Very shaky, misshapen characters, but three characters nonetheless. *Mother of Kai*.

Ping realized it was meant to be a question. Who was Kai's mother?

Ping wrote an answer in the earth. *Lu Yu*.

Gu Hong wrote more characters. *Color. Ancestry. Cause of death*.

239

Ping felt her face burn with shame. She didn't know what color LuYu was. She had never seen Kai's mother in full daylight. In Ping's memory she was just gray. She knew nothing about where Kai's mother had come from. And, worse still, she had died from neglect and misery. At Huangling, Ping hadn't had any power to change the conditions that the dragons lived in, and it wasn't even her job to care for them, but she could have done more.

*Don't know*, she scratched in the dirt.

Ping had many questions she wanted to ask—how did the dragons at Long Gao Yuan die? Why did Danzi leave them? Couldn't she have a more useful role in the haven?—but these were all difficult questions, and she didn't think it was the right time to ask them. Instead she asked a simple question. *Dragons dig holes?* She indicated the craters around them. *No*, was the reply. *Caused by fire dragon turning in his sleep.* Gu Hong scratched more characters in the earth. It was a slow method of communication, but gradually Ping learned about the huge fire dragon that the dragons believed lived far below the earth's surface. His breath was so hot that it melted rocks. Underwater streams were heated by the molten rock. At a few places in the world, this water found its way to the surface, and hot springs burst out of the ground. In these special places, the fire dragon protected the earthly dragons. Ping didn't think they had much faith in his powers of protection, as there was always one dragon on guard duty, day and night.

The beautiful colors of the water were caused by the different moods of the fire dragon when he breathed on the rocks. Kai had told Ping that the pools had different properties depending on their color. The yellow one was a healing pool; the purple one, cleansing; the white was for strength and rejuvenation.

Jiang came to help her mother into her favorite pool. Ping was relieved that she had a way of communicating directly with the dragons, even if it was slow and laborious. She wondered how Gu Hong had learned to write.

Ping left the dragons to have their afternoon snooze and continued to explore the plateau. She was worried about the cold weather that would be arriving in a month or two. The dragons would sleep for most of the winter. Ping wasn't sure if they would wake up to hunt from time to time. In any case, a lot of their prey would be hibernating as well. The coming winter would be a long and lonely one for her. She didn't want it to be a hungry one as well. Like a squirrel, she had to collect a store of food. She had started gathering berries and mushrooms and laying them out to dry, but that wouldn't be enough. She sat in the afternoon sun and made a snare out of dried grass stalks so that she could catch rabbits and pheasants. She practiced by throwing it around rocks.

Ping was looking for rabbit burrows on the northern end of the plateau when she found a cave burrow-
ing into a low, grass-covered hill. Bushes almost hid its
entrance. She ducked her head and entered. Daylight
filtered through small holes in the roof. It wasn't as
dingy as the caves at the other end of the plateau, and
Ping wondered if it would make a better home for her.
Then she noticed something at the back of the cave. A
large flat rock was positioned in the center, and several
objects were arranged on it. She moved closer. As her
eyes grew used to the dimness, she could make out
what some of them were. There were three lumps of
jade, not carved or fashioned into any shape. They
looked like they had been cut from rock. There was a
large stone that had split in half to reveal a forest of
amethyst crystals inside. There was a mother-of-pearl
seashell, and several strings of dragons' teeth. Ping
caught her breath. In the middle of the display were
three large oval stones.

"Dragon stones," she whispered.

The thought of young dragons in the haven brought
a smile to Ping's face. When the eggs hatched, she
would have a purpose. She could help the females raise
the little ones. Kai would be very excited to have other
young dragons to play with. She was reaching out to
touch one of the dragon stones when the back of her
neck prickled. Her stomach ached as if indigestible
food lay rotting in it. Her skin turned cold despite the

warm air. Ping's joy at finding the dragon stones drained from her until there wasn't a drop left. Despair filled the empty space. She gripped her stomach as the pain increased. It was so intense, she doubled over.

Ping hadn't felt the sense of dread for a long time, not since she'd been in the presence of the necromancer. All through her travels, she had expected it. She'd waited to feel it when the imperial guards on the Great Wall had turned nasty. When she first saw the Ma Ren, she'd thought she might experience it. But the sense of foreboding had never come. Not until now.

There was someone outside the cave who meant Kai harm. She swung around expecting to see a necromancer or a dragon hunter or a squad of imperial guards. A deafening roar echoed around the cave. Whatever was outside, it wasn't human. Ping didn't know what she was about to face, but she didn't want to be cornered in the cave.

She staggered outside, still clutching her stomach. The pain threatened to make her lose consciousness. She fell to her knees. A large, dark shape towered over her. It was a dragon. A black one.

The black dragon was big—bigger than Danzi, almost as big as Gu Hong. He crouched on his haunches, ready to spring. His legs bulged with huge muscles. A long puckered scar cut across his belly, and the tip of one of his horns was broken off. His eyes weren't brown like the other dragons', but blood red.

The limp carcass of an antelope hung from the talons of his right forepaw. The black dragon bared his teeth and snarled. Ping would never have believed that such a sound could have come from a dragon.

Before she had time to react, his paw swiped her across her face, knocking her to the ground. Her ears were ringing from the blow, but she heard a deep, angry voice in her mind.

"Humans should not enter the treasure cave!"

The dragon's red eyes were glowing with anger.

She heard another more familiar dragon cry. It was Kai's. He ran and stood between Ping and the black dragon. He spoke in the dragon voice Ping couldn't understand, but she could tell he was trying to defend her.

Ping clutched Kai to her. When she had confronted the necromancer and the dragon hunter, the foreboding had felt full of greed—greed for gold, greed for power. This time the sensation was laced with hatred for her. When Kai had appeared, the sensation had grown even stronger. The black dragon hated Kai as well. Ping couldn't understand how he could feel such malice toward another dragon.

The other dragons were gathering around. The yellow and white dragons seemed intimidated by the black one. Gu Hong was slow to arrive. She hobbled forward, with Jiang cowering behind her. Gu Hong was the only one who wasn't afraid of the newcomer. She raised herself up and roared at him. The black dragon's muscular legs rippled, and Ping thought he might leap at the old one, but he didn't. He lowered himself onto all fours and growled from deep in his throat. The old red dragon might not have been able to fly or see well, and she probably couldn't walk very far, but like the others, the black dragon had respect for her.

"Humans are not permitted in the treasure cave," the black dragon said to Kai. "Make sure your servant stays out."

"He says—"

"You don't have to tell me what he said, Kai. I heard him in my mind."

Kai fussed around her, and she leaned on him as she got to her feet.

"I am no one's servant," Ping said. "I am Kai's Dragon Keeper."

The black dragon snorted. "A female can't be a true Dragon Keeper."

"Did Ping hear him?" Kai asked.

Ping nodded. "Who is he?"

"His name is Hei Lei."

Gu Hong roared again. The black dragon snarled back. He threw the dead antelope at her feet, then walked away toward the white pool. Hei Lei meant Black Thunder. It was a good name for him. The two yellow dragons crept forward and picked up the antelope, carrying it between them. They took it into one of the caverns.

Ping touched her right cheek and examined her hand. There were four lines of blood from where Hei Lei's talons had raked across her face.

"He means you harm, Kai. My second sight told me."

"Hei Lei is not friends with anyone," Kai replied, "but he wouldn't hurt another dragon."

"I felt the sense of dread. It was stronger than ever before."

"Hei Lei is very angry," Kai said. "But with Ping, not with Kai."

Ping watched Hei Lei crouch at the edge of the white pool and drink the water. The pain in her stomach was fading. It was now no worse than the discomfort she'd felt after eating too much at an imperial banquet. She went to the falls and washed her face. Kai followed her.

"Perhaps one day Ping will understand all the dragons," Kai said hopefully.

In the past, intense anger had improved Ping's second sight. She wondered if it was Hei Lei's anger that enabled her to understand him. Perhaps at first she would be able to comprehend the dragons only when they experienced strong emotions. She hoped that gradually her mind would be able to hear more and more of their speech.

The dragons didn't sleep as soon as it got dark, like birds and other creatures of the earth. Every evening so far, they had gathered together at the orange pool at twilight. The beginning of the gathering was heralded by the sudden spurt of boiling water as the fire dragon sprayed hot water into the evening air. The females waded into the water. The males sat on the surrounding rocks. They spoke in low dragon voices. Sometimes one or two chose not to take part. Some might decide to go to the sleeping cave before the gathering was finished, even while another dragon was still speaking. Kai never missed a moon gathering. He soaked up every sound the dragons uttered.

That night the fire dragon's jet of water sprayed into the air, but none of the dragons moved. Ping went over to Kai.

"Why isn't there a gathering tonight?"

"There is no moon," Kai replied.

Ping looked at the black sky. There were thousands of stars, but no moon. On moonless nights the dragons went to their caves as soon as night fell. Left alone in the darkness, Ping thought again of the winter to come. She had no lamp oil to bring light to the long hours of darkness. She wondered if she would be permitted to light a fire after dark, but she wasn't sure the dragons would allow it.

Ping went to the falls and had a warm bath with only the stars watching her. At least she wouldn't be cold during the winter.

The next evening, there was just the thinnest sliver of

moon floating in the star-spangled sky, but the dragons gathered again. Kai had told Ping that the female dragons acted as a council. It was they who made decisions, settled disputes, and decided on punishment if any dragon ever did anything wrong.

The fire dragon heated the water in the orange pool when he was in a thoughtful mood. The dragons believed that this helped them make just and correct decisions.

"Ping must not drink from the orange pool," Kai had told her.

"Is it poisonous?"

"No. The dragons think that if humans touch it, the properties of the pool will be disturbed."

The dragons' glow was barely noticeable in the light of the slender moon. Hei Lei crouched on the rocks with Tun. Kai seemed reluctant to join them while the black dragon was there. Hei Lei spoke in his deep dragon voice, using the sounds that Ping couldn't understand. As he spoke, the females, one by one, turned to glance at Ping.

"What is he saying?" Ping asked.

"Hei Lei wants Ping to leave the haven," Kai said calmly. "They are listening to his argument before they make a decision."

Ping's heart started to race. "What argument? What have I done wrong?"

"Hei Lei thinks that because Ping is a female, Ping can't be a proper Dragon Keeper," Kai told her. "He thinks female humans are even more untrustworthy than males."

"But Lao Longzi said that Dragon Keepers were welcome in the dragon haven."

"Not anymore," Kai said.

"Not since the massacre?"

Kai nodded, then clambered over to the rocks and sat next to Tun.

Ping had imagined that her right to stay with Kai was beyond question.

Hei Lei answered the female dragons' questions at length. Ping was not invited to speak on her own behalf. She longed to know what they were saying about her. She listened to the chinking sounds, hoping that they would start to make some sense. She searched for some way of reaching inside the dragons' minds with her second sight. It didn't help; within the minds of the dragons, she could feel a shield preventing her from hearing their thoughts. She caught Gu Hong's eye. The red dragon was aware of her probing.

After Hei Lei had finished speaking, the six female dragons sat in the pool in silence. There was no discussion—or none that Ping could hear. If there was any debate it was by thought. But a decision was made. Gu Hong said a few words. Kai came back to translate her pronouncement.

"Ping can stay," Kai said. "For the moment."

Hei Lei snorted and walked away. Ping felt weak

with relief, but she wished the female dragons hadn't found it necessary to take so long to decide.

"You didn't seem worried that they might have sent me away," Ping said to Kai.

"Kai trusts the dragons to make the right decisions."

Ping wondered what Kai's reaction would have been if their decision had been different. She wasn't convinced he would have objected.

Ping's cheek was sore. The talon scratches on her face weren't healing. She fetched the pot of red-cloud herb ointment from her cave and smeared a little on the scratches. The female yellow dragon was standing at a distance.

"Sha wants to know if you are all right," Kai translated.

Ping had never been able to get close to the shy yellow dragon before.

"Sha is our healer," Kai said. "She thinks water from the healing pool will help Ping's wounds."

"Tell her I have red-cloud herb ointment."

Ping could see that Sha was interested in what she was doing, but was too timid to come closer.

"Come and have a look, Sha," Ping called out, even though she knew the yellow dragon couldn't understand her. She smiled and beckoned to her.

Slowly, shyly, the yellow dragon came to Ping.

"Tell her I used this ointment to heal Danzi's torn wing and his arrow wound."

Kai explained to Sha. The yellow dragon moved closer and sniffed the ointment.

"Tell her I also used it on your dragon stone before you were born."

Kai hesitated.

"Go on, tell her." Ping wanted the dragons to know what a good Dragon Keeper she'd been.

Kai started to tell Sha, but before he finished, the yellow dragon darted away and disappeared into her sleeping cavern.

"What's wrong?" Ping asked Kai. "What startled her?"

"Sha and her mate, Tun, would like to have a family," Kai said.

Ping could feel his sadness.

"She has laid three dragon stones."

"The ones in the treasure cave?" Ping asked.

"Yes."

"Then she is blessed. They will have a family when the eggs hatch."

Kai shook his head. "The dragon stones were gray when they were laid."

Ping had thought it was the dim light in the cave that made the stones look gray, but that was their actual color.

The dragon eggs were dead.

# CHAPTER NINETEEN

# NINE IS BETTER

It didn't take long for the news to spread among the other dragons that Ping had upset Sha. Gu Hong sent for her. She scratched more questions in the dirt. She wanted to know who had raised Kai and why his dragon stone had been ailing. The questions Gu Hong asked always seemed to prove what a bad Dragon Keeper Ping had been.

"Didn't you tell the dragons that I raised you?" Ping asked Kai when Gu Hong had finished quizzing her.

"No."

"Why not?"

"They think it is wrong for a dragonling to be raised by a human—especially a female. They think Kai must be . . ." He searched for the right word.

"Tainted?" Ping suggested. "Like food cooked with rancid oil?"

Kai nodded slowly.

"I didn't know they felt that way," Ping whispered.

Ping couldn't sleep that night, she was so angry with the dragons. She'd raised Kai well, considering she'd had no training. All she'd had to guide her was the little information Danzi had given her before he flew away. The dragons didn't know about the months she'd spent on Tai Shan caring for baby Kai with no help. It hurt Ping to know that Kai was ashamed of his upbringing. He was a strong and intelligent young dragon. He was eager to learn, and his shape-changing skills were better than any of the other dragons'. He was fearless when he played the rough games with the older dragons. Ping could have stayed in the comfort of Beibai Palace, but she hadn't. She'd risked her life and brought Kai to them. What more did the dragons want? They didn't realize how hard she'd tried to replace Lu Yu, his dead mother. Ping also felt guilty. She'd upset Sha, reminding her of events she was trying to forget. It was almost dawn when Ping finally fell asleep.

She slept later than usual and came out of her cave just in time to see Hei Lei fly off on a hunting expedition. Kai was already training with Tun. Even Gu Hong was up.

Ping's feeling of dread had faded completely, but she was relieved Hei Lei had left. It was wonderful to see Kai living with other dragons, learning from Tun, being fussed over by the females. But she knew that they thought he was unnatural in some way. She could watch over him for her lifetime, but then what would happen? Could she trust the dragons to treat him well?

Or would they always consider him to be an outsider? Ping wished she could glimpse Kai's future. She wished she had a bundle of yarrow stalks and the *Yi Jing*, so that she could ask it what she should do.

Danzi had once told her that Dragon Keepers could read the future. Long ago, when people had first tamed dragons, they had noticed that after many years of close contact with the creatures, young men developed the ability to foretell coming events. That's why emperors had decided to keep dragons, so that their keepers could predict the future for them.

Ping hadn't tried to develop that skill. She'd never really wanted to know what the future held. If there was nothing but sadness and misery ahead, she didn't want to know. Even if the future was full of happiness, she thought it was best not to know. How could she concentrate on the present? She was afraid she might neglect her duty while focusing on what lay ahead.

Ping's mind tied itself in knots whenever she thought of this. People hadn't learned to read the future for the good of their dragon charges—it was a skill they had cultivated for their own advantage. Her second sight told her when her dragons were in immediate danger, and that was all she'd needed to know. Foretelling the future was a skill she'd thought she could do without. Until now.

She needed to be sure that the dragon haven was the right place for Kai to live. She had done what Danzi thought best, but he hadn't known how the dragons' lives had changed. She had to know if Hei Lei was a threat to Kai. Ping sensed that his anger hadn't disappeared but was seething inside him. One day it would burst out, like over-fermented wine exploding out of a sealed jar. One day Hei Lei would fly into a deadly rage, Ping was sure of it.

She focused her mind and tried to sense what the future held. There was something there, something as difficult to grasp as mist. Whenever she thought she was close to reading the feeling, it evaporated. There was nothing substantial, so surely that meant she had nothing to fear? But she couldn't forget the intensity of the dread she'd felt when she'd first met Hei Lei.

She went to see Gu Hong. *Is Kai safe here?* she wrote in the earth.

The old dragon scratched characters next to Ping's. *Of course.*

Ping tried to think of a way to express her concerns. *Hei Lei wants to hurt Kai.*

Gu Hong shook her head.

"Hei Lei is not a bad dragon."

Ping heard the words clearly in her mind. She looked around. The words hadn't come from Gu Hong. Kai was off playing with Tun, and Hei Lei was away hunting. Jiang was the only other dragon close by.

"You can speak to me," Ping said to Jiang.

"Yes. Not all dragons can make their thoughts

understood by humans, only those who have lived with a Dragon Keeper."

"So you have had a Dragon Keeper, Jiang?"

"Yes."

"And Hei Lei?"

"Yes."

"Then why does he dislike me so?"

"You must ask Hei Lei."

Ping knew that would be a waste of time. "I'm sure he means to harm Kai."

"My mother says he will not. It is humans he hates, not dragons."

Ping suspected Hei Lei hated humans so much because of the massacre at Long Gao Yuan, but the other dragons had also suffered there. They had escaped from whoever killed the Dead Ones, yet only Hei Lei was filled with hatred. She wanted to ask Jiang what had happened, but she knew she'd be wasting her time. Getting a straight answer from a dragon was never easy.

Ping heard the jingling sound of Kai's laughter. He had beaten Tun in the game of hide-and-hunt for the first time—though Ping suspected the yellow dragon had allowed him to win.

Gu Hong spoke. Jiang translated for Ping.

"You may leave the haven if you wish," she said. "But we will not let Kai go."

Ping hadn't had any real intention of taking Kai away, but now she knew for certain that it wasn't possible. She looked out at the mountains stretching to the distant horizon in every direction. If they tried to escape, the winged dragons with their dragon sight would easily track them down. In any case, Kai would never agree to leave.

No matter what she envisaged for the future, Kai's life was no longer in her hands.

Gu Hong scratched more characters in the earth. *Nine good.*

Including Kai there were nine dragons. Nine was an auspicious number. It symbolized long life, everlasting happiness. For a species threatened with extinction, it was the best number.

"Now we are nine, all will be well," Jiang said. "Hei Lei is quick to anger, moody and unfriendly, but he is loyal to us. His maleness is needed. He has much *yang*. There are too many females in our cluster. Hei Lei balances our excess of *yin*."

But as time passed, Ping saw that Jiang and the others were wary of the black dragon. She wasn't the only one who was happier when Hei Lei was away. The plateau was a more cheerful place when he wasn't there. As soon as he returned, the dragons were a little on edge, as if they were worried that they might upset him. Ping remembered the *Yi Jing* reading. There was still one line of the divination left. It was the sixth and last line left— and the only inauspicious line. *When a dragon is arrogant, there will be cause for regret.* She had no doubt which dragon that would be. Hei Lei. She would have to watch Kai more closely. She looked around to see where he was and found him swimming in the yellow pool.

Kai was a better swimmer than any of the other dragons. The yellow and the red dragons were competent, but the whites just paddled across the pools like dogs, never putting their heads underwater.

Kai loved to demonstrate his skills in the water. He dived, he did somersaults, he leaped up into the air like a flying fish and plunged back down again. The three white dragons and Sha watched his displays, encouraging him with a high-pitched chattering noise.

"Does this plateau have a name?" Ping asked Jiang, relieved that she could converse easily with at least one of the dragons.

"No. Names are dangerous," Jiang replied. "If you give a place a name, it becomes known. If a place is never named, no one can ever speak of it."

Lao Longzi had told her that the name of Dragon Plateau should never be written down, never spoken aloud. That hadn't been enough to save the dragons from whatever happened there. Their new home didn't even have a name.

The yellow pool was Kai's favorite. He had told Ping that in one place it was deeper than the length of the Serpent's Tail. The other dragons waded cautiously into the shallow end of the yellow pool only when they needed its healing properties.

Lian threw a stone into the deep end, and Kai dived to retrieve it. He was underwater for a long time, but eventually he broke the surface with the stone between his teeth. All the young females gathered around to praise him. Ping felt pride for her dragon swell in her chest.

"But if they aren't comfortable underwater, what happens when they hibernate in the pools during winter?" Ping asked Kai, when he had finished showing off.

"They don't sleep in pools in the winter," Kai told her.

"They don't hibernate?"

"Not anymore."

Ping thought that they might not need to hibernate because they could keep warm in the pools, but the males didn't spend much time in the warm water. In fact, Ping had never seen Hei Lei enter any of the pools. He didn't bathe. He cleaned himself by splashing water from the purple cleansing pool over his scales. She wondered if he could swim at all.

The following afternoon, Hei Lei returned with a dead animal hanging from his talons. It was a wild ox, so big it would feed the dragon cluster for several days. The yellow dragons took the ox from Hei Lei and cut pieces from it. Ping had no sense of dread, but her stomach was unsettled. Perhaps Jiang was right and the black dragon's hatred had been directed at her, not at Kai. Perhaps she had misread the message her second sight had given her. In the past, her enemies had always been after her dragons, not her.

The black dragon dug his teeth into the raw meat and ripped off a chunk. Blood dribbled down his chin. Hei Lei was aggressive and unpleasant, but he did provide well for his cluster. Without him, the dragons would go hungry. There was no reason to expect that all dragons would be nice. There were people Ping liked and those she disliked. Why should dragons be any different?

She went to collect her share of the meat. She could tell that Hei Lei enjoyed her being dependent on him for food. She would have liked to say she didn't need it, but she was hungry.

She picked up the meat. Hei Lei snarled as she took it.

"We should make her work for her meat," he said, addressing the dragons. "I could use a slave to trim my talons and clean my cave."

Ping ignored him. She turned to go and cook her meat.

"Though, on second thought, I wouldn't want her in my cave. Everything she touches turns bad," Hei Lei continued. "She allowed the whelp to become contaminated by contact with humans. Eating cooked meat and cakes. He's not a dragon, he's a tame pet. No proper Dragon Keeper would permit such things."

Ping felt her anger boil, but still she said nothing.

"I suppose it's not even her fault. It was Danzi who chose her. A female keeper. No other dragon has ever been so stupid." He laughed. "It's no wonder the whelp turned out bad."

Ping tossed her meat angrily into the cooking pool, but she didn't respond. She wouldn't give Hei Lei that satisfaction.

When the meat was cooked, she tried to make her meal as civilized as possible. She cut it up with her bronze knife and added herbs and the leaves of a bitter green plant. She ate with her chopsticks.

Hei Lei continued to provoke her. The other dragons sat in awkward silence. None of them dared stand up against Hei Lei.

"Humans have only ever wanted us for what we can do for them," he said.

"The people of the Empire know that dragons are special creatures, different from other wild animals," Ping replied, trying to form a reasonable argument. "They believe that their lives are in your . . . paws. Every spring, people all over the Empire offer gifts to dragons in the hope that they will bring the rain."

"As I said. They only honor us because we are useful to them."

"They hang painted images of you on their walls." Ping tried not to allow any anger into her voice. "The Emperor has embroidered dragons on his robes."

Lian, Bai Xue, and Sha were trying to follow the argument, but they couldn't. Jiang translated Ping's words for them.

Bai Xue spoke.

"She says the humans are angry with us because there is no rain," Jiang said. "She has seen them throw iron and chinaberry leaves into lakes and rivers."

"If their crops don't grow, their children will die," Ping said. "They do whatever they can to stop that."

Sha spoke to Jiang.

"What did she say?" Ping asked.

"She wants to know if the drought is very bad."

"Even before summer, wells were drying up and ponds shrinking. The crops will have withered. It will be a long, hungry winter. Many will not survive, and it is always the children and the old ones who die first."

That evening at the moon gathering, Lian and Sha spoke much more than they usually did. From the tone of their voices Ping knew they were arguing for some sort of proposal. It sounded like there was a disagreement. Ping had never seen the quiet female dragons roused before. The gathering lasted for several hours.

"What were they discussing?" Ping asked Kai after the dragons had left the pool.

"Lian and Sha want to bring rain to the Empire," he said.

"But they can't do that."

"Dragons can make rain," Kai said.

Ping thought that the dragons had come to believe the stories that people told about them. Now Kai was starting to believe these legends, just as he believed in the fire dragon under the earth.

"They can't," Ping insisted. "Danzi made it rain, but there had to be clouds to start with. He flew up and spat on the clouds. His saliva made the rain fall from the clouds."

"Dragons can make rain."

"How?"

"They make clouds with mist from their breath. Many dragons breathe mist together on a high mountain. The wind carries the cloud over the land. Moisture from the air is drawn to the dragon cloud. It gets bigger and divides into other clouds. When the clouds get heavy with water, rain falls."

Ping didn't know whether to believe Kai's story or not. "When did you learn this?"

"At the moon gatherings."

"Why didn't you tell me?"

"Ping didn't ask."

She sighed with frustration. Sometimes Kai was just like his father. "What did they decide at tonight's gathering?"

"They will not bring rain."

Ping sat out in the moonlight after Kai had gone to bed. She thought of all the desperate people they had met on their journey west, the cracked fields, the withered crops, the hungry children. It would be worse now. People would be dying. Did the dragons really have the power to put an end to their suffering?

# CHAPTER TWENTY

# SCALES IN MOONLIGHT

Ping watched Kai as he played hide-and-hunt. His skills were improving. She could tell that Tun and Jiang were no longer allowing him to win. It was an aggressive game. In fact, it wasn't a game anymore. Each dragon was trying hard to win, and though they stopped short of seriously harming each other, they didn't worry about inflicting wounds. The three white dragons watched the games. Lian always seemed to be cheering Kai on, and this attention made him even more reckless. He was covered in purple scabs where the other two had scratched or bitten him. Kai was proud of his battle scars and counted them before he went to sleep each night. Ping once caught him sharpening his claws on a rock.

"That's not a nice thing to do," she'd said. "You might hurt one of the other dragons."

"Tun showed me how to do it," Kai said defiantly. "All male dragons sharpen their claws."

That wasn't the sort of thing Ping had imagined Kai would learn from the older dragons.

While they were young, it was customary for male dragons to help the females with their chores and not begin their training until they were fifty years old. Ping wasn't sure if it was because Kai had exceptional skills or because of the shortage of males that his training had started so early.

She didn't feel like being with the dragons, so she decided to go up to the northern part of the plateau. Her winter food store was still not large enough. She took a digging tool she'd made from a piece of bone, hoping to find roots and the edible fungus that grew underground. She breathed in the air. It was good to be away from the smell of the pools and to feel grass beneath her feet.

Ping found herself missing the company of other people more than she had when she and Kai were living on Tai Shan. There, her days had been filled with caring for a baby dragon. She thought of Jun. She missed his company. She imagined him picking mulberry leaves with his family and neighbors to feed their silkworms. They would be eating the mulberries, too. Ping's mouth watered at the thought of the sweet, juicy fruit. The berries on the bushes around her were sour to taste, and chewy.

She found a few roots near the edge of the plateau. They were quite tasty when cooked and mashed with herbs, and made a welcome change from boiled meat. The northern edge of the plateau sloped down gradually before it ended abruptly in a cliff.

A little way down the slope, Ping could see the broad leaves that meant more of the edible roots were growing beneath the ground. She carefully edged toward them. It was a good patch, and there was no danger as she was still several *chang* from the edge of the cliff. She inched farther down the slope. Then she tripped. She staggered and thrust her foot down to regain her balance. The ground gave way beneath her, and she found herself falling into a gaping hole. She grabbed hold of a clump of long grass on the edge and just managed to stop herself from falling in. Her feet scrabbled to find a foothold, but the earth crumbled away. She looked down. The hole wasn't naturally formed. Sharpened spikes of rock had been set upright at the bottom. It was a trap that had been hidden with a covering of interwoven twigs and leaves.

Ping could feel the grass that she was clinging to uprooting. The trap yawned beneath her. Then the air was full of leathery wings as three dragons appeared above her.

Tun, Shuang, and Bai Xue flew at her so fast she thought they were attacking her. Without thinking, she held up her hands to protect her face from their talons, letting go of the grass. Tun dug his talons into the back of her jacket as she fell. He lifted her up and flew off over the edge of the cliff. There was nothing between her and the mountain slopes many *chang* below. Ping gasped as Tun let go of her jacket. She thought he was going to drop her, but he was just transferring her to his other paw. He flapped his wings and took her back to the plateau. Then he did drop her, none too gently, on the hard white clay. Ping lay gasping for breath.

The dragons stood around her as they had when she first arrived.

"Ping cannot leave," Jiang said sternly.

"I wasn't trying to leave. I was just collecting food."

"Do not go over the lip of the plateau," Jiang said. "There are traps all around the perimeter of our haven."

"You are lucky that the traps were made to keep humans out—not in," Hei Lei said.

"You triggered one of the trip wires," Jiang explained. "They are there in case anyone gets past the spiked pits that ring the plateau."

"So you would kill any person who happened to stumble on your home by accident?"

"If a human found the dragon haven, it wouldn't be accidental."

"But not all people mean you harm."

"All humans want to tame us," said Hei Lei. "They want to turn us into pets, just like you did with the whelp."

The other dragons shifted uncomfortably, but Hei

Lei turned away. It was midday, so Tun and Sha brought out the day's ration of meat. Hei Lei joined the others, and they ate in silence.

Ping couldn't eat. She was still shaken. She thought about what Hei Lei had said. He believed that dragons were better off living in the wild, but Ping wasn't so sure. In the haven, the dragons didn't really do anything. They slept, lolled around in the pools, ate, and then slept some more.

As the dragons finished eating, they went to their caves one by one to sleep. Even Kai had got into the habit of having an afternoon nap. They were wise and powerful creatures, but they had no reason to use their great wisdom.

"So is this all you're going to do?" Ping asked irritably.

Jiang was the only dragon who was still awake.

"You eat, you sleep, you bathe. Don't dragons need some purpose in their lives?"

"Do birds need a purpose, or snow leopards?"

"No, but dragons are more than beasts. They are wiser, they can communicate with people. There has to be some reason for that."

Jiang didn't reply, but Ping wouldn't let it rest.

"Hei Lei said Dragon Keepers turn dragons into tame animals. But look, you do it yourselves. You're just like huge, scaly oxen."

Ping had finally stung Jiang to anger.

"How we live is not the business of humans." Jiang turned from her and walked to the cave.

"Perhaps not, but that doesn't mean I can't have an opinion on the matter," Ping called after her.

Ping hadn't realized that Hei Lei was nearby, listening. "What do you suggest we do?" he asked.

It was the first time he had spoken directly to Ping. She could tell he was glad that Ping had angered the placid red dragon.

"You say you can make it rain," she snapped. "If you can, why don't you do it?"

"We don't help humans."

"It isn't only people who die of thirst and hunger when there's drought. All the creatures of the world need water to live."

"We have all the water we need."

"Why did Heaven give dragons the power to bring rain if not to use that power? Dragons are one of the four spiritual beings. The phoenix and the *qilin* have already disappeared from the earth. Whatever powers they had have been lost to us. There are only dragons and tortoises left. Heaven put you on the earth and gave you unique powers for a reason."

"You are just a little girl. You are not qualified to speak of such great matters," Hei Lei snarled.

"I have a tongue, I can speak."

"What have humans done to deserve our protection?"

"Nothing. People were given the honor of bonding

with dragons, and they abused the privilege. I don't blame you for choosing to live apart from people, but you still have a job to do in the world. If you don't do it, you will change. You will become wild creatures, no different from eagles or leopards. Magnificent creatures, to be sure, but you will lose your wisdom."

Hei Lei snorted and stomped off. Ping stood alone, seething with frustration. Her bitter words echoed in her ears as if they were still in the air around her, trying to find someone who wanted to listen to them. She shook her head. She might as well have talked to herself.

Ping's anger was still festering when the dragons woke from their nap. Kai spent time with the females most afternoons. They told him which plants and insects should be gathered for food and healing. They taught him how dragons conserved plants and populations of animals and insects, so that they never took too much and risked a food source dying out. Whenever an animal was killed, a portion of it was kept aside to be cut into strips, soaked in one of the sulphurous pools, and then dried in the sun for use in winter.

Ping had been allowed to join the female dragons when they were teaching Kai. Even though she couldn't understand what they said, she had enjoyed sitting with the females. But she'd caused so much fuss that day—tripping the intruder alarm, upsetting Jiang—that she thought she had better keep to herself.

The role of female dragons in the cluster was

crucial. Ping already knew that they acted as decision makers. They also looked after the treasure cave and memorized dragon lore so that it could be passed on. Kai loved spending time in the treasure cave, touching the precious objects and learning their histories. One of the most important jobs for the female dragons should have been to care for unhatched eggs and dragonlings. But there were none.

Ping waited until she could speak to Jiang alone.

"I'm sorry I spoke so harshly to you," she said.

"You do not know our history," the red dragon said. "You do not know what humans did to us at Long Gao Yuan."

"Tell me," Ping said. "Then I will know."

Jiang said nothing, but she didn't walk away. Finally she spoke.

"There was not one dragon hunter, but many. For some reason they all put aside their rivalries and banded together. I don't know how they discovered our haven. They waited for winter to begin. When we had been asleep in our pools for just a few days, they crept up to Long Gao Yuan. We had grown careless. We had stopped keeping watch. The dragon hunters had a sorcerer as an ally. He had prepared a strong sleeping potion to put in the wells. The hunters didn't want to poison us—our organs would have been worthless. Instead they wanted to paralyze us so that we were easy prey, unable to fight back. In those days, we all spent

the winter in the wells. All except Hei Lei. Black dragons never hibernate in water. He was sleeping in the
cave when they came. He attacked the dragon hunters
but there were too many of them. The potion paralyzed
us for a few hours. The dragon hunters had prepared
many iron weapons—swords, spears, hooks. Some
were sharp and shiny, others had been left to rust. The
hunters attacked us while we slept, hacking us to
pieces one by one. The sharp weapons killed outright,
the rusty ones made unbearably painful wounds."

Ping wept as Jiang continued the tale.

"Just seven were able to resist the potion enough to
escape. Hei Lei was badly wounded, so was my mother.
It was her last flight. She flew only a short way, then
crashed to the ground. But winter was deepening, and
the hunters couldn't risk staying to track down those
who had escaped. They were content with their kill. It
was difficult enough for them to carry away their awful
plunder. They left the bones."

Ping couldn't speak. She searched for words as the
image of the pile of bones at Long Gao Yuan swam in
front of her eyes. She couldn't think of anything to say.

"We no longer hibernate; we have to stay alert. And
no humans were allowed in our haven—until you came
along."

The fire dragon's jet of steaming water spurted into
the air. Jiang turned and made her way to the orange pool.

Ping sat thinking about Jiang's story. She felt drained

and miserable. The sky was darkening; she shivered. She had been in the dragon haven for almost a month. Summer was nearly over. The days were still warm and cloudless, but they were getting shorter, and after sunset, the breeze had a sharp edge to it. A full moon slowly rose above the jagged black peaks of the distant mountains.

Kai was looking up at the night sky. "It's the dragon moon," he said. "Tonight all the dragons will take part in the gathering. It will last until the dragon moon fades into dawn. Each dragon will take a turn to speak."

The moon hung above them, pale yellow, like some sort of luminous fruit. It seemed so close that Ping felt she could reach out and pluck it from the sky.

"Kai is going to speak at a moon gathering for the first time," the little dragon told her.

"What will you speak about?" Ping asked. She could tell by the tone of his voice that it was an important occasion.

"Kai will tell them the story of the dragon who redrew the riverbeds for Da Yu after the great flood, and the tale of Ying Long, the dragon who fought alongside the first emperor in the battle against the rebel Chi You."

"Don't they know these stories?" she asked.

"They know parts of them, but not the whole stories."

Ping felt a swell of pride. She had taught those stories to Kai.

"Also tell them about Father and Kai being dragons of the Empire," he added.

Ping half wished Kai would keep silent about those times. The little dragon had experienced imperial comfort, but he had also endured pain and distress at the hands of the Emperor. So had Danzi. It was Kai's life story, though, and he was entitled to recount it as he wished.

The steam rising from the gathering pool had an orange tinge to it. It drifted eerily across the moonlit plateau. The dragons, all of them, slowly walked through the mist toward the pool. Kai followed them. For the first time, the males climbed respectfully into the orange waters.

Ping imagined them telling the stories of their long lives and yearned to hear them. They each spoke longer than on other nights. Ping wrapped herself in her bearskin, ready to sit out the night with them.

The dragons glowed brighter under the dragon moon. Sitting together in the moonlight they looked like an outcrop of strangely-shaped rocks, glittering with minerals. The red dragons' scales blushed rosy pink. The yellow dragons were flecked with gold as the moonlight reflected on the texture of their scales. The white dragons' scales were speckled with silver. Hei Lei's scales were lit with streaks of steely gray, like glints from a polished sword. Kai glowed from head to foot. His scales were luminous green, like a jade vase that was lit from within. Ping wished she could wade into the pool and that the orange waters would magically give her the ability to understand what the dragons were saying. But she hung back as she always did, sitting at the entrance of her cave, watching the magnificent creatures from a distance. She had to be content with the knowledge that she was the only person who had ever seen such a sight.

When his turn came, Kai's dragon voice was clear and confident. The other dragons listened carefully to what he had to say. When he had finished, they asked quiet questions, which Kai answered confidently.

When it was Sha's turn, to Ping's surprise, the yellow dragon stood up and made a sound like she had never heard before. It was a melodic sound, as if Sha were singing, but it was more like a drone, a humming. It was achingly sad. Ping thought she must be singing to her dragonlings, who had died before they were hatched. It made the hairs on the back of Ping's neck stand on end.

Hei Lei's voice was deeper than the voices of the other dragons. He spoke firmly and without pause. He didn't speak as long as the others, and there was a silence after he finished, as if the others were pondering his words.

Gu Hong spoke next. Her speech was more faltering, her voice soft. Ping had wanted to sit up all night, but the sound of the dragons' voices lulled her to sleep.

# CHAPTER TWENTY-ONE

# TEETH, TALONS, AND TAIL

Ping woke with a start. It was still dark. There was a pain in her stomach. A sharp pain that made her cry out. Her heart thudded in her chest. She struggled to her knees, but she couldn't stand up. She'd never felt such pain. It radiated from her stomach all over her body to the tips of her fingers and toes. It felt like her bones were being ground to powder. The pain shut out everything else. She couldn't move. She could barely think. Deep breathing helped her to clear the pain from a small space in her mind.

A loud noise had awakened her. She could still hear it. Two dragons were roaring. Arguing. One of the voices was more familiar to her. It was Kai's. The other belonged to Hei Lei. The dread had returned. The black dragon wanted to hurt Kai. He wanted to do more than hurt him—he wanted to kill him.

She had so little control over her second sight. What was the point of knowing that Kai was in danger, if the warning was so painful it left her unable to protect him? Ping focused her mind and tried to concentrate her *qi*. She had to use it to reduce the pain. Previously, she had always directed her *qi* power outward at someone or something else. She had never used it to attack something within herself. The dread felt solid in her stomach. She surrounded it with a sphere of *qi*, squeezing it tighter and tighter until all the pain and discomfort was in one small, concentrated lump. It still hurt, but she could move. She staggered to the edge of the pool.

Kai and Hei Lei were face-to-face in the orange pool. They glowed in the moonlight—Kai, bright green, Hei Lei, glittering gray. Tun and the female dragons had all climbed out and were watching from the rocks. The two dragons were still arguing. None of the others were trying to stop them.

"What's happening?" she asked Jiang.

"Kai disputed something that Hei Lei said."

Ping knew that that was a serious breach of the rules. The dragons never interrupted each other at a gathering.

"What? What did he say?"

"It was about Dragon Keepers. Hei Lei said that dragons would have been better off if they'd never made an alliance with humans. Kai said that wasn't true."

Ping concentrated hard. She desperately wanted to

be able to hear what Kai and Hei Lei were saying. But it didn't work. The sounds they made were still unintelligible.

As Kai glared at Hei Lei, Ping saw hatred in the little dragon's eyes. She'd never seen that before. He spoke again, but this time she heard his words in her head. He was allowing her to listen.

"Father believed that if it wasn't for the bond with Dragon Keepers, dragons would be just like oxen and goats. They would have no wisdom." He was repeating what he'd heard Ping say. She wished she'd kept her mouth shut.

Hei Lei made a sound like bells ringing. He was laughing, but it wasn't a happy sound. Ping felt his red eyes drilling into her.

"The humans who want to kill dragons are not Dragon Keepers," Kai continued. "They are bad people, greedy and stupid. Dragon Keepers are special people."

Hei Lei snorted. This time he too spoke so that Ping could understand him.

"Your father was deluded," he spat. "He couldn't make a decision unless he consulted his keeper. Without a human he was like a sheep without a shepherd. He was just a beast."

"Father was wise and good."

"He was weak. Danzi was the leader of this cluster once," Hei Lei said. "I challenged him, but he was too cowardly to fight me. After one swipe of my talons he gave in. That's why he left Long Gao Yuan."

Kai stood in stunned silence.

"You didn't know that, did you?" Hei Lei gloated. "He left to save his own scales. He was too weak to stand up to humans, and too spineless to accept my challenge."

Kai reared up on his hind legs.

"Kai will challenge Hei Lei!" he said. "Kai will fight to defend Father's name."

Kai was so small, even on his hind legs, he didn't reach Hei Lei's shoulders. Ping would have smiled if the situation hadn't been so serious. She was waiting for Gu Hong to put an end to the argument, but the old dragon was silent.

Ping turned to Jiang. "Gu Hong is the leader. Why doesn't she . . ."

"She is not our leader," Jiang interrupted. "She is our elder. We respect her, but she doesn't lead us. We have been without a head dragon since Danzi left. Hei Lei wants to take the leadership, but we females don't want him as leader."

"But you're not going to let Kai challenge Hei Lei . . . ?"

"No one can stop him," Jiang said.

Ping felt her insides dissolve. "You must. It's not fair! Look at him, he's a baby."

"We don't have the power to stop a challenge once it has been laid down."

Ping was aghast. "But he has no horns, no wings. Hei Lei will kill him."

Jiang spoke to the other female dragons. They all shook their heads firmly.

"Hei Lei must accept the challenge or leave. Those are his only options," Jiang told Ping. She then turned to the black dragon. "Do you accept?"

Hei Lei nodded his great head. Ping tried to run to Kai, but Tun stopped her.

"Can't I just say something to him?" She desperately wanted to put her arms around the little dragon.

Tun took no notice of her plea.

"Kai," Ping called out. "Tell them you didn't mean it. Withdraw your challenge."

"Kai must defend Father and defeat Hei Lei."

Whether that was because of the dragons' rules or his own stubborn pride, Ping didn't know.

The female dragons were speaking together.

"Hei Lei, please don't hurt him," Ping begged.

"I wasn't the one who challenged," the black dragon said. "I have to defend myself."

The females finished their discussion.

"Teeth, talons, and tail," Jiang told Ping. "Hei Lei is not permitted to use his horns or his wings."

Ping could find little consolation in that. She suddenly remembered the sixth line of the *Yi Jing* reading. *When a dragon is arrogant, there will be cause for regret.* She had always thought Hei Lei would be the arrogant one.

But it was Kai. She had no doubt there would be cause for more than regret. There would be cause for pain, death, and despair.

"Kai must choose where the challenge will take place," Jiang said.

Kai didn't hesitate. "There," he said, pointing a talon at the rocks alongside the yellow pool.

Ping thought there would be some ceremony to start the fight. She thought that one of the dragons might speak, but if there was a signal to start the combat, Ping didn't see it.

Kai leaped at Hei Lei. He was still in midair when Hei Lei's tail swiped him. The tail caught Kai in the chest and knocked the breath out of him. He fell into the pool with a splash. Hei Lei peered into the opaque water, waiting for Kai to appear. Minutes passed, but Kai didn't resurface. Hei Lei gingerly climbed into the shallow end of the yellow pool. Then he yelped and leaped up onto the rocks again. His right hind leg was bleeding. Kai had bitten him while he was underwater. The surface of the water broke, and Kai reappeared. Despite her revulsion at the sight of dragons fighting, Ping felt a surge of pride. The first blood was Kai's.

Hei Lei had been calm so far, confident of an easy defeat, but Ping sensed that his anger, never far below the surface, was about to erupt. He hadn't been expecting Kai to be a real opponent. The black dragon waded back into the pool. Kai lunged at Hei Lei, raking his talons across the black dragon's shoulder. Purple blood sprang from deep cuts. Ping was now glad that he'd been sharpening his claws. Hei Lei dug his talons into Kai and picked him up by the scruff of the neck. Kai dangled from his talons as if he were a rabbit or a fawn. Ping sensed Hei Lei's savage strength. She fumbled for her pouch and took out the dragon-stone shard. She wanted to be ready to go to Kai's aid, and if she took on the black dragon, she would need every *shu* of strength she possessed.

Hei Lei raised Kai's small body, ready to throw him against the surrounding rocks. Ping cried out. The sound distracted the black dragon. He hesitated. In that moment Kai twisted around and whacked Hei Lei in the face with his tail. Hei Lei let go of Kai in surprise. Kai disappeared beneath the water again. It was no accident that the contest had ended up in the yellow pool. It was Kai's favorite environment, and one where Hei Lei was completely uncomfortable. Kai had lured his opponent there.

Hei Lei's anger exploded. He had kept his temper under control until then, but he was no longer a reasoning dragon. He was a wild animal. He swept his front paws through the water, trying to find Kai, then jumped and growled angrily. Kai had bitten him again. Hei Lei's grasping talons found Kai and dragged him up out of the water. This time he hurled him against the rocks, but his anger made him rush the throw. Kai was winded and bruised, but not seriously hurt. Hei Lei pounced on Kai, sank his teeth into his flank, and tore off a hunk of Kai's flesh. Purple blood, bright in the moonlight, splashed on the rocks.

Ping tried to rush to Kai, but Tun and Jiang held her back.

"You have to stop him!" she yelled.

Hei Lei dug his talons into Kai's wound. The little dragon howled with pain. Hei Lei threw Kai again. This time his aim was better, and Kai screamed as his body was dashed against the rock. The pain weakened the shield around Kai's mind. Clasping the dragon-stone shard, Ping saw into areas of his mind that she'd never had access to before. Reading his raw thoughts that hadn't formed into words, she knew he'd broken a bone in his left foreleg. He sank back beneath the surface of the water with a groan.

Hei Lei waded around the pool. The more Kai evaded him, the more furious Hei Lei became. Ping realized that Kai had chosen to fight in the yellow pool for another reason. It was the healing pool. He had known Hei Lei would hurt him. He was gaining time, allowing the healing waters to soothe his wounds. But the yellow waters couldn't mend bones, not in a few minutes, anyway.

The surface at the other end of the pool rippled. Hei Lei plunged into the water. He thrashed about. Kai had lured him into the deepest part of the pool. Hei Lei tried to find a footing, but the water closed over his head. He flailed and splashed. He couldn't swim. Kai dived under again. Ping knew dragons couldn't drown, but Hei Lei hated the water. He was trying to stop himself from sinking. Ping couldn't see Kai, but she knew he was darting around underwater like a fish, biting and scratching the black dragon as he floundered hopelessly. Hei Lei finally found his feet and pulled himself into the shallower water again.

This time he used his huge tail to sweep the pool. Ping held her breath.

She had penetrated the shield around Hei Lei's inner thoughts as well. She glimpsed a young man and a younger black dragon on Long Gao Yuan. She grasped the shard with both hands. Her second sight was growing stronger. She saw deeper into Hei Lei's mind. She knew why he hated humans so. Lao Longzi had told her about a young Dragon Keeper. He had been Hei Lei's keeper. The black dragon had loved and trusted the young man. Together they had flown off on adventures that the other dragons disapproved of.

Hei Lei's trust had been misplaced. His Dragon Keeper had left him, run away after a pretty young woman he'd met in an inn on one of their escapades. Hei Lei had learned that humans couldn't be trusted. The betrayal had left him bitter. His anger had turned hard and sharp and had lodged in his heart like a splinter of steel. He'd decided that dragons were better off without humans. He couldn't trust his Dragon Keeper to keep the secret of their hideout. He decided he had only one choice. He had tracked down his Dragon Keeper and killed him.

Ping was roused from this second hand memory when the black dragon suddenly spoke.

"The contest is over," he announced. "Proclaim my victory."

The other dragons stood in stunned silence.

But Ping could read Kai's thoughts. He wasn't defeated, not yet. Beneath the surface of the water he was calming himself, getting rid of his anger so that he could shape-change. He shape-changed into a rock and then slowly raised himself out of the water, a hair-breadth at a time. His movement was so slow that even the keen-sighted dragons didn't notice it. When Hei Lei's back was turned, Kai took on his true shape and pulled himself up onto the rocks on the opposite side of the pool. He made a rude sound with his lips that sounded like someone farting. He waggled his head and stuck out his tongue like a cheeky child. Hei Lei was incensed. The black dragon had many skills, but shape-changing wasn't one of them. The huge dragon suddenly launched himself across the pool toward Kai. It was too far for him to leap, and he didn't want to fall into the water again. He unfurled his wings and flapped them once. The other dragons, who had been perfectly silent until now, all cried out together. Hei Lei had broken the rules of the challenge.

The black dragon fell on Kai, digging his talons into the little dragon's neck. Ping shook off the other dragons and ran around the edge of the pool. This time no one stopped her. She launched herself at Hei Lei, but he knocked her aside with a sweep of his tail, as if she were no more than an irritating fly. Hei Lei still had Kai in his talons. But Ping's charge had given Kai time to think. He suddenly shape-changed into a vase. Hei Lei wasn't expecting it. The shock of unexpectedly touching a shape-changed dragon made men faint, and though it wasn't enough to knock Hei Lei out, it made him stagger. His grip on Kai loosened.

Kai ripped himself from the dragon's talons, tearing his hide. He dropped to the ground, landing on all four paws. As soon as his paws hit the ground he ran behind Hei Lei. Blood was pouring from his fresh wounds, but he didn't falter. The black dragon shook his head to clear away the dizziness.

Kai ran up Hei Lei's huge tail and clambered up his back. The moonlight reflected off his scales in a way Ping had never seen before. The tips of the scales were glowing with a new iridescence, like the feathers of a peacock. They gleamed green, red, white, black, and yellow. All the colors shimmered, even the black, which flashed like polished ebony. The dragons cried out in wonder. Ping couldn't believe this magnificent creature was her own little dragon. She moved closer.

Hei Lei reared up on his hind legs and struck out

with both front legs. But he couldn't reach behind him. Kai clamped the talons of his hind legs around Hei Lei's neck. No matter how much he shook his head or reared up, Hei Lei could not dislodge Kai. His front paws could swipe at him and his talons could dig into Kai's hide, but he could do little more than scratch him.

"What's happened to Kai's scales?" Ping asked Jiang.

"He is a dragon of five colors." Her voice was full of awe. "I have never seen one before."

Hei Lei tried to reach Kai with a back leg, like a dog scratching its ear. Kai swung his weight from side to side to put him off balance, so that Hei Lei was forced to put his paw down to steady himself.

"What does it mean?" Ping asked

"Kai is born to lead," Jiang replied. "If a dragon of five colors claims the leadership of a cluster, no one can challenge him."

· CHAPTER TWENTY-TWO ·

# RED DAWN

Kai was gloating over having gotten the better of Hei
Lei, despite the blood pouring from his wounds. Ping
was horrified by the bloodlust she saw in his eyes. What
the seer had said when he'd written out the final line of
the divination flashed into her mind. "Read it only
when you are faced with your greatest difficulty, when
you experience your worst moment." She'd thought
her worst moment was when Tun had taken Kai away
from Long Gao Yuan, but it wasn't. This was it. Things
couldn't get any worse. Only if Kai died. And that
could happen at any moment. Ping ran to her cave. She
pulled everything out of the saddlebag. She found the
calfskin crumpled at the bottom and opened it out with
fumbling fingers. The six readings were on one side.
She turned over the calfskin and read the single line of
characters again. The ink strokes had faded over the
months, and she could barely make them out in the
moonlight. *A cluster of dragons without heads. Great good*

*fortune.* Ping angled the calfskin this way and that. The words still made no sense.

Though Kai could hurt Hei Lei, he couldn't kill him. But in the black dragon's fury he might kill Kai and the other dragons. He might tear off their heads in his rage. But how could that be deemed good fortune? Ping remembered the terrible pile of bones at Long Gao Yuan. If Hei Lei killed them all, there would be no more dragons in the world. Surely that wouldn't bring good fortune. She didn't have time to ponder the details. It didn't matter what the *Yi Jing* said, she couldn't bear the thought of a world without dragons.

The other dragons were standing like statues on the rocks, watching the combat but not daring to try and stop it. Ping ran toward the fighting dragons. Hei Lei was shaking his great head from side to side, roaring and raging, bashing his head against the rocks in an attempt to dislodge Kai.

Kai reached his front paws around in front of Hei Lei's face. The little dragon's sharpened talons glittered in the moonlight, his iridescent scales gleamed. Ping gasped in horror. She felt Kai's pleasure as he dug his talons around Hei Lei's eye sockets. Hei Lei cried out in pain and terror. Kai was about to rip out the black dragon's eyes.

"Stop!" shouted Ping.

She stood in front of Hei Lei. The black dragon couldn't see because Kai's paws were covering his eyes.

He reached out, feeling for Ping. She moved closer, within his reach. The black dragon grasped hold of her, digging his talons into her flesh. She cried out in pain.

"Ping." She heard Kai's voice in her head for the first time since the combat began.

"A dragon leader needs wisdom, not the ability to kill," she said. "Get down, Kai. Hei Lei will release me if you stand aside."

Hei Lei loosened his talons.

"But the challenge; I have to defend Father."

"Forget the challenge. I would rather Hei Lei kill me than see another dragon die. You are so few. Every dragon is precious. Don't do it for my sake. Do it for the Dead Ones. They wouldn't want any more dragons to die."

Kai unhooked his talons from Hei Lei's face and climbed down the black dragon's back.

Hei Lei put Ping down.

Ping turned to Kai, expecting him to be angry that she had prevented him from making his first kill, but the battle anger had drained from him. Weak from blood loss, he collapsed into the pool.

Ping waded into the water. Whether the pool was sacred or poisonous she didn't know or care. She had to get to Kai. The young dragon floated on the surface of the yellow water. His scales had lost their iridescence. She took him in her arms.

Hei Lei's huge body had sagged. The puncture

wounds around his eyes were bleeding. It looked like he was weeping tears of blood.

Ping could still see into the black dragon's mind. She saw him killing his Dragon Keeper with one blow, so the young man died instantly. But there was something that he was still shielding—something even more terrible. Something he didn't want anyone to know about.

Holding the dragon-stone shard, Ping concentrated and saw through Hei Lei's final shield to his innermost thoughts, a dark place full of despair. Killing his Dragon Keeper hadn't been enough. Hei Lei's young Dragon Keeper had taken the woman up to Long Gao Yuan. He had shown her the hidden way up to the plateau behind the Serpent's Tail falls. She had kept the secret for many years, but in her old age she had told a dragon hunter where many dragons could be found, in exchange for three pieces of gold.

The hunter hadn't rushed up to Long Gao Yuan. He had laid his plan carefully. He sent messages to other dragon hunters he knew. They had been rivals before, but with the prize of so many dragons in their sights, they agreed to band together.

Ping looked up into Hei Lei's eyes. The red glow had faded, his anger had been replaced by sadness. He had been so proud of his mischievous young Dragon Keeper. The only other Dragon Keepers he'd known were old and dull. He had loved his cheerful attitude, his playful pranks. The massacre at Long Gao Yuan was the fault of his Dragon Keeper. And he had chosen the man.

Tears filled Ping's eyes, and they weren't for Kai. She knew he was strong enough to survive his wounds. They were for Hei Lei.

Ping tried to lift Kai out of the water, but couldn't. The other dragons gathered around. Tun came forward and pulled Kai out.

"Kai can walk," the little dragon said.

Ping helped him to his feet. The dragon moon had disappeared from the sky. The day was dawning with a bloodred stain on the horizon. Slowly Kai limped along, his broken leg dragging behind him. He looked small and weary and wounded. His scales weren't gleaming with the five colors now; they were dull. He didn't look like a leader of a dragon cluster. Instead of returning to his bed in the main dragon cavern, he limped to Ping's cave.

The other dragons wouldn't enter. There was barely room for one of them anyway. They quietly brought things to the cave mouth for Kai—straw for a bed, animal skins, meat. Sha brought two of the jade healing stones from the treasure cave, and Ping placed one at his head and one at his tail, just as the yellow dragon instructed.

"I'm going to light a fire," Ping said. "I need to make an herbal remedy for him."

None of the dragons objected. Ping lit a small fire

and made staunchweed tea. She bathed Kai's wounds with water from the healing pool. They were not as bad as she had expected. The yellow water had already stopped the bleeding and cleansed the wounds. Ping took out the remains of her nightgown, washed it in the yellow pool, and tore it into broad strips. Then she bound them around Kai's wounds. The one where Hei Lei had gouged a chunk out of his right flank would leave a nasty scar, but the other wounds would heal well enough. Then she set the broken bone in his hind leg and asked Sha to find a good straight stick to use as a splint. The young dragon understood her. Ping could speak to all the dragons with her mind now.

When the herbal tea was ready, she started preparing some broth with the meat that the dragons had brought, adding more medicinal herbs that she had picked on the plateau.

Ping sat at Kai's side, spooning the herbal tea into his mouth. Sha poked her big yellow head into the cave.

"I would like to learn about human ways of healing," she said. "I can see why dragons allowed humans to be their keepers long ago. Your hands are dexterous, and you have useful knowledge of the world."

Ping smiled at the shy dragon.

After Kai had eaten a little of the broth, he slept. Ping went outside and breathed the morning air. The sky was pink now. The other dragons had all gone to their caverns, except for Tun.

"Do you believe that Kai is your true leader?" she asked. It was the first time she'd spoken to him.

He nodded his great yellow head. "He is a dragon of five colors. No one can dispute it."

"But he is too young."

"He will not take on full leadership until he is five hundred years old. Until then, the council will help him make decisions. Gu Hong will advise him. But his opinion will still carry the most weight."

It was a great responsibility for such a small dragon.

Ping went back into her cave and lay down next to Kai. Her mind was swirling with thoughts. Kai had been arrogant, but he had survived. Why did the *Yi Jing* reading say there would be cause for regret? Kai had been revealed as the dragons' true leader. Hei Lei had released the secret that had been poisoning him for so long. Kai's arrogance had actually led to good things happening. Ping thought that her buzzing mind would prevent her from sleeping, but the terror of the night and the strain of reading the dragons' thoughts had exhausted her.

When Ping woke, the morning was well advanced. Kai was still sleeping. It wasn't until she had eaten a little food and made herself some ginger tea that she looked again at the crumpled calfskin. She could read the characters clearly now. In the daylight, the six characters were as she had seen them in the pale moonlight the night before. She sipped her tea. What a night it had been. Now she knew why it was so important for Kai to have come to the dragon haven. He was their leader, their future. Overnight he had transformed from a juvenile green dragon to a dragon of five colors, the leader of the last cluster of dragons in the empire, maybe even the world.

Ping looked at the calfskin again. She hadn't misread the characters, but she had misinterpreted their meaning. A character could have more than one meaning. *Wu shou* could mean "without heads." It could also mean "without a leader." *A cluster of dragons appears without a leader. Great good fortune.*

The cluster had struggled without a leader for many years. They had become weak and purposeless. Now they had a future leader. That was good fortune.

Jiang was the only dragon who had emerged from the cavern.

"Where's Hei Lei?" Ping asked. "I'll tend to his wounds as well."

"He has gone," Jiang replied.

"Gone where?"

"He failed in his challenge to lead the cluster. He also broke the rules of the combat. He has flown away to live alone. He's too proud to live under Kai's leadership."

Ping found that this news didn't give her any pleasure.

"Now we are eight again," said Jiang.

Eight was a very inauspicious number.

For three days Ping cared for Kai in her cave. She made food and herbal remedies for him. She tended his wounds. She told him stories as she had done when he was a dragonling. The dragons visited one by one, sitting outside the cave mouth and speaking to Kai with their strange chinking sounds. Ping was relieved that she had something to do again. On more than one occasion, she had to stop herself from feeling glad that Kai had been injured.

Ping hoped that the dragons would realize she could be useful and allow her to have a role in the dragon haven. Perhaps they would accept her as a member of the cluster. She could communicate with all the dragons now. No other Dragon Keeper had achieved that. She liked the idea of having eight dragons to care for. As far as she knew, no other true Dragon Keeper had cared for more than one dragon. She would complete the nine.

On the fourth day, Kai got up and limped outside. The females chattered like starlings as he emerged. They each reached out to touch him. He went to the purple pool to wash. Then he spent the rest of the day moving from the yellow healing pool to the white rejuvenating pool.

Tun and Shuang had to take Hei Lei's place and hunt

for food. Neither was as big or as strong as Hei Lei, but they hoped that together they could provide for the cluster. The long flights exhausted Tun, and the prey they brought back was smaller. There was enough to eat, but rarely any left over to dry for winter.

Ping spent long hours searching the plateau for mushrooms and edible roots, but her additions to the winter store were only small. She wanted one of the winged dragons to take her farther afield to find fruit, nuts, and green vegetables that could be dried for storage, but they refused, as they didn't want to risk being seen by other humans.

When he was well enough, Kai joined the dragons for a moon gathering. The meeting didn't last long, but Jiang told Ping that the council had agreed that Kai was their leader. There was no debate. He was the first dragon of five colors for three generations. But because of his youth, it was decided that the female council would continue to make decisions for the cluster until Kai's horns grew.

"Did Danzi know that Kai is a dragon of five colors?" Ping asked Jiang after the gathering.

"He couldn't have. It is the blood of battle flowing through Kai's scales that has made them show their true colors for the first time. But Danzi's father was a dragon of five colors. Though he didn't inherit the trait himself, he would have known there was a chance that Kai would."

"Kai should take a new name now that he is leader," Gu Hong said.

"Kai doesn't want a new name." He had overheard. "Kai wants to keep the name that Father gave."

"All dragon leaders take a new name," Jiang said.

"I've got an idea, Kai," Ping said, picking up the stick that she'd used to write messages to Gu Hong in the clay. "You can still call yourself Kai, but you can write it differently."

The dragons gathered around as she drew a character in the clay.

"This character is pronounced *kai*, but it means 'triumphant' or 'victorious.' You can still be Kai Duan, but now it means 'triumphant beginning,' to signify the beginning of your reign as leader."

Kai nodded. He clasped the stick in his talons and made a shaky copy of the character.

"Yes, Kai likes that name."

Gu Hong turned to Ping. "You are free to bathe in the pink pool."

The other dragons nodded.

Ping wasn't convinced that the minerals in the pink pool were harmless to humans, but she figured that her hot falls were pinkish, and they hadn't harmed her. Plus she didn't want to offend the council. She knew it was a great honor.

The nights were starting to get cool. Ping bathed in the

pink pool each evening and found that she slept well afterward. It was a small, shallow pool, not much bigger than a bath. As she sat in it, she would close her eyes, relax completely, and allow her thoughts to clear. An image of the dragon haven would form in her mind. It wasn't the usual view that she saw as she walked around it. It was from above, as if she were flying over. It was a peaceful sight. The dragons were going about their business. Some were flying away, others hovering as they prepared to land. They looked purposeful. It was a vision of the future.

Ping didn't believe in the dragons' story of a fire dragon beneath the earth. She had read about hot springs in the library at Beibai Palace, so she knew that the earth itself made the hot springs. She also knew that minerals dissolved in the water made the pools different colors. Whatever minerals turned her bathing and drinking water pink, in combination with the dragon-stone shard, had enabled her to penetrate the mind shields of the dragons. They were also improving her ability to read the future.

"Why don't the dragons bathe in the pink pool?" Ping asked Jiang one evening while she prepared for bed.

"It is not correct," the red dragon replied.

Ping sighed. Why was it always so hard to get a straight answer from a dragon?

Each evening the image of the dragons' future

became clearer. She could see Kai growing up with the other dragons. She searched her visions looking for herself, but she was never there. Of course, she didn't know when the image would become reality. It might have been hundreds of years in the future. She might have lived out her entire life at the dragon haven and been buried there somewhere. She tried hard to persuade herself of this, but she couldn't fool herself. She knew what the image was telling her.

Ping stopped bathing in the pink pool for a while.

"Why don't you bathe anymore?" Jiang asked her.

"No reason," Ping replied.

It didn't make any difference, though. She couldn't remove the image that had formed in her mind. She had seen the future of the dragon haven. The dragons were going about their lives in peace and harmony. She wasn't there.

• CHAPTER TWENTY-THREE •

## ALONE

Kai now spent most of his time with the other dragons. They each had things to teach him. Ping tried to keep busy, but she found herself spending a lot of time sitting with Gu Hong. Even though Ping could now hear the old dragon's voice in her mind, Gu Hong still preferred to write out their communications in the earth. Conversation with the old red dragon was slow, but Ping wasn't short of time. They had chosen a sunny spot where the earth was brown and easier to write on than the hard white clay that surrounded the pools.

*Dragonlings born in captivity usually die*, Gu Hong wrote. *You reared Kai well. No one else could have done it.*

This was high praise from the old dragon, but Ping could read her unspoken thoughts now. She didn't want any humans in the dragon haven—not even Ping. The same thoughts had formed in all the dragons' minds.

*Why didn't Danzi bring Kai's dragon stone here himself?* Gu Hong asked.

301

Danzi had headed in the exact opposite direction. He'd gone to Ocean and then across to the Isle of the Blest. He couldn't have gone any farther away.

*He said he wanted to leave the world of men and live on the Isle of the Blest,* Ping wrote. *He was going to take Kai as well, but at the last minute he changed his mind and left him with me.*

*He was a long time in captivity; perhaps his mind wasn't as clear as it used to be,* Gu Hong wrote.

Ping remembered the old dragon as she had last seen him. His scales no longer reflected the sun, but were dull and faded. His eyes had taken on a yellowish cast. But although Danzi was weary of body, his mind had stayed sharp. Ping believed it was his pride that had stopped him from bringing Kai himself. He had lost the leadership of the cluster. He hadn't wanted to come back and face Hei Lei again.

That evening, while Ping was bathing in the pink pool, she had a vision of herself. It was in the future, and she was somewhere that she didn't recognize. She was in a house writing on calfskin. Something that smelled good was bubbling on a stove. There was a dog wagging its tail. Someone else was there, too. She tried to see who it was, but the image faded. Whether that was her true future, or just a possible one, Ping didn't know.

Ping now knew why the sixth line of the *Yi Jing* reading said there would be cause for regret. Hei Lei had been right all along. Humans had no place at the dragon haven. She had to leave Kai.

At the moon gathering that night Sha and Lian spoke again about bringing rain. They were outnumbered. Tun and the rest of the female dragons wouldn't agree.

"Kai should decide," Lian said.

Kai shook his head. He had been ready to fight for his position as leader, but he wasn't yet ready to make such important decisions.

"It is too hard," Kai said to Ping later. "Kai feels sorry for the humans who are dying of hunger, but also understands that the dragons cannot forget what humans did to the cluster. Dragon hunters killed the white dragons' parents, Tun's sister, Shuang's mate, their companions."

"I don't blame them for not wanting to help humans," Ping said.

"Sha and Lian want to help. Jiang thinks we are too few. We could only make a small cloud; it wouldn't be big enough to bring rain to the whole Empire."

Ping decided that now was as good a time as any to tell Kai her plans.

"The dragons don't want me here, Kai," she said.

"Kai makes the decisions. Ping can stay."

"I can hear all their voices now. I know what they are saying. They don't want any humans in the haven."

"They don't mean Ping."

She scratched him under the chin. "I have to go, Kai."

Kai sighed. He was silent for a while and then he turned to her. "When?"

"Soon."

"Ping could wait until Kai is bigger."

"I can't teach you what you need to know to be a wild dragon."

"Just wait a little while longer . . . till Kai is five-times-ten."

Ping smiled, fighting back tears. "I'll be too old to climb back down the mountains then. I think it would be better for me to leave before winter sets in."

He made a low, sad sound. "Who will look after Ping?" he asked.

"I'll look after myself, Kai."

She scratched the bumps on his head where his horns would one day grow. When they did she knew she would be long dead.

Once she had voiced her decision to leave, there was no reason to delay. Tun offered to carry her back to where he had found her. She would then have at least two months to reach a town or a village where she could spend the winter. She packed some food, but without Hei Lei to provide for them, the dragons' winter store was low, so she didn't take too much. The female dragons gave her a pair of shoes they had made from dragons' scales, stuck together with their saliva.

"They will not wear out," Jiang said.

Ping had a gift for the dragons. "I think Danzi's mirror should be kept in the treasure cave," she said. "My life is like an eye blink compared to yours. I could keep it, but what will happen to it after I die? No one else will understand its significance." She paused. "I would like to keep Kai's dragon-stone shard, though."

"You will be remembered in our lore," Jiang said. "Ping, the last Dragon Keeper, will be revered at every dragon moon."

"We won't forget what we have learned from humans," Tun said. "But now it is time for us to live without them."

"Take care of Kai for me," Ping said. She couldn't stop the tears from falling. "He might be a dragon of five colors, but he is still very young."

Sha and Lian stood on either side of the little dragon.

"We will watch over him," Sha said.

"Don't let him get lazy," Ping said. "Just because he's your future leader doesn't mean he shouldn't do his share."

Ping touched Kai for the last time, feeling the familiar roughness of his scales, the spiky points of his dorsal spines. She put her arms around Kai's neck. Her tears ran off his scales. He made the sound of a cracked bell tolling.

Ping hoisted the saddlebag onto her shoulder and turned to Tun.

"I'm ready," she said.

"Wait." Ping felt Kai's talons catch the back of her worn jacket. "Ping should wait till spring."

She turned back to him. "No, Kai. It's never going to be easy for me to leave you. Now is a good time."

"Take this." Kai winced as he pulled out one of his scales. "At dragon moon, Ping will dream of Kai."

Ping took it from him. It was smaller than Danzi's scale, and brighter. It lay like a piece of jade in her hand. In the daylight, the other colors at its tip weren't visible. She would only be able to see them in the moonlight.

"I don't have anything to give you," she said.

"Ping has given Kai so much."

She dug into her pouch. "You keep this." She handed him the silk square. "If you keep it out of the sunlight the characters won't fade anymore."

Kai took the silk square from her. He held it up so that it fluttered like a flag.

Ping climbed onto Tun's back. Jiang had fitted him with a saddle of woven grass. She wound a rope around Tun's neck and then around Ping's waist to secure her. Ping grasped the dragon's horns.

"Just one more thing," Jiang said. The red dragon spat in Ping's eyes. "If you don't know where our haven is, you can never be forced to give up the secret of its location."

Ping rubbed her eyes, but that only made them more sore. She opened them again. She couldn't see anything. She felt Tun take off. She had hoped to watch

Kai waving good-bye with the silk square until he shrank to the size of a dot. She heard him cry out, that mournful sound of copper bowls crashing together. Tears soothed her eyes, but they didn't bring back her sight. She felt the wind on her face. She knew for certain she would never see Kai again.

The air was colder than it had been when Tun had carried Ping to the dragon haven. The tears on her face turned to ice crystals. She shivered. In a month or two it would turn cold in the mountains. She didn't know where she would go when Tun left her. She didn't know where she'd be spending the winter, the rest of her life. Loneliness overwhelmed her like an ocean wave. She called out to Tun to take her back. But her words were whipped from her mouth by the wind and scattered in the sky.

Tun seemed to know exactly how long the effect of the dragon saliva in Ping's eyes would last. Just as she started to make out the blurred outline of mountains below, he began to descend. By the time the dragon's paws touched the ground, she could see again.

Tun didn't linger. As soon as Ping had untied herself and climbed down from the dragon's back, he was ready to take off again. He touched her with the pad of a paw and made a chinking sound, which sounded like a friendly farewell. She could no longer read his thoughts. Then he flapped his wings and was soon no more than a speck in the sky.

Ping looked around. Tun had put her down in the exact spot where he had found her. She was hundreds of torturous *li* from the nearest village. If she was lucky, she might chance upon a tribe of wandering yak herders. If she was very lucky, they might take her in for the winter. Her life was in the hands of Heaven.

Ping hadn't felt cold for months. It was barely autumn, but the wind had a sharp chill to it. Ping had no winter clothes. She looked up at the sun and started to walk. She was doing what she least wanted to do, but she knew it was right. It was a strange feeling.

Ping had the dragon scale shoes and enough food to last her for more than a week. She had a sharp knife, a snare she had woven from grass stalks to set traps for rabbits, and a pair of fire-making sticks. She had a bearskin to keep her warm at night. Her heart was heavy with the loss of Kai, but she knew he was in the safest place he could possibly be. One day she would find out what she was supposed to do with her life. The heartache would pass. In the meantime she had to focus on her journey. She had to find her way to a village or town where she could spend winter. She had enough gold to pay for lodgings. She could perhaps earn more as a storyteller or a scribe. That was one possibility for her life. There would be others. She tried to create a thread to lead her to the nearest village, but she had already lost her second sight.

A week passed. Ping walked through the mountains without seeing another human being. The wind turned icy. She needed something warmer to wear. Just as that thought formed, she caught sight of movement out of the corner of her eye. It was a rabbit. She had walked all day and was hungry. She still had dried meat and nuts in her bag, but after weeks of eating boiled meat, the thought of a roasted rabbit made her mouth water. She could save the dried meat for leaner times. And the skin would be useful. One or two more rabbits and she would have herself a warm vest.

The rabbit was about two *chang* away, nibbling on a tuft of yellow grass. The wind was in her favor, and the animal had neither heard nor smelled her. Ping took out the snare and got down on her hands and knees and crawled toward it. The rabbit was concentrating on eating the juicy grass. She moved closer, inch by slow inch. She wanted to pounce on the creature in case it hopped away, but she forced herself not to.

Ping gathered the snare into a loop in her left hand. Then she threw it. Her weeks of practice had paid off. Her aim was good. The loop fell over the startled rabbit's head, and she pulled it tight. The rabbit leaped up at least two feet and turned in midair. As it landed, it darted off. Its strength took Ping by surprise. It yanked the snare, and before she had time to react, the snare slipped through her fingers.

Ping jumped to her feet and ran after the rabbit. She

wanted the meat, but she wanted the snare more. It was an important part of her winter survival kit. She raced after the rabbit, stumbled on a rock, and felt her ankle turn. She fell, tumbling down a slope. Her body crashed against rocks until it landed at the bottom of a gully. She hit her head.

It was peaceful in the gully. Ping was glad that she had stopped tumbling. She was quite comfortable lying where she was. There was soft grass beneath her. The wind was blowing higher up but couldn't find its way down into the gully. The air was still and not as cold. Her ankle wasn't broken, just twisted. She'd be okay once she'd had a nap.

When Ping woke up, it was dark. She was cold. Her ankle hurt. She lay awake, shivering until dawn. She tried to get to her feet, but the pain in her ankle was too strong. She had to find a branch to use as a crutch. The problem was, she was still too high up in the mountains for trees to grow. She tried to crawl out of the gully, but it was too steep, and the pain made her weak.

It felt colder than it should have been for early autumn. The sun should have been overhead by now. She looked up at the sky. There was a cloud. A gray cloud. It was quite large. She felt a few drops of icy rain on her face. It seemed the dragons had decided to make rain after all. She could almost see the cloud growing before her eyes as it gathered the moisture from the air. The raindrops turned to flakes of snow. She would have laughed if she hadn't been shivering so much. The cloud might grow and grow until it brought unseasonal rain to the people of the Empire. That would be wonderful. But there on that mountain, it might end up being the death of Ping.

It stopped snowing after a few minutes, and the cloud broke up and drifted away. But the day didn't get any warmer. She tried again and managed to stand. Then, using rocks to support herself, she hobbled up the hillside. But when she reached the top, the wind blew her off her feet. She slid back down the slope. She was better off sheltering in the gully. She ate the last of her dried meat and nuts, collected some of the thin layer of snow to quench her thirst, and wrapped her bearskin around her.

It wasn't the cold that kept her awake, it was her ankle. The pain hid in drowsy corners of her mind, ready to jump out and wake her every time she started drifting off to sleep.

The next morning Ping didn't move. She couldn't think of any good reason why she should. She didn't know where she was going, or why. She didn't know what she was going to do with the rest of her life. Perhaps her life was over now that Kai had found his place in the dragon world. She had done her duty.

As she drifted in and out of consciousness, she

thought about her family. She could go to them and see
if they could find a place for her in their household. But
they didn't need her. What about her friends? She could
go to the Emperor and ask him if he could give her a
job to do. But she had already refused his offer of love.
She could go to Jun's village and see if he had returned
to his family. But what if he hadn't? She couldn't bear
to find out that she had been responsible for his death.
All in all, the best course of action seemed to be to stay
right where she was, to sink into a warm, comfortable
sleep and never wake up again. That seemed like an
excellent plan.

The sky darkened. There's another cloud, Ping
thought. The dragons have been busy. She looked up at
the sky. It was a very black cloud, and it was moving
strangely. She realized it wasn't a cloud at all. It was a
black bird. A large black bird. It swooped down closer.
And then Ping saw that it wasn't a bird, either. It was a
dragon—Hei Lei.

That was a different way to end her life, killed by a
dragon.

Ping felt the dragon's talons dig into her shoulder
and haul her up the side of the gully. Her ankle banged
against a rock. She cried out.

"Can you climb onto my back?" Hei Lei said.

Although she had lost her second sight, she could
still understand the dragon. His red eyes no longer
looked fierce. They looked like wounds.

"What for?" She wondered if he was planning on flying her to a great height and dropping her.

"So that I can take you to a place where humans live."

"You're not going to kill me?"

"No."

Ping pulled herself up onto the dragon's back. She had no rope to secure herself. Instead she looped the strap of her bag around the dragon's horns and then over her head and around her waist.

"I'm—" Before she could finish, the dragon had taken off.

She was glad she could see the view. This would definitely be her last dragon flight. She didn't know where Hei Lei was taking her, and she didn't care. Below, the mountains stretched in every direction like a huge length of crumpled cloth. Then they were up above the clouds in the sunlight.

"You like flying?" Hei Lei asked.

"I love it."

Hei Lei's great wings flapped up and down on either side of Ping. He was flying against the wind, but he didn't falter. She felt her spirits rise. Perhaps she wouldn't die just yet after all.

After flying for several hours, the clouds disappeared. The mountains softened to hills. She could see a village. Hei Lei flew lower.

"Aren't you worried that people will see you?" she asked.

"No, I often fly above human dwellings. I can take on the colors of my surroundings. From below, I look the same color as the sky."

He had the mirage skill, just like Kai.

Ping wondered why the black dragon visited inhabited lands. Knowing his dislike of people, she couldn't help but think the worst.

"I come here in spring," Hei Lei continued. "The pomegranate blossom in this region is the sweetest."

Ping smiled to herself. She would never have guessed that Hei Lei had a sweet tooth.

He landed neatly on the top of a hill.

"I will leave you here," he said. "There is a human nearby who will help you."

Ping climbed down. Just as the black dragon was flexing his wings to take off again, Ping reached out to touch his scales.

"Hei Lei," Ping said. "Thank you for saving me."

The dragon made no response.

"Go back to the dragon haven," she continued. "Gu Hong is old. Kai is young. The dragons need you. They need your strength, your *yang*." Hei Lei didn't say anything. "And the people of the Empire need rain. The dragons only managed to make a shower yesterday. Without you they can't make enough clouds."

The black dragon took off.

"Eight is twice-four," she called out to him. "It's a very inauspicious number. Nine is better."

# CHAPTER TWENTY-FOUR

# GREEN

Ping looked around. She could see no sign of life or the village she'd seen from the air. She had no food, no water, and thin clothes. The earth was so dry, there were cracks wide enough for Ping to put her hand in them. It was chilly. She didn't think Hei Lei had deceived her, but a dragon's idea of "close" to a village might be a lot different from a human's. She found a branch she could use as a crutch.

Before long, signs of human habitation did appear. There were empty fields, a dead ox. Ping's heart soared when she saw a house, but when she got close she realized it had been abandoned.

Ping started walking . . . again. It seemed that she'd spent a large part of her life walking without knowing where she was going. Her ankle hurt, and she knew she wouldn't get far on it. She felt frustration rise in her. She'd had enough of living at the whim of others—masters, emperors, dragons. She was tired of it. She wanted to be in control of her own life for once.

She saw something on the next hill. A plume of smoke. Whether it was coming from a chimney or a grass fire, she didn't know. Either way it was something to walk toward.

As Ping drew closer, she could see that there was a village on the hill. If there was smoke, at least one person was still living there.

It was a village of about twenty houses. As she walked through the open gate, several thin faces turned toward her. They weren't welcoming. Ping could guess what they were thinking. Another mouth to feed. Raised voices drifted from a barn. Two donkeys were tied up outside. A farmer came out of the barn.

"I don't care how much gold you have," he was saying. "Hay is worth more than its weight in gold. I can't sell you any."

Another man followed him out of the barn. He looked as if he were about to argue, then he caught sight of Ping. Ping's heart began thudding. It was Jun. A smile broke over his face. He was wearing a thick winter gown, and he looked thinner than the last time she'd seen him. Ping suddenly wished she wasn't wearing a threadbare jacket and trousers with the knees worn through. He ran over and hugged her.

"Thanks to Heaven! You're alive. I'd almost given up hope."

Ping clung to him and found that she couldn't speak.

"Are you injured?" Jun asked. "You look terrible. And where did you come from?"

"I dropped out of the sky," Ping said, smiling through tears. Hei Lei had known exactly where he was leaving her.

Jun looked around. "Where's Kai?"

"I had to leave him," Ping said.

"You found the dragon haven?"

Ping nodded. "It wasn't on Long Gao Yuan."

"Where was it?"

"In a faraway place. I don't know its name or where it is. I could search all my life and never find Kai again."

Ping hadn't allowed herself to think about the little dragon after she'd left the dragon haven. Now her unhappiness overflowed. She buried her face in Jun's gown and cried. She sobbed until she had no strength to cry anymore. It took a long time. The villagers grew tired of watching and went back to their business. Jun stood holding her, stroking her back until all the grief had emptied from her heart.

The barn was the only accommodation available in the village. Jun had some food supplies, a warm jacket. Ping had a little dried ginger left. A village woman gave them a kettle of boiling water to make tea.

Ping sipped her hot drink. "What happened to you after Kai and I climbed up the Serpent's Tail?"

"I tried to climb the cliff myself, but I couldn't. I had the strength, but I couldn't fit into the narrow space between the cliff and the falls like you and Kai. I reached about two *chang* before the water washed me off the wall and I fell."

"But you didn't wait for us," she said.

"I couldn't," Jun replied. "A large yellow dragon picked me up in its talons, carried me for many *li*, and dumped me in the middle of nowhere."

Ping smiled. "That was Tun."

Ping and Jun took turns recounting their adventures. Jun had bought the two donkeys so he could search for Ping, but it had been difficult to buy enough food to keep him and the beasts alive.

"Everyone is hungry," he said. "No one has any food to spare. I don't know how we will survive."

Ping told him about the dragon haven—the dragons, the colored pools, the bubbling mud, the talk of making it rain. It all sounded like a story she'd made up. They talked until after midnight.

The sound of excited voices woke Ping the next morning.

She went outside. The villagers were staring into the distance, shading their eyes from the early morning sun. They were pointing at the horizon. Gray clouds were huddled there. Jun came and stood next to her.

"They're big clouds," Ping said. "Hei Lei must have gone back to the dragon haven and helped the others make mist."

"You believe that?"

Ping nodded. "Yes."

The sun shone on the underside of the clouds, turning them from gray to deep purple. The villagers watched, worried that the sun would frighten the clouds away. A rainbow appeared over a distant hill, its colors as pallid and translucent as dragonfly wings.

"There must be a shower of rain over there," Jun said.

The band of cloud loomed closer. The colors of the rainbow grew stronger until they were as brilliant as those of an embroidered gown. They could see it clearly now—a column of steady rain falling on the next hill. The sun still shone stubbornly over the village.

"The dragon!" one of the villagers shouted.

Ping looked up in the sky, but there were no dragons there. The villagers ran into the barn and emerged again with a dusty bamboo shape covered with faded silk. Four men held the shape above their heads and danced around the village. The silk that covered the bamboo was tattered and faded, but it was still recognizable as a dragon.

The clouds continued to move steadily toward them, dark and heavy, until at last they blotted out the sun. The rainbow disappeared. The villagers cheered. Lightning zigzagged across the sky. There was a crack of

thunder. Large drops of rain were falling on the villagers' upturned faces. Before long the rain was pouring from the sky. No one took shelter. They danced in
the rain.

Ping was riding on one of the donkeys. She no longer
had to hide. They could travel along good roads. With
the help of the donkeys, they would reach Xining
before winter set in. The rain was still coming down, as
it had been for two days. The hills were already tinged
with green. Ping wore a bamboo hat that kept her head
dry, but the rest of her was soaked to the skin. She
didn't even think of complaining. Jun was leading the
other donkey, which carried their baggage. His hair
was wet through. Water was dripping off the end of his
nose.

"You don't think your dragon friends will get too
carried away and cause a flood, do you?"

"No. They'll know when to stop—when the lakes
are full and all the rivers are flowing again."

It was too late to sow grain. There would be some
grass for the animals to eat, and people could plant
winter vegetables, but it would still be a tough winter.
Hopefully the people would survive through it. Ping
was sure there would be good rains next spring.

"So where do you want to go?"

"I don't know."

"Kai is in his right place—in the world of dragons,"

Jun said. "Now it's time for you to take your place in the world of people."

The world of people frightened Ping. "I've never had a place there. I've been looking after dragons since I was four years old."

"Now you'll discover how you should be spending your own life," Jun said.

The rain slackened and then stopped. Ping got down from the donkey and dried Jun's face with her sleeve.

"You make it sound easy," she said.

"You could go to Chang'an," he said. "The Emperor would give you an imperial post. You could live a grand life."

Ping shook her head. "That's not the life for me."

She couldn't imagine returning to Beibai Palace, either.

"What about your family? You could live with them."

"No. I'll visit them from time to time, but there is no place for me with them."

"Do you like mulberries?" Jun asked.

Ping smiled at him and nodded. He was the only friend who had ever come back to her.

Jun put his arms around her and kissed her.

Ping remembered the vision she'd had of her own future—a comfortable home, a life shared with someone.

"Your mulberry trees will be flourishing in this rain," Ping said.

For the first time in her life she could choose what she wanted to do. Jun held out his hand, and Ping took it. They walked together leading the donkeys.

Three weeks later, Ping looked up at the night sky. There was a full moon. A dragon moon. She took Kai's scale from her pouch. It glowed luminous green in the moonlight. As she turned it this way and that, the tip of the scale glittered red, black, yellow, green, and white. She lay down to sleep, holding the scale to her breast.

She dreamed of a dragon, a green dragon, a happy dragon. He swam in colored pools. He learned how to hunt. The jingling sound of his laughter filled the air.

# GLOSSARY

CHANG
A measure of distance equal to about seven and a
half feet.

HAN DYNASTY
A period in Chinese history when the emperors all belonged
to a particular family. It lasted from 202 B.C.E. to 220 C.E.

HAN FOOT
A measure of length equal to about nine inches.

JADE
A semiprecious stone also known as nephrite. Its
color varies from green to white.

JIN
The measure of weight for gold.

JUJUBE
A name for the fruit known as the Chinese date.

LI
A measure of distance equal to about three tenths of
a mile.

QI
According to traditional Chinese beliefs, *qi* is the
life energy that flows through us and controls the
workings of the body.

QILIN
A mythical Chinese animal with the body of a deer,
the tail of an ox, and a single horn.

RED PHOENIX
A mythical Chinese bird that looks a lot like a peacock.

SHU
A drop; a very small amount.

YI JING
An ancient Chinese book used for divination. It is
also known as the *I Ching*. This book is three or four
thousand years old.

# GUIDE TO PRONUNCIATION

The Chinese language includes many sounds unlike any sounds in English. The Chinese words in this book are written in *pinyin*, which is the official modern way of writing the sound of Chinese characters using the Roman alphabet. The *pinyin* system was introduced by the People's Republic of China in 1958 and has since been adopted worldwide. In *pinyin*, words aren't always pronounced the way you might think. Here is a guide to help you pronounce them properly.

| | |
|---|---|
| Bai Xue | Buy Shware (rhymes with *bear*) |
| Beibai | Bay buy |
| Cai | Tsai (rhymes with *buy*) |
| Danzi | Dan-za |
| Hou-yi | Ho-yee |
| Jiang | Jee-ang (jee as in *jeep*) |
| Ji Liao | Jee Lee-ow (rhymes with *now*) |
| Jun | Jun (u as in *butcher*) |
| Lao Longzi | Low (rhymes with *now*) |
| | Lung-za (u as in *butcher*) |
| Lao Ma | Low (rhymes with *now*) |
| | Ma (rhymes with *far*) |
| Lian | Lee-en |
| Liu Che | Lee-oo (oo as in *loop*) |
| | Chuh (as in *church*) |

| | |
|---|---|
| Long Kai Duan | Lung (u as in *butcher*) |
| | Kai (rhymes with *buy*) Dw-ahn |
| Lu-lin | Loo (rhymes with *shoe*) lin |
| Ming Yang | Sounds just like it looks |
| Ping | Sounds just like it looks |
| Sha | Shar |
| Shuang | Shwang (rhymes with *bang*) |
| Tai Shan | Tai (pronounced as *tie*), Shan |
| Tinglan | Ting-lan |
| Tun | Twun (u as in *butcher*) |
| Xiong Nu | Shee-ung Noo (u as in *butcher*) |
| Yangxin | Yang Shin |
| Yi Jing | Yee Jing |

# ACKNOWLEDGMENTS

I have been known to throw the *Yi Jing* when faced with a difficult problem (using coins not yarrow stalks), though I'm pleased to say it wasn't necessary during the writing of this book. Ping's *Yi Jing* reading is based on the first chapter of that ancient Chinese book, which is more often written as *I Ching* and known in English as *The Book of Change*.

I read several translations of this chapter, then made my own interpretation with the help of my minimal knowledge of the Chinese language and the great online dictionary and translation aids at http://www.mandarintools.com/.

Chinese, with its four tones and many homonyms (words that sound the same but mean different things), is a fascinating language. I spent many hours (sometimes pleasurable, sometimes infuriating) using the online dictionary while working out the punning place names on Danzi's map.

I am indebted to all the historians, researchers, and translators whose labor has enabled me to learn about ancient China. For a full bibliography of sources used, see my Web site at www.carolewilkinson.com.au.

Though some sources say that the Chinese puzzle *qi qiao ban* (Seven Cunning Pieces—known in English as Tangram) is ancient, while writing this novel I discovered that the current view is that it is not. I decided to use the puzzle in my story anyway. Texts of the *Yi Jing* have turned up in Han dynasty tombs, so maybe one day someone will find an ancient Tangram set.

I would like to thank Vicky Deresa for her invaluable help with the three place-name puzzles and Danzi's four-character message. I would also like to thank Haiwang Yuan for telling me the Chinese version of "out of the frying pan into the fire."

Thank you to Andrew Kelly and Alison Arnold of black dog books once again for their wonderful editorial assistance, creative support, and friendship. Thanks also to everyone else at black dog for reading drafts.

I'd also like to thank Blue Boat Design, especially Rob Davies, for another gorgeous cover, Julian Bruère for his meticulous maps, and William Lai for his beautiful calligraphy. There were some tight deadlines for this book, so I am particularly grateful to my husband, John, and my daughter, Lili, for putting up with more than usual angst as I wrote it.

Finally, I'd like to thank all those readers of the previous two books in the Dragon Keeper series who took the trouble to write to me. Their enthusiasm and encouragement have been inspiring.